WITHD

Praise for Sha

'More fun than a girl's night out!'
OK!

'There are only two words for Shari Low:
utterly hilarious'
Carmen Reid

'Totally captivating and it felt like I'd lost a new best
friend when it came to the end'
Closer

'Shari Low writes with humour and skill about the
complicated subtleties of adult relationships. A gentle
warning to smug marrieds everywhere'
Dorothy Koomson

'Great fun from start to finish'
Jenny Colgan

'Compulsive . . . This is a hilarious read'
Sun

'Absolutely hilarious. A brilliant read that keeps your
attention right up until the end'
Bookbag

Over the years, **Shari Low** has been a nightclub manager, a sales rep, run health clubs and lived in Amsterdam, Hong Kong, Shanghai, London and Los Angeles. She has been fat, thin, in love, out of love, back in love again, then out of love (this could go on for a while), a wife, a mother, good at reading bedtime stories, rubbish at football, obsessed with travelling, addicted to eBay and blessed with a group of fantastic friends.

Shari now lives with her lovely husband and two very funny sons near Glasgow. She has published seven novels and writes a weekly opinion column for the *Daily Record*.

And she's currently medium-sized, in love and looking for a bargain break to New York or Sydney.

To find out more about Shari, visit her website at www.sharilow.com

Temptation Street

Shari Low

piatkus

PIATKUS

First published in Great Britain as a paperback original in 2010 by Piatkus

A CIP catalogue record for this book
is available from the British Library.

ISBN 978-0-7499-5295-2

Typeset in Baskerville MT by Palimpsest Book Production Limited,
Grangemouth, Stirlingshire
Printed and bound in Great Britain by Clays Ltd, St Ives plc

Papers used by Piatkus are natural, renewable and recyclable
products sourced from well-managed forests and certified
in accordance with the rules of the Forest Stewardship Council.

Mixed Sources
Product group from well-managed
forests and other controlled sources
www.fsc.org Cert no. SGS-COC-004081
© 1996 Forest Stewardship Council

FSC

To Emma Beswetherick, my very, very favourite
book chick.

And to John, Callan and Brad. Everything. Always.

Prologue

'Right, here are the rules. No work talk, no arguments. Joe, feel free to molest me under the table at any point and, Suze, if you order a salad, I'm leaving.' Melissa raised a loaded eyebrow in the direction of her sister-in-law sitting directly across from her. 'Calories. Lots of calories. Look at it as being a gesture of friendship and solidarity.'

Suze smoothed down invisible wrinkles on her replica Hervé Léger body con dress and raised her champagne glass in the direction of the self-appointed master of ceremonies. Calories were definitely on her agenda but she had a feeling that the majority of them would be ingested in liquid form. 'For you, anything – I'll prepare my internal organs for incoming stodge. Oh, and Karl –' she turned to her husband, who had barely said a word since he'd sat down ten minutes before '– I'm up for some of that under-table action too, if you're so inclined.'

Melissa and Joe saw Karl's easy grin, the playful nod. Only Suze noticed the flicker of hesitation that came before it. Another sip camouflaged her sinking heart. It hadn't been like this last year. Or the year before. Same date, same restaurant, same people . . . different husband. Back then he'd needed no encouragement to let his hands wander and his affection show. But there was no time to brood, because, almost by some kind of weird, fraternal osmosis, her brother-in-law was adopting the jovial, gregarious role normally filled by her husband.

Joe slipped an arm around Melissa's shoulders, lifted his glass and thrust it into the air above the centre of the table. 'Happy Anniversary to all of us. Suze, you've put up with my brother for ten years now and I want you to know that we will be applying to have you officially recognised for such a monumental sacrifice. We were thinking they could maybe name a street after you or a public holiday.'

'I want a street. And there had better be a Prada in it.'

As the laughter rose, Mel winked across the table at her sister-in-law, followed up with a surreptitious 'wow, what's got into him?' gesture just out of Joe's line of sight. Her shy, reserved husband would normally be the last one to make public declarations and grand gestures. And he wasn't done yet . . .

'And Mel, my gorgeous Mel – eight amazing years. I love you so much and I hope we have another sixty.'

Mel felt the tap on her tears flick to the 'on' position and headed off the potential pathetically gushy moment with a kiss, a huge smile and a return to the four-way toast that was still dangling in midair between them. 'To us,' she echoed. 'Another year gone and many, many more to come.'

Several of the nearby diners heard the clinking of the glasses and watched as the two couples celebrated their special occasion. It was the perfect scene, four attractive twenty/thirty-somethings, all radiating the kind of happiness that only love and intimacy can bring.

It was no wonder then that no one knew. No one knew that one of them was deeply unhappy. That one of them had done a terrible thing. That one of them was about to commit an act that would blow their perfect little foursome apart.

And no, when it came to anniversary dinners for four, there would be no more years to come.

One

'The gear stick! The gear stick! Aaaaaargh!'

There was a startled pause before they both collapsed into fits of laughter, dissipating the frenzied passion that was responsible for the steam that clouded every window. Bending her head to avoid car-roof-inflicted concussion, she un-straddled him and manoeuvred into the passenger seat, her hot, damp flesh sticking to the leather upholstery.

'Wow,' he said, his tone somewhere between relief and amusement as he prised himself out of the gap between the two front seats. 'That gear stick got way, way too personal there. That wasn't the kind of threesome I ever imagined having.'

'Do I have to call an ambulance?' she asked. 'Only, this might take some very creative explaining.'

'Nope, think I'll live, although any future possibility of fatherhood might just have plummeted.'

Slowly, gently, he extricated himself from the space between the two front seats and used his finely toned thigh muscles to propel him to the right. As he slumped with a relieved sigh behind the wheel, two things suddenly struck her. The first was the absurdity of the image: two people sitting in a car, chatting casually as if this was the most normal

3

thing in the world. Which it might have been if they weren't both entirely naked. The second thing was that he'd just mentioned the 'F' word. Fatherhood. OK, so it was a glib, throwaway comment, but it twanged an emotional string and cast a momentary shadow of seriousness that just about cancelled out the gear stick/naked driver hilarity.

Fatherhood. She tried to swat the thought out of her head. She wasn't going to go there. Hadn't they agreed that this was just a bit of fun, purely physical, no strings attached? She was going to disregard what he'd said. Ignore it. Forget he'd ever uttered the word. Unfortunately, the message didn't reach her mouth, which was at that very moment blurting, 'Is that something you want? To have children, I mean.'

The sigh escaped before he could stop it. Bugger – why had he even joked about the kids thing? Didn't he bloody know better than that? Hadn't he learned a woman's normal reactions and personality could transform when set against the thumping of her biological clock? Right on cue she was looking at him all expectantly, waiting for some kind of profound or romantic answer. The truth was, he didn't have one and he had no intention of going down that road. That wasn't what this was about. It had nothing to do with futures and families and forward planning. It had nothing to do with dreams and hopes for the rest of their lives. It was completely removed from any kind of mental or emotional depth and, as far as he was aware, she felt that way too. Their day-to-day lives were about other people, commitments, responsibilities and vows, but this? Right at the very beginning they'd agreed that this would only be about one thing and he had no intention of changing the game plan.

His 'emotional depth' alarm – primed to scream like a klaxon at the first sign of anything resembling deep and meaningful conversation – had been activated and he immediately deployed diversionary tactics. Reaching over, he tenderly pushed his hand around the side of her neck, caressing her temple with his thumb, before slowly pulling her towards him.

'Baby, when I'm with you I don't think about anything except how incredibly, beautifully, shaggably sexy you are.'

4

He pressed his lips down on to hers and she automatically returned the gesture, an involuntary groan escaping as she did so. Mission accomplished. Panic averted. No casualties, no prisoners.

Normal service was resumed and once again the meeting was all about the one thing he liked best.

The weekend it all started . . .

Two

'Are you absolutely sure that you want to go through with this?' The question tailed off as the receiver slipped from Mel's grasp. 'Bollocks! *Hang on a minute, Suze*,' she yelled as she followed her falling phone into that dark, terrifying void into which she knew no one should ever go without thorough mental and physical preparation.

'Sorry, hon. Dropped the phone in the washing basket. I'm now speaking to you while inhaling the aroma of socks. Anyway. So. Are you sure?'

'I am. I have to know and this is the best and quickest way to find out. And don't breathe like that.'

'Like what?'

'Like that. You're breathing in a disapproving manner, I can tell.'

'I'm not – it's the sock fumes. Although, I do. Disapprove, that is. I'm not judging you, Suze, you have to do what you think is right and I'll support you all the way, but I just can't help thinking that there's something a bit, well, *immoral* about it all. You have to admit it's kinda seedy.'

'It isn't seedy, it's empowering. It's being proactive. It's

9

taking control. And, although it's put me on the emotional level classified as "shitting myself", I still think it's better than carrying on while alternating between oblivion, denial and blind bloody worry. I just . . . I just have to know.'

Melissa heard the crack in her friend's voice and succumbed to a wave of sympathy.

Suze regained her composure. 'You haven't said anything to Joe, have you? Promise me, because you know what they're like – he wouldn't be able to stop himself giving Karl a heads-up.'

Tossing Joe's favourite shirt into the washing machine drum, Mel subconsciously nodded as she acknowledged the truth in Suze's words. Karl and Joe were the closest brothers that she had ever encountered. They worked together, they socialised together, played five-a-side football for the same team. They were, in short, inseparable. Like the Kray twins only without the propensity for crime and with perfectly formed bodies, courtesy of three gym sessions every week – which, of course, they did together. Joe's sense of family loyalty had been one of the things that attracted Mel to him in the first place. Having grown up an only child, she'd relished the fact that Joe came as a package deal with two parents who welcomed her into their family with open arms and a brother only two years older who treated her like the sister he'd always wanted. The icing on the Happy Families cake was Karl's wife Suzanne, who'd made the transition from sister-in-law to closest friend within months of their meeting.

Karl and Suzanne's marriage had always been the more volatile one, oozing passion and excitement that occasionally morphed into drama and emotional overload. But Mel knew that Suze's latest suspicions that Karl was being unfaithful were surely unfounded. He couldn't be. Karl was a decent guy, just like his brother.

'I haven't told Joe, I promise. I don't tell him everything, you know.'

'Yes, you do.'

'OK, I do, but, honestly, I didn't tell him about this. It'll come to nothing, Suze. There's no way Karl is doing anything behind your back – he'd never do that.'

'That's what all wives say . . . right up until the husband buggers off with the secretary and the next thing they know Mrs Denial is living in a one-bedroom bedsit while the mistress is screwing him six times a night in the marital bed and booking a fortnight in Marbella with his credit card. I know at heart he's a good guy, Mel, but I'd be stupid to ignore the warning signs. You have to admit that he was really quiet at our anniversary dinner, and you know Karl, normally we have to beg him to stop singing when the waiters are turning the lights out. He's changed . . . and I need to know why.'

Mel closed the washing-machine door with a bang and pressed the eco-wash button.

'Are you absolutely sure it's not just some kind of mid-life-crisis thing?'

'Karl's only thirty-one,' Suze replied.

'So it could be a premature mid-life crisis.'

'The only thing that's premature these days is –'

'Noooooooo – don't say it! I have to face my brother-in-law at weddings, christenings, birthdays and special occasions that involve giblets – don't give me mental images that could cloud the way I look at him for ever!' Sensing that she wasn't winning this battle, she decided to go the pleading route. 'Don't do this, Suze, please.'

'I have to. I'm a control freak – being in possession of all the facts is in the job description.'

Mel's stomach started flipping in synchronisation with the smalls that were swooshing around in front of her. She

11

hated drama. She hated crisis. She felt torn in two – on the one hand, she wanted to be supportive to her best friend, but, on the other, she was terrified that events could go all Jeremy Kyle and the next thing she'd be visiting her in-laws in separate houses on alternate Sundays.

There was a pause before psychic Suze sighed, 'Stop chewing your lip.'

'I'm not!' Mel blurted, through well-chewed lips. She absentmindedly prepared the next load, making a molehill of whites in front of the whirring machine. 'So when's it going to happen?'

'This weekend sometime. I've given the agency details of Karl's schedule for Friday, Saturday and Sunday and they'll decide when to approach him. They don't tell the wife in case she turns up, watches events unfold, then takes a baseball bat to the husband if he falls for the bait.'

'I can see why that wouldn't be a good thing.' Bra. Bra. Thong. Thong. Bra. Nightdress. T-shirt. Bra. The washing molehill was approaching official mountain status.

'I've told them to send a brunette with long legs and breasts like space hoppers. He always says that's his type.'

'But you're blonde and flatter than Holland.'

'And now you understand my seedlings of doubt.'

Mel sighed wearily. This was all her fault – she was the one who'd pointed out the newspaper feature on a new agency called 'Honeytrap for Hire – For Wives with Suspicious Minds and Wandering Husbands'. For a substantial fee, they specialised in sending gorgeous babes to attempt to seduce husbands in a kind of twisted, warped fidelity test. She'd thought it was absurd. Crazy. Ridiculous. Unfortunately, her sister-in-law thought it was the answer to her deep-rooted doubts about her husband's monogamy. As a result of that one article, Suze's bank balance was £500 lighter, Melissa now had a large dose of nervous anxiety, and the unwitting Karl was in line for what might just be the most memorable – and potentially expensive – chat-up of his life. This was bizarre. Surreal. This was the kind of stuff that happened on American reality shows right before a bloke with a microphone burst in and confronted the cheating partner in front of two million salivating viewers. This didn't happen to people she knew and definitely not to family.

Suze loved Karl. Karl loved Suze.

Melissa loved Joe. Joe loved Melissa.

Sure, the national fifty per cent divorce rate gave a clue that one of the couples was likely to hit a bump along the way, but Mel had always assumed that they'd defy statistics. In fact, she still did. There was absolutely no way Karl would cheat. Never. She absolutely believed in her brother-in-law. He would rebuff the Special Agent Fake Slapper, the agency would give Suze the good news and they'd all laugh about this in fifty years time when the four of them were living in the two halves of semi-detached sheltered housing, sharing two sets of false teeth and talking about the good old days when they could still get around without the aid of a motorised scooter.

Nevertheless, she decided to make one last attempt to derail the train to Temptation Street. 'Please, Suze – just talk to him. Can't you go down the "calm reasonable discussion and honest revelation of your fears" route?'

Suze sighed. 'It would never work. What's he going to say? "Yes, love – I'm shagging someone else. Glad we got that out in the open. Now what's for dinner?" Are you kidding? He'll deny, deny, deny and then I'll be no further forward. And the stalemate will come with the added bonus that, if he's innocent, he'll resent my suspicions and lack of trust until the end of time. Nope, I honestly think this is the best thing to do. If he does the dirty I'll have concrete proof, and if he doesn't then I'll know my fears were unfounded without him ever realising that I doubted him. Doddle.'

Melissa slumped down on top of the washing pile. There were many words that sprung to mind, but 'doddle' wasn't one of them.

'Dread' and 'apprehension', on the other hand, definitely were.

Three

Suze pressed the disconnect button on her phone and thumped her head down on to the kitchen table. A little too hard.

Rubbing the new tender spot on her forehead, she flicked on the black Dolce Gusto coffee maker that sat perched on her granite worktop, a raven-coloured stone pitted with thousands of tiny gold flecks. Karl and Joe had built this house with their own bare hands, assisted by the bare hands of several employees of Marshall & Sons, the building company that their father had founded and that they had inherited when their mother had finally dragged him off to a life of forced retirement in a bungalow on the edge of an Ayrshire golf course. Karl was the suit in the operation, running the business side of things, while Joe headed up the workforce. The perfect men to know when you discover a breathtaking acre of land on the outskirts of Whitecraigs, a beautiful, well-heeled suburb on the south side of Glasgow. Normally it would have been way out of their financial reach, but, by bargaining for the plot and then doing the work themselves, they'd created a beautiful home for the kind of money that their neighbours spent on their matching his 'n' hers Lamborghinis. They'd planned every inch of the home together. Their forever home. The room Suze stood in now was a testimony to a husband with a gadget obsession, a wife who favoured minimalist chic and the kind of pristine tidiness that could only exist in a child-free area.

Child-free area.

Suze felt a pang of regret as the shouts of last night's argument screeched back into her head.

It was the kids one again. Again. Again.

Karl: I want to start a family.

Suze: Well, I don't. I'm not ready yet.

Karl: We need to compromise.

Suze: There is no compromise on this.

She stared aimlessly out of the kitchen window, her eyes unfocused, not even absorbing the aesthetic pleasure of the Swiss Alpine summer house or the immaculately groomed lawn. When did being married become so damned difficult? He was everything she'd ever dreamed of – smart, funny and handsome in a young Richard Gere fashion (post-*Pretty Woman*, but before he chummed up with the Dalai Lama and pissed off China). Ten years they'd survived in the closest thing you got to blissful harmony outside of a Country & Western ballad. OK, maybe that was a slight exaggeration – there had been a few memorable blow-outs but they'd always been immediately followed by the kind of making up that involved nudity and frantic sweating.

But the last year? Carnage. It just seemed like they were morphing into two different people. Gone were the bride and groom who were absolutely in synch, agreeing that children were something they might think about at a later date. No pressure, no breeding deadlines. In fact, they weren't even sure that the day would come when they would want to start a family. All that had mattered was that they had 100 per cent confidence that they were meant for each other and would work life out as they went. But that was then. Now it seemed like they were independent souls with nothing in common, opposing views on everything and lately there had been a loss in appetite for any of the nude frantic stuff. Much as she understood why Mel insisted this was just a temporary bad patch, deep down Suze knew it was much more than that. This felt like the approach to the end of the road. Like the forewarning of a parting of the ways. She'd give *anything* to get back to where they used to be but . . .

Her thoughts were violently interrupted by the sensation of warm liquid spreading down her right leg. Shit! The coffee cup had overflowed, flooded the worktop and was now running down her Canadian oak units on to the cream travertine floor via her brand new Diesel jeans, which were – naturally – white.

And – naturally again – Karl picked that very instant to walk in the front door. Suze spun around and watched as he turned and headed for the floating glass and oak staircase on his left, with just the briefest glance across their open-plan living area to where she was standing.

'Hey, Suze, it's me – just heading up for a shower, be down in five,' he announced as his perfectly formed buttocks disappeared out of sight.

Her immediate conclusions said it all really. His nonchalant tone made it clear that he didn't even care enough about the fight last night to prolong the friction with a sulk of a decent length and severity. But, on the other hand, there was no kiss, no warm greeting, no idle chit-chat. Their whole lives these days consisted of forced politeness and the kind of fleeting conversations more suited to flatmates than husband and wife. This blatant disregard had resulted in the depressing realisation that he paid her so little attention these days that he had not even noticed that the alleged love of his life was standing in their kitchen looking like someone with overwhelming incontinence issues.

Yep, they were doomed. In her heart of hearts, Suze knew it was over . . . she just didn't fully understand why.

But she had a sinking feeling she was about to find out.

Four

Even in the crowded bar, heaving with Friday-night, demob-happy suits, it wasn't difficult to spot him. The tall brunette with the hourglass figure took another look at the photo in front of her. Yep, it was definitely him, although he was better looking than in the picture and much more of an attractive package than her usual targets. She'd been on enough of these assignments now to know that the guys were usually delusional twats in their forties or fifties, with three things in common: money, success and ego. This one didn't look like he came into any of those categories. In fact, he looked quite ... well, nice. Normal. No apparent dress-sense bypass. No facial hair. No dodgy dancing to the eighties soundtrack that was blaring from the speakers. And – quick visual scope of the armpit area – no obvious perspiration problems.

Always a bonus.

She mentally repeated her rules as she stuffed the photo back in her silver, customised MaxMara clutch and brushed imaginary lint off of her red curve-skimming shift dress. Do not initiate conversation. Do not blatantly flirt. Look approachable. Look gorgeous. But most of all, look very,

very alone. Stomach in, chin up, shoulders back, very best wiggle on, do not fall off these bloody ridiculous heels between here and the target.

She checked her watch – 8 p.m. – early enough perhaps to get this one done and move on to one of the others that were on standby for that night. So many cheating bastards, so little time. She gave the target another once-over and made a silent wager with herself – one new pair of Gucci bondage boots said that this one wouldn't fall for her. She just had a feeling. He looked too straight, too laidback. He wasn't scoping the place for hot tottie, he wasn't sucking in his stomach muscles and he hadn't spotted that she was strutting towards him wearing a bra that enhanced her cleavage to proportions that could be seen from space.

She reached the marble bar without injury or embarrassment and slipped into the gap beside him, careful not to even glance in his direction. Outright seduction crossed the line between availability and entrapment and she'd been doing this job long enough to know that, if he was of a mind for some on-the-side action, then he'd make it obvious, with or without her encouragement.

She caught the eye of the shaggy-haired bartender and wondered once again why males in the 18–22 age bracket apparently held the conviction that showing off the top of their pants elevated them to sex-god status.

'A glass of red wine, please. House is fine,' she said in a breezy voice (happy, endearing, and the choice of wine screamed 'low maintenance'), through a wide, perfect smile, courtesy of the whitening treatment that her shady accountant had assured her could be classed as an occupational necessity and was therefore tax-deductible.

100. 99. 98. She looked at her watch and quietly sighed, looking around her as she did so. 95. 94. 93. She made a point of pulling her phone out of the small bag that she'd

casually positioned on the bartop. She checked the screen, and then shook her head despondently as she replaced it. 82. 81. 80. A flick of the hair and an anxious look in the direction of the door. 69. 68. 67. The barman flushed slightly as she winked in thanks for the drink that had appeared in front of her. 61. 60. 59. £6.75! For a glass of plonk? Bloody hell, whoever owned this place should be wearing a mask. She concealed her outrage with another flash of the pearlies as she handed over the cash. 47. 46. 45. The mark's (it had taken her ages to use the industry lingo without feeling like she was acting in a really bad BBC drama) eyes would be flicking towards her now, taking in the show. That thought wasn't borne of conceit, but of experience gained on a hundred other nights that started exactly like this. 34. 33. 32. Cue a deep, mournful exhalation, with slumped shoulders for added effect. 26. 25. 24. She knew he would be staring now. And wondering why the room seemed a little hotter than before. 19. 18. 17. Another sip of her drink. Another glance towards the door. Another check of her watch. Another sigh. 10. 9. 8. She pushed her half-empty glass towards the other side of the bar, picked up her clutch and jutted her chin out in a decisive manner, making it very obvious that she had decided to leave. 3. 2. 1.

'Whoever you're waiting for must be crazy not to show up.'

Bingo! There it was. One hook. One line. One utterly predictable sinker.

She offered up a shy, sheepish smile in his direction. 'If I give you his number, will you call him and tell him that?'

'Definitely. Or I could buy you another drink and we could muse over our character flaws that have resulted in both of us being passed over on the same night?'

'You've been stood up too? Wife or girlfriend?'

'Brother. You?'

'Blind date. To be honest I didn't hold out much hope.

He is an accountant who likes hill walking. I'm thinking that he'd resent my spending on superficial things like high heels and holidays in the sun.'

Ooh, his eyes glistened when he smiled. But of course, she made that observation in a purely professional capacity. Ditto the fact that he was well over six feet tall, and now that she was up close she could see that he had that whole wide-shoulder, narrow-hips thing going on, the obvious result of dedication to the gym and a direct contradiction to the fact that they were standing in a city that was definitely in the running to be the fried-food capital of the universe.

His beautifully cut charcoal suit sat perfectly over a white open-neck shirt and shoes that were almost certainly of Italian origin. Actually, if she hadn't been reliably informed that he was Glasgow born and bred, she may well have deduced that the rest of him had its roots in the Mediterranean too. She loved the humour and the gregariousness of Scottish men, but there was no denying that they commonly sported light-brown or ginger hair that contrasted against a complexion that was so pale it was tinged with a discernible hint of blue. Not this guy. His jet-black hair was short, neat and the perfect frame for his olive-green eyes and eyelashes that could dust shelves.

The background beat of an old Madonna track barely registered as they made their introductions, the false name par for the course.

'Saffron? That's really unusual. I've never heard that before.'

'Duran Duran.'

'Pardon?' Oooh, and he had a very sweet little line between his eyebrows when he was puzzled. Another purely professional observation.

'Simon Le Bon called his daughter Saffron. It's just one of millions of completely inconsequential and utterly trivial things that I know.'

'Give me your favourite.'

'Cows make more milk when they listen to music. Unless of course it's Madonna, in which case they just shout, "Cover up your pants, woman – you're in your fifties."'

As laughter tilted his head back, she repositioned her bag to what she hoped was the perfect angle. The video camera had a pretty good range, but she always liked to ensure that as much of him was in shot as possible. Hopefully, the sound would be crystal clear despite the background noise. The wives were always so much harder to convince when it was just the honeytrap's word against his.

'Can I buy you a drink?'

OK, so he was being friendly, nice, sweet. It didn't mean that she'd been wrong in her initial prediction that he would resist her charms, it just meant that he'd been brought up to have good manners. The Gucci bondage boots were still safe. She made a play of hesitation before gingerly nodding.

'Thank you. Do you always buy drinks for strange women in bars?'

'Never. And you are definitely strange. Stunning but strange.'

Oh, crap. A tiny wave of Gucci-boot denial symptoms began to rise. There was something in the way he said it – too smooth, too innocent. He was either incredibly genuine or an incredibly good liar – and, in her line of work, the 82 per cent proof of guilt statistic made the latter the most likely option.

While the fashion victim behind the bar poured them another round of drinks, target number one noticed that the people on the other side of him were leaving and immediately claimed custody of their barstools, pulling one of the chrome and black leather seats round for her to climb on to. Chivalrous. Thoughtful. If he could add 'faithful' to that list, then his wife was a lucky woman. She briefly wondered what had instigated his wife's call to the agency. Was he behaving oddly? Had she found incriminating evidence? Was she paranoid? Insecure? Irrational? Or just perceptive and cautious?

A couple of hours later, she was getting closer to the answer. They'd shared a bowl of nachos and done the whole 'career' chat (he was in construction, she was in human resources); they'd done the favourite movies (Him: *Fightclub, Smokin' Aces*. Her: *Pretty Woman*, although she didn't feel it wise to admit that this resulted in a secret – and thankfully brief – teenage ambition involving gainful employment in the sex industry); and they'd worked their way through music, books and holiday destinations. It was getting less like a kind-hearted consolation occasion and more like a first date with every passing minute. The bondage boots were becoming a faded dream when instinct told her it was time to wrap things up and test whether or not he would put the nail in the 'innocent interaction' coffin.

'I should go,' she said, feigning reluctance. 'It was really nice to meet you and thanks for defusing my public humiliation.'

'That's OK. I've really enjoyed meeting you too.'

Her feet groaned as she slid off the stool and back on to four-inch stilettos, and it was only when she reached for her bag that she realised his arm was in front of it. Oh, arse, when had that happened? She'd been too engrossed in Mr Gorgeous to notice that he'd been blocking the lens. Still, hopefully, they had enough to go on and the most important bit wasn't what had already happened, but what would or wouldn't come next.

Suddenly, his hand covered hers and his mouth went into blurt mode. 'Can I ask you something?'

'You want another useless fact so that you'll ooze witty repartee at dinner parties?' she offered with a grin.

'Close. I was . . . I, er . . .'

Don't do it! Don't do it! she silently screamed. Some of

her colleagues loved it when the mark succumbed, seeing it as something between a vigilante success for womankind and a personal validation of their own irresistibility. But not Saffron. Her reaction usually sat somewhere between pragmatism and detachment – however, this time she was erring towards disappointment. There was something about this one, something . . . attractive. Something that made her think that transferring to that fictitious job in human resources and making this a real date wouldn't be too much of a hardship.

'. . . wondering if I could see you again. Maybe have dinner?'

And there it was. The top half of the guillotine had been raised, he was on his knees with his neck perfectly positioned in the carved-out semi-circle, and she was holding the rope. Time for the final act.

'Sure, I'd love that,' she said, beaming, before pausing, as if she'd just been struck by a ridiculous thought. 'I hope you don't mind, but can I just check something? It's just that, well, I've been burned before in this situation.'

'Sure, anything.'

The rope was slipping . . . slipping . . .

'You're not married, engaged or already seeing someone, are you? Sorry if that's too blunt, but I just wanted to check.'

The untrained eye wouldn't have noticed the fleeting look of panic that crossed his eyes, the split second pause or the jaw-clenching resolution of someone who was preparing to lie.

'I'm separated. Have been for a long time. We've both moved on and put it behind us, but I haven't met anyone else yet. Until now . . .'

Ugh, he was good. The effortless duplicity instantly cancelled out every positive thought she'd had, so much so that she almost smiled as she mentally let go of that rope, and the top half of the guillotine came crashing down . . .

Five

'You've got Stacey and her 32 double-humungous in changing room one, a bit of an unusual crotchless knickers in changing room two and the woman over there has her gusset in a twist about a basque that she says is incorrectly sized.'

'I've told you before, Cammy, straight men should never use the word "gusset" – it's just wrong on every level.'

'You're right. I'm away back to the testosterone section to beat my chest and grunt in a manly fashion.'

Mel laughed as she watched her sales director walk off with an exaggerated cowboy swagger towards the stands that were laden with Calvin Klein and Armani boxers, then she nipped into the office-cum-staff-room area behind the sexy-nightwear stand to ditch her coat and bag. A quick brush through her russet-coloured locks (inspired by Debra Messing, circa *Will & Grace*), a rapid dab of nude lippy, a smooth-down of her purple, boned pencil dress (looked designer but bought for £50 on eBay) and she was back out into the midst of the rich, opulent, deep reds, golds and blacks of the shop floor. The concept behind the design of her beloved lingerie boutique had been a fusion of French vintage chic and gothic seductiveness – overstuffed Louis XV-style bergère armchairs, elaborate chandeliers, gilt fixtures and dramatic clashes of colour – but the end result sat somewhere between a Parisian, eighteenth-century whorehouse and the place that brocade came to die. Mel adored every sumptuous, magnificent inch of it.

'There's no way this is a 40DD. I've been a 40DD for years and I can't get it to even meet across the tits,' she of the twisted gusset announced to everyone within earshot.

How many other people had a conversation to rival that one as a starter to the working day, Mel mused as a surge of contentment focused her mind on the job in hand. Or rather, in at least two hands. Or possibly two small hammocks.

Like a highly trained craftsman, Mel surveyed the scene in front of her and mentally estimated the scale of the problem – there was no way on earth that the assets of the platinum-blonde, fifty-something woman in front of her were even a fraction less than a 44F. Tact and diplomacy came into play as she retrieved a specimen of the correct size from a nearby shelf. 'I'm so sorry about that – it's the new French range. The quality and cut is exquisite but I do think the sizing is definitely on the small side. Why not slip into changing room three over there and try this one – I'm sure it'll be perfect for you.'

Sails deflated of wind by Mel's soothing, reassuring tones, the blonde harrumphed in a mollified manner and headed off to try on La Femme Dangereux in a racy shade of scarlet.

A smile played on Mel's lips. This is why she loved her shop. Well, technically it belonged to Suze, Joe and Karl too, but, although it was a joint venture, she was solely responsible for every inch, penny and thong of it.

La Femme, Le Homme had been open for two years now and was one of a kind in Glasgow. Situated across the road from her flat in an old converted court building on the slightly less exorbitant edge of the upmarket shopping district, Merchant City, it specialised in gorgeous underwear for both men *and* women. It was a huge gamble at the start. Business managers, industry insiders and marketing consultants had repeatedly warned her that women would be too embarrassed to shop for their undies in the same store as big hairy-arsed men. Likewise those 'big hairy-arsed men' wouldn't want to browse the Y-front section with women only a few yards away.

In fact, the opposite had turned out to be true.

The shop had become a magnet for all types of blokes. There were the metrosexuals who wanted good-quality underwear that came with the added bonus that there were invariably hot-looking chicks across in the female section. It was a huge hit with the bashful middle-aged blokes who wanted to treat their wives to something delectable but were too embarrassed to go into a shop that just sold ladies' stuff. And yes, there was the very occasional perv who just wanted a cheap thrill, but they had mostly been weeded out thanks to the photo stills taken on the surveillance camera at the front door and aligned on a bulletin board in the back office in what was the lingerie equivalent of the Sex Offenders Register. One sign of a familiar face and Cammy was enlisted to suggest gently that the culprit shop for his pleasures elsewhere.

The female section of the shop was every bit as successful. In a society where it was perfectly acceptable to go clubbing in little more than a bra and boy shorts, the girls who frequented La Femme had absolutely no embarrassment about sharing the space, and, in fact, the abundance of attractive men in the male section was often an incentive

28

for clients to deliberate loudly and at length between two equally attractive and sexy garments. Countless times Mel had watched with amusement as a girl approached a hot guy, held up two gorgeous ensembles and then asked him which one he'd prefer his girlfriend to wear. No girlfriend? Oh, that's a shame. Would you like to grab a coffee? Honestly, they were wonderfully, hilariously shameless. An invitation to her first customer wedding had yet to drop through the gilt letterbox, but Mel knew of at least three or four couples who had hooked up over the unisex-briefs rail.

A quick glance around assured her that everything was in place, switched on and tidy. But then, wasn't it always when Cammy was in charge? It had been a happy day when he'd charged in carrying two large cardboard boxes of late stock, tripped over a bra rack that was waiting to be mounted and ended up in a seriously convoluted position involving 250 miscellaneous G-strings and a kettle. That morning they could have renamed the shop Bedlam Central – twenty-four hours until opening and there was still a week's worth of work to be done. Karl and Joe and a few of their guys were still wiring, painting and plumbing (one of the perks of a family construction business); Josie the sexagenarian cleaner was screaming, 'Yer a no-good wanker!' at a vacuum cleaner; Suze was lying on the floor trying to put a display of peephole bras in size order; and Mel was having a hot flush in the corner, while arguing with American Express over the credit-card terminal that had just turned a test transaction of a tenner into an account deduction of ten grand. And now she had a potential accident liability case on her hands. What was the going rate for two broken legs inflicted on a FedEx delivery guy?

Apparently, it was a cup of tea, half an hour of grov-elling and a tearful request not to sue. Or it might have been the peephole bras that did the trick. Either way, half an hour later, Cammy, having regained the feeling below his knees, announced that they were his last drop-off of the day anyway and pitched in to help, obviously spotting a killer job opportunity when he saw one. It worked. His charm, diligence and good humour landed him a temporary post in the blokes' section. Two years later, he was still there and traded his managerial title – awarded after six months of devoted employment when he moved to the position vacated by Suze – for his self-penned accolade, Director of Sack and Crack Support Services.

At least a dozen of her regular customers (both male and female) were hopelessly in love with him, a situation that she reckoned boosted profits by at least five per cent.

Oh, and Josie, the outrageous cleaner with the complete inability to edit anything that came out of her gob, was now a full-time assistant with the complete inability to edit anything that came out of her gob. But, like Cammy, the customers adored her.

'Don't panic, I'm here!' she announced as she stormed in the door with a dramatic flourish. As always, she was dressed in black from head to black spike-heeled leather boots. ('When you get to my age, it's one funeral after another so you're as well being dressed for it,' she'd once glibly informed Mel.) 'Cammy, love, try to restrain yourself – I know I'm looking irresistible today.'

'Will do, Josie – but if you see me walking with a limp . . .'

Roaring with laughter, Josie passed Mel, pausing to give her a kiss on the cheek as she headed to the staff room.

Mel was still smiling when her first paying customer of the day materialised from changing room one.

'I'll take these and three bottles of the strawberry nipple oil please.'

'Hey, Stacey, good to see you! How's things?' Stacey

Summers, pole dancer, weekly customer and absolute sweet-heart with a body any woman would kill for – with or without the fruit-flavoured nipples – emerged from a fitting room. She was just one of the wide spectrum of women that Mel had come to know and genuinely like – everything from strippers, to lawyers, to dinner ladies to members of the local WI (and no, that particular group's cash transactions couldn't be traced back to them).

Stacey leaned over to give Mel a hug. 'Knackered. It's only two weeks until I go to LA so I'm pulling double shifts to make some extra money. I swear to God, my buttock muscles are about to snap.'

'It'll be worth it, hon – if that arse isn't in the next *Baywatch* movie, there's no justice in this world.'

'That's exactly what I've been telling her,' announced a voice from the back. The platinum blonde with the dangerous corset joined them and placed the silky number on the pile on the counter. 'And I'll take this too, love – you were right, this one fits perfectly. They don't half make them small those French.'

Stacey rolled her eyes in amusement. 'Mel, this is my mum, Senga. Mum, this is Mel.'

'Pleased to meet you, Senga. Your girl is gorgeous,' Mel said with a smile.

'Aye, looks just like me when I was that age. Think I could get away with some of your erotic dancing now I've got my sexy basque here?' She cackled, giving Stacey a playful nudge that almost sent her flying into a table of Elle Macpherson's bras and matching cami-knickers.

'And to think I was worried that it might be a bit embarrassing shopping here with my mother,' Stacey deadpanned.

Mel smiled and took twenty per cent off the total bill. Stacey had brought in so many new customers over the years that she deserved the discount. Besides, the dancer

31

needed every penny she could muster for her trip to Hollywood. She'd been invited there by a recent customer in her club who claimed to be a big-shot producer in the States, and had decided to take him up on his invitation to audition for a small role in his next movie.

The general consensus was that there was a) a fifty per cent chance that he was a fraudster; b) a thirty per cent chance that he wanted her to appear in a movie with a title along the lines of *The Plumber Plunges Deep*; c) a nineteen per cent chance that he'd sell her to international sex-traffickers; and d) a one per cent chance that he was legit and genuine and that he really did think she had the perfect look for the part. Time and the local Blockbuster store would tell.

Pink glossy La Femme bags in hand, Stacey and her mum were just about out the door when Cammy spotted them.

'Bye, Stacey . . . and remember, if they're looking for a young stud to play the handyman, I'm the very guy.'

'No chance, love,' she bantered, 'they like them good-looking out there.'

Her mother's chuckles could be heard all the way down Ingram Street.

The door had barely shut when it swung open again and Suze entered at speed.

'What? What is it? What's happened? Oh no, don't tell me . . .' Mel blurted.

'Nothing! Nothing! Just had one too many espressos this morning and had to get out of the salon before anxiety made me spontaneously combust and short circuit the sunbed tubes. By the way, that new bloke from *Blaggart* is in and he has hairs where no man should ever have hairs.'

'More information than I need there, Suze,' Mel replied with a grin. The truth was she had a bit of a thing for the new guy in the cop show, *Blaggart*, a young, hard-nosed detective with authority issues and a bad-boy lifestyle. Yep, if she wasn't married she would definitely . . . Anyway, back to the present.

'The new uniform is great, Suze. For a frazzled basket-case you're looking pretty gorgeous.'

The scarlet cheongsam, coupled with red kitten heels, was Suze's new choice of work-wear for the staff in her salon, Pluckers, next door. When it had become clear that La Femme, Le Homme was going to be a success, the girls had invested in the adjacent empty unit, and Suze, a trained beautician, had moved in there to manage it. Now it was a thriving hub of plucking, tweezing, freezing and beauti-fying that embraced the same principles as La Femme, Le Homme – unisex, funky, trendy, with a hugely diverse clien-tele.

Before Suze could reply, a voice interjected from the side. 'I'll have these please.'

It took Suze and Mel a few seconds to process the situ-ation, but the bullet points were: exceptionally tall female, long black curls, holding several pairs of crotchless knickers in various colours, well dressed, huge hands, deep voice, pearls wound around neck balancing delicately on what was definitely an Adam's apple.

Mel didn't even bat a false eyelash as she took the purchases and wrapped them in tissue, before ringing up the cost on the till. The customer paid by credit card (account holder name on card: George Dullard) and then waltzed out of the shop with a sunny smile.

'That may be up there in the running for most unusual event of the day,' Mel mused.

'Nope, that is.' Suze was pointing in the direction of the window, through which they had the perfect view of Mr Crotchless Knickers meeting up with what was obviously her/his partner, the one who had just come out of the unisex beauty salon next door.

They paused for a long, lingering snog on the pavement.

'Bloody hell, and I really fancied that guy from *Blaggart*.'

As the lovebirds strolled off into the seething metropolis, Suze decided that the audience's attention had been diverted from her plight for far too long. 'Hello? Sister-in-law in a flux here!' she demanded.

'Sorry, Suze, so have you heard anything yet?'

'They just phoned, said I've to go into their office this afternoon to discuss it.'

'So what does that mean? What's to discuss?' Mel's brow furrowed in consternation. She was sure her brother-in-law would never cheat. There couldn't possibly be anything to report.

'They wouldn't tell me on the phone. Said it's company policy to discuss everything face to face. Wouldn't even give me a hint as to whether I should be relieved or crushed, so I thought I'd just go for blind fucking panic until I see them.'

'Honey, it's going to be fine. They're going to say that absolutely nothing happened and you're going to go home, love Karl, and never ever tell him that you're a suspicious cow whose morals are in the gutter,' she joked, in a vain attempt to defuse Suze's panic.

Wearily, Suze rested her head against the bosom of a mannequin wearing a sheer leopard-print negligee over matching chiffon pants. 'You're right, I'm a horrible person who deserves nothing but scorn. But what if he fell for it? I know it's a bit late but the consequences of this are just beginning to sink in. I mean, what if this is it, Mel? What if it's all over?'

Six

Think diversionary thoughts. Think diversionary thoughts. Need new Hoover bags. Must check filters on cooker hood. VAT return to be done by Saturday. Husband is shagging another woman. Nooooooo. Car needs MOT. And new tyres. And one of those air-freshener thingies. And . . .

'How can I help you?' asked the heavy-set bloke behind the big old mahogany security desk at the front door.

Suze's first rational, cohesive thought (right after her simultaneous urges to faint and make a run for it) was: Fuck, he looks like something out of *The Sopranos*.

'I'm here to see Gloria Winters at Honeytrap.'

Sopranos guy now looked at her with a depressing mixture of pity and scorn. Great. What little scraps of self-possession and dignity she had left had now been battered to death by public humiliation.

'Sixth floor, first door on the left.'

The creaky old cage-style elevator, typical of the ancient, architecturally beautiful buildings in Glasgow's city centre, trundled upwards at a snail's pace, as if trying to protect its inhabitants from their fate for as long as possible. Why had this ever, ever seemed like a good idea? Mel had been right, it was certifiably insane. But Suze had been so sure, so convinced . . .

Trundling, still trundling, she gave herself an internal bollocking. This had to stop. All her life she'd been impulsive, spontaneous, sometimes even reckless. If something seemed like a great idea, then bam! It was done. Buying the salon, nipping off for weekends in Paris and throwing parties for thirty people with only a couple of hours' notice had worked out great. The orange leather sofas that lasted six weeks in the living room and the trekking holiday to Nepal (she didn't even own shoes that had less than a three-inch heel) not so much. Likewise the flirtation with Botox and the cream suede trousers.

Oh, and the bit about sending another woman out to seduce her husband.

The sound of her rapping on the glass partition of the door echoed down the hall and made her teeth rattle. Or perhaps that was just fear.

Why had she come alone? Mel had offered to be with her and provide support, but the knowledge that the solidarity would come with an overtone of disapproval had made her refuse. For a moment she wished she could be just like Mel: optimistic, sweet, caring, and in possession of a glass that was interminably half bloody full. Sure, her sister-in-law could be overcautious and entirely too trusting, but she always saw the best in people, and in every aspect of her life she found a way of overcoming the negatives and returning to a balanced state of calm, happiness and karmic zen.

But Suze? Already today she'd been frantic, terrified, indignant, furious, bold, courageous, panicked, confident, defiant and insecure . . . and it was only four o'clock.

Hoover bags. MOT. Air-freshener thingy.

She just needed to know, then everything would get back to normal and she could start to focus on making her marriage work again.

'Mrs Marshall?' *Sopranos* guy's only slightly less scary sister looked up from her desk as Suze entered. 'Just go on through – Gloria is ready for you.'

Ready for what? Ready to set my mind at ease? Ready to ruin my life?

With grey hair that was pulled back into a loose pony-tail and curves that were on the rotund side of bodacious, Gloria Winters looked like the kind of rotund, jolly woman who normally spent the day at home cooking biscuits for a large collective of grandchildren. In fact, she'd informed Suze on their first meeting that she was a hard-nosed ex-policewoman who had survived the sexism that was rife in sixties and seventies law enforcement, overcome the death of two husbands and the desertion of another and raised three children almost single-handedly while dealing with financial stress, childcare issues and the worst of Glasgow's criminal underbelly. Suze had tried not to appear freaked out when Gloria confided that she missed the good old days.

'Would you like a coffee? Water? Anything before we get started?' she asked, as Suze settled into one of the two black leather chairs in front of the huge teak desk.

'Unless you've got Prozac or a bottle of gin under there, then I'd rather just begin,' Suze replied with a half-hearted smile. She scrutinised Gloria's face for clues – did she look concerned? Jubilant? Like a woman who was going to announce that no illicit activities had taken place? Or did she look like she was about to deliver the speech of doom and then slip Suze the number of a decent, affordable hit-man? Her throat spasmed.

Hoover bags. MOT. Air freshener.

Don't cry. Don't you dare cry.

'OK.' Gloria took a deep breath and adopted a very businesslike tone.

Suze didn't expect anything else, given that Gloria had advised from the start that she liked to keep all inter-actions strictly professional as she was there to be her clients' investigative adviser not their new best friend.

'As you know, an agent was sent to meet your husband at Club 80 last night . . .'

Suze had a sense of déjà vu and then realised that listening to Gloria was like settling down to an episode of *Crimewatch*. And incidentally, dear Lord, why had her nerves suddenly moved to the outside of her skin. Do not throw up.

Gloria reached for the remote control that lay next to the telephone on the right-hand side of her immaculately ordered work-space.

'Saffron is one of our most experienced girls and was able to engage your husband in conversation almost imme-diately on entering the premises.'

Oh, fuck, she was going to throw up. A vice had appar-ently now attached itself to her abdominal muscles and was twisting them in a circular motion.

The press of one of Gloria's chubby fingers sparked the plasma TV screen on the wall into life. The picture was grainy at first, the angle odd, but Suze could clearly see a male and female from the neck down. The action zig-zagged fiercely as Gloria fast forwarded then paused.

The room started to spin around Suze's head. OK, don't panic. He was just talking to her. Doesn't mean he did anything wrong. Doesn't mean he betrayed her. Doesn't mean . . . Oh, fucking hoover bags. Don't cry. Don't cry.

'The conversation up until this point has been largely general interaction and casual conversation with no specific overt flirting or comments that one would consider to be unacceptable.'

Suze resisted blurting out that, in the case of her husband, *any* fucking conversation with a female who looked like Saffron would, in her estimation, be deemed unacceptable. Bastard. How could he? Please don't do this, Karl, come on . . .

Her silent screams at the TV were interrupted again by the voice from *Crimewatch*. 'However . . .'

Nooooo, don't say however! However can't be good!

'. . . at this point the interaction escalates to a level that you may find uncomfortable.'

For the first time in years, tears swam in the bottom of Suze's eyes, preparing to gush in torrents that no water-proof mascara would be capable of withstanding. She didn't do tears. She didn't do hysterics. Normally she got by on equal doses of jaded cynicism and fatalistic acceptance of reality. But now, yep, she was definitely going to cry. If only she'd brought Mel.

Gloria pressed the play button again.

The screen cleared and this time the side profiles of two figures could clearly be seen. Suddenly, a flesh-coloured mass covered the camera. A hand? An arm?

'Can I ask you something?' the male was saying now. Oh dear God, make it be 'What time is it?' or 'Can I have directions?' Preferably followed by '. . . back to my beloved wife who's sitting home waiting for me.'

Shit, why was that obstruction there? She wanted to see his face, see every line, ever nuance as he stepped into the land of the cheating scum.

'Close. I was . . . I, er . . . wondering if I could see you again. Maybe have dinner?'

Suze gagged, her constricted throat snapped shut and she squirmed as trickles of sweat ran down her back. Head between knees – she definitely wanted to put her head between her knees.

He'd done it. He'd done it. And it was so, so wrong. Wrong.

It was . . . wrong.

The woman was speaking again now. *'I hope you don't mind, but can I just check something? It's just that, well, I've been burned before in this situation. You're not married, engaged or already seeing someone, are you? Sorry if that's too blunt, but I just wanted to check.'*

The flesh-tone mass that was partially obscuring the lens moved now and attached itself to one of the female's hands. Her other hand was busy reaching to her mane of chocolate-brown hair and casually tossing it back from her face, just in time for the fatal blow.

Suze gasped.

The passing glimmer of confusion melted away, replaced by comprehension. She saw everything now, saw it all so clearly, saw the life that she'd had up until now slip away because after this she knew one thing – nothing would ever be the same again.

'I'm separated. Have been for a long time. We've both moved on and put it behind us, but I haven't met anyone else yet. Until now . . .'

A scream stuck in her strangled larynx and suddenly she was so, so glad that she'd come alone. Because that face on the screen, the one that belonged to someone who was taking his marriage and tossing it into the skip for the sake of a well-stacked brunette he'd never met before was the face of someone she adored.

But it wasn't *her* husband.

It was Mel's.

Seven

'Are you stealing stock again? Only I'm going to have to ask you to return it because if the owner finds out she'll go ballistic and, trust me, you don't want to see that – she's a dragon.'

Mel pulled her head out of the large cardboard box in the middle of the office and raised an eyebrow in the direction of her insubordinate employee. 'Someone has to road-test the products, and don't take this the wrong way, my sweet, but I don't think you've got the legs for it.'

Slouched against the doorway, Cammy almost spurted his mouthful of Diet Coke. 'Don't underestimate me – you've no idea how great my legs are. And go for the pale blue, it'll look great.'

Mel held up two bra and knicker sets, identical designs – satin balconette with lace trim and matching briefs – one in peach and one in blue. She then took a brief second to acknowledge how weird yet absolutely normal it seemed to be talking to a man other than her husband about what pants she was going to wear. 'You think?'

She thrust the peach one back in the box. He was right

– with her pale complexion and red hair, peach sometimes tended towards the insipid, whereas blue said 'I'm a tomboy, come and get me.' Actually, it said £39.99 for the set, but trying out the product was a vital part of the job. How could she comment on comfort and durability if she didn't actually wear the products that she sold?

Josie breezed in and enveloped Mel in a huge bear hug. 'Right my darling, I'm off – *arrivederci, ciao, tagliatelle.*'

'Can't believe you'll be away for a month – we're really going to miss you.'

When Josie had first booked time off for her annual sojourn to visit her son and his family in Rome, it had seemed like ages away, yet it had come around so quickly.

'I know, Mel, but I have to go. He's going to be devastated when I pop my clogs and he discovers there's nothing in the will, so I have to give him some kind of happy memories to hold on to ... even if it means living with his overbearing, excruciatingly loud wife for a month. No idea why he'd go for a woman like that.'

Her forty-Lambert-&-Butler-a-day raspy laugh filled the shop as she hugged Cammy and headed out into the Saturday-night city-centre throng.

Mel returned to the serious business of de-tagging her new knickers. Joe would love these. But then, she could wrap three rolls of gaffer tape around her body and he'd love that too. From the moment they met, he had made her feel like the sexiest woman on earth. Well, perhaps not the *exact* moment that they met ... at that particular time, she'd been in the reception of a hotel complex in Fuengirola, begging the manager to open the gift shop so that she could buy balm for the third-degree burns (in hindsight, perhaps just a light scorch) that she'd managed to incur despite having been in the sun for a mere hour and a half while wearing a two-inch layer of SPF 60. She'd made several decisions there and then. From then on, every holiday would involve skis. If the manager didn't find the little old man who worked in the shop within the next thirty seconds, she was prepared to serve time in a Spanish prison for smashing the window. And the tall dark-haired guy standing next to her at the reception was gorgeous.

Ten minutes later, the old man with the shop key had arrived, by which time she and Joe were chatting. Twenty minutes later, she'd agreed to go for a stroll along the beach. It was an incongruous sight – a tall, dark, tanned demigod strolling along with a redhead whose skin matched her hair colour and whose burned thighs were forcing her to adopt the bow-legged gait of a rodeo cowboy.

The subsequent transformation of that Club 18–30 holiday romance into a lifelong commitment went something like:

A) Overexposure to sunlight.
B) Use of local Spanish pain medication renowned for its numbing, analgesic effects: called Sangria.
C) Late-night fumble, abandoned due to pain medication wearing off.
D) Long, romantic night of shared confidences and deep conversation – remembered by both of them as a slurred rant of nonsense that lasted until they both conked out on balcony chairs.
E) Mel waking up next morning looking like the lead role in the *Rocky Horror Show*.
F) Joe thinking she was adorable.
G) Snog. Another fumble.
H) One-week romance, tearful farewell at airport, six-month long-distance relationship.
I) One-way ticket from Lewisham to Glasgow Central.
J) Tearful farewell to beloved parents, whom she now

phoned once a week and visited for occasional weekends.

K) Arrival in very cold Glasgow.

L) Marriage

Eight years later, they were still happy and she thanked God every day that he'd equipped Joe with an attraction gene that went for size-fourteen curves and legs that could really do with being three inches longer.

Cammy pulled his black leather jacket off a chrome hook on the wall and shrugged it on.

'So who is it tonight then? Anneka or Anna?' She couldn't help the grin that went with the question.

To Mel's endless amusement, Cammy was simultaneously dating two women with such similar names that he had an unfortunate habit of getting them confused at the most inopportune moment. There was Anna, a tall, lanky brunette and one of the city's most popular models. And then there was Anneka who was, er, a tall, lanky brunette. And a model. Not that he was doing anything illicit. Apparently, the New York dating system had found its way to Glasgow (via *Sex and the City*), thus Anna and Anneka knew all about each other and were perfectly comfortable about the fact that the relationships were 'non-exclusive', a status that Mel was sure was just another way of saying 'I like you, but not enough that I don't want to see what else is out there'.

'Anneka. We're going out to Mar Hall for the night – charity fashion show. Anneka is donating a dozen struts up and down the catwalk.'

'Staying over?'

He nodded.

'Lucky you,' she said wistfully. Mar Hall was a beautiful country-house hotel on the outskirts of the city, overlooking

44

the river Clyde. Joe had taken her there for her birthday last year and they'd spent the most glorious twenty-four hours of her life basking in luxury and tranquillity.

'Who's lucky?' The voice came from behind Cammy, swiftly followed by the rest of Joe Marshall. The two men shook hands.

'I am, apparently. Night at Mar Hall tonight.'

'With the Barbie twins?' Joe joked.

Cammy laughed. 'Just one of them. I've told you before mate, we're *non-exclusive*, not *all-inclusive*.'

Joe switched his attention to his wife. 'Nice undies – stock or take-home?'

'Take home,' Mel replied playfully.

'God, I love your job.'

Cammy tutted in mock indignation. 'I'll have you know *I* picked those out for her – some credit here please.'

'Wow, you're needy.' Joe laughed. 'Thank you, Cammy – I'll persuade her to give you a pay rise.'

'Excellent. And tell her to be a bit more complimentary about my legs please,' he added as he turned and headed for the front door.

'Be nicer about his legs,' Joe commanded, like it was the most natural thing on earth.

Mel rolled her eyes. 'I'll do my best. Night, Cammy!'

'G'night. See you Monday.'

'Don't ask,' Mel said, as Joe crossed the room and took a bottle of water from the mini-fridge. He was wearing her favourite outfit – tan work boots, jeans, plain white T-shirt. The image went straight to her hormones and she realised with a surge of longing that she could shag him right there and then . . . if it wasn't for the security cameras, obviously.

'You almost ready, babe?'

Waving the blue underwear set in front of her, she

45

nodded. 'Both I and this beautiful example of the superior stock purveyed by this very store will be ready any minute.'

Joe was leaning against her desk now, so she squeezed in beside him to switch the computer off then bent down to get her handbag from the floor. Suddenly a jerking motion pulled her to the left.

'Er, Joe, you do realise that your hand appears to have slipped down the back of my skirt?'

She'd been pulled in close to him now, her back against his front, his lips bearing down on the back of her neck.

'I noticed.'

Small kisses started on the exposed section of her shoulder and worked their way upwards, his hand gently pulling her hair back so that his tongue could slowly trace its way up behind her ear.

'And you do realise that you're now licking my person while I'm in my place of work?'

'I noticed,' he repeated, his breathing heavy now as he pulled her even tighter to him and she felt the pressure of his hard-on squeezing into her back.

Her brain disconnected immediately and allowed her hormones to have full control of her faculties. His free hand was slowly, inch by inch, working her skirt upwards, sending shooting signals of thrill and ecstasy through her tummy.

'And, if I'm not mistaken, my darling wife, this is ovulation week, so it's mandatory that we get it on several times over the next few days.'

Her gasp was enough of an answer.

'Then I think, unless you have any objections, that I'm going to have to attempt fertilisation on this desk before we go home.'

The surge of pure pleasure started somewhere around

her toes and shot upwards, making pitstops at weak knees, tingling nethers, clenched buttocks, hard nipples and the vocal cords that groaned with sheer joy as she nodded.

'Hang on, hang on!' Despite the fact that her skirt was around her waist now, exposing her black lace-top hold-ups and matching cami-knickers, her natural caution kicked in. Breaking free from his clutches, she reached over to switch off the security system. There was no way she wanted this captured on film. Making love to your husband in the privacy of your own office – sexy. Making love to your husband and then taking the chance that the shop could get burgled and the tape stolen and posted on the internet for everyone including parents, granny and former school-teachers to get a close-up view of your muff? Terrifying.

Strutting back over to him, she grinned seductively. 'Now, what was that you were saying about fertilising your wife?'

Joe reached out and pulled her towards him again, kissing her hard and urgently. An involuntary guttural sound came from her throat as she fumbled with the belt on his jeans, before finally wrestling it open and pulling down his zip. She reached inside, feeling the . . .

Brrrrrrrrrrriiiiinnnnnng. The phone made her jump, and she automatically withdrew her hand, eliciting a yelp from Joe as the large onyx costume ring on her hand scratched a part of his anatomy that was looking for action of an entirely different kind.

'Damn! Sorry, babe, sorry, I . . .'

The two of them collapsed into laughter.

Brrrrrrrrrrriiiiinnnnnng.

'Let me just . . .' She reached over to get the phone but suddenly Joe's hand caught hers and guided it to his chest, where he held it tightly on top of his heart.

Brrrrrrrrrrriiiiinnnnnng. 'I love you, Mel. You know that, don't you?'

47

His sincerity took her breath away. It was one of the things she loved most about Joe – he never, ever left her in any doubt about how much he adored her.

Brrrrrrrrrrriiiiinnnnnng.

'And you know I love you right back.'

A clicking noise announced that the answering machine had kicked in and in the background Mel heard her own voice. 'You've reached La Femme, Le Homme – please leave a message and we'll get back to you just as soon as possible.'

All notions of answering the phone now extinguished by lust, her attention had returned to the injury that she'd just inflicted on the love of her life. 'Honey, you do realise that I'm now going to have to kiss this better?' she purred, her head disappearing downwards, downwards . . .

'Mel, it's me.' Suze's voice filled the office and immediately Mel shot back up, far too quickly, the top of her head catching Joe's chin and sending his head thrusting backwards with yet another loud yelp.

'Shit! Sorry! Shit! Shit, there's blood. Oh my God, I've knocked your teeth out. I'VE KNOCKED YOUR TEETH OUT!'

Joe was bent over now, his hand clutched over his mouth, speckles of blood now dripping through his fingers, the rest of his face contorted in pain. Mel reached for the first thing that came to hand and dabbed away the blood. 'Shit, sorry, Joe. Oh my God!' Her eyes were filling up now. Why, oh fucking why was she so fucking clumsy? Now her gorgeous, perfect husband had no teeth and it was all her fault.

'It's OK, it's OK! My teeth are fine.'

Oh dear Lord, thank you.

'I just bit my lip, that's where the blood is coming from,' he slavered, pink saliva running down over his already swelling lip.

48

'Joe, I'm so, so sorry.' A single tear popped out and ran down her right cheek, as she grabbed his cold bottle of water from the desk and held it against his mouth to stop the swelling. How had a romantic, spontaneous act of love between a man and woman somehow managed to turn into grievous bodily harm? And what was worse, *he* was crying now. She'd made a grown man cry! He was . . . hang on.

'Joe Marshall, are you laughing at me?'

She reached over and pulled the medicinal Evian away from his face to see that, yes, indeed, the man with a lip that looked like a Cumberland sausage was laughing at her.

'Mel, you are a complete fucking nightmare.'

Her expression switched from outrage to sheepish. 'I know.'

He reached out to her and wound her into his arms. 'But I love you, babe. Even when you assault me.'

Her eyes were drawn to the pile of fabric that she'd initially used to stem the blood flow. Oh, crap . . .

'And so you should,' she jested. 'What other woman would use sexy blue silk knickers to mop up your wound? At least we'll get to see how they stand up to a boil wash. C'mon, let's go home. Before I inadvertently kill you or maim you for life.'

One by one, she flicked off sockets and lights and was just about to set the alarm code when something struck her. 'Suze's message – what did she say?'

Joe shrugged. 'No idea. I was too busy trying not to pass out from blood loss.'

She nudged him playfully in the ribs – with the emphasis on playfully. She'd done enough damage for one night.

Beep. 'First new message, received today at six fifty-five p.m.'

'Hi, Mel, it's me.' Pause.

49

They looked at each other, Mel doing the female thing that went along the lines of: *'It's Suze, she sounds a little strange, she must have been for the results of that honeytrap thing. Did she sound elated, or traumatised, or sad, or devastated? Must call her back, really worried about her, will go over straight away if she needs me.'*

Meanwhile, Joe was doing the male thing, the one that stopped analysing anywhere past, *'It's Suze.'*

'Hang on a minute, love, let me call her back.'

Experience told him that there was no point in arguing. As much as he was close to his brother, Mel and Suze had developed a bond that was just as tight.

Suze's home number rang out, so Mel tried the mobile. Same result. 'Hi, Suze, it's just me, returning your call – buzz me back when you pick this up.'

Must be in the shower. Or the bath. Or maybe gone for a run, sadistic fitness freak that she was. Or perhaps making mad passionate love to Karl because she'd just discovered that he hadn't been unfaithful in any way whatsoever. Yep, that was it. Now they could put the whole thing behind them, forget it had ever happened and get back to where it used to be.

Suze loved Karl. Karl loved Suze.

Melissa loved Joe. Joe loved Melissa.

She punched in the alarm code and flicked off the office light and, as she reached for her husband's (slightly blood-splattered) hand, she just knew that everything was going to be absolutely fine. Because they all loved each other. And nothing could change that.

Eight

Suze stared at the ringing phone, willing it to stop. The four glasses of Merlot that she'd consumed before working up the courage to call Mel a few moments ago now didn't seem enough to deal with this. She doubted there was enough wine in Glasgow to deal with this. What was she going to say? She'd thought through a dozen different outcomes of the whole honeytrap thing, most of them involving the attachment of electric probes to her husband's genitals while he slept, but never in all the crazy fucked-up outcomes could she have predicted this one.

Joe. Her darling little brother-in-law. It was so easy to see how the mistake had been made. Only eleven months apart in age, Joe and Karl could easily have been twins. Standing next to each other, you could see the differences: Joe was an inch or so taller, Karl a little broader; Joe wore his hair slightly longer and Karl already had a few whispers of grey. But apart? They were mistaken for each other all the time.

She didn't even realise she was refilling her wineglass, too busy trying to process the questions that screeched through the synapses of the brain cells that weren't yet too soaked in France's finest to function.

Why had Joe been in the bar on his own that night? The brothers had a standard Friday-night routine – circuit training then over to Club 80. Joe would stay for one beer, Karl usually met up with some of the guys from the five-a-side team and stayed a little longer. Had there been a change of plan? Karl hadn't mentioned anything but, then, Karl barely told her anything any more, so that wasn't too surprising. Hang on, while Joe was busy letting his dick do the talking, where was Karl? He'd been out all night and when he came home he'd said something about being sore from too much exercise. Or had that been a lie? Was this all one big twisted lie?

Why in the name of wandering fucking penises would Joe ever, *ever* have even considered cheating on Mel? Was this the first time? Or had he done it before? Were they both having affairs? Were the Marshall brothers simultaneously shagging their way around the single female population of the city? How did she even begin to deal with this? And the biggest question of all – how would she tell Mel? *Could* she tell her? She'd even contemplated denial – deny, deny, deny. Deny that there had been anything wrong, deny that the honeytrap mission had been carried out. She could say that when she got to the office they'd informed her that the mission had been aborted because . . . because . . . the honeytrap girl had copped off with someone else before she got to Karl. Tut, tut, you just couldn't get decent sex bait these days.

Another slug of wine. She felt sick as the red liquid sloshed into her stomach. If she could rewind the last week and call the whole thing off, then she knew, without a single doubt, that she would. This was information that she didn't want to possess. Oblivion was a far, far more appealing

52

option than this. Nothing could take away from the absolute certainty that this was going to destroy her best friend. And it was all her fault. Mel had warned her not to do it, begged her to change her mind, but, oh no, she didn't bloody listen. She was 'Sort-it-out Suze'! A take-charge, no-nonsense, know-the-facts, bolshy fucking idiot whose doubts about her own marriage had now veered off like a drugged-up joyrider and crashed right into the roundabout sign-posted 'Mel & Joe's Eternal Bliss'.

She couldn't do this. She couldn't. But then . . . How could she not? She choked as another gulp of wine took her oesophagus by surprise. How could she let her best friend be with someone who would cheat on her at the drop of a 32GG's hat?

Joe. Bastard. Perhaps she should tell Karl first and find out if he knew. She could make up some story as to how she'd found out and grill Karl on whether this was a regular occurrence. Maybe Karl could have a word with him, thump him around the head with a blunt object and tell him not to be so bloody stupid. Wasn't that what big brothers were for? Yes, that could work. Karl could sort out Joe, Joe would return to being faithful lovely husband of the year, Mel would never need to know any different and they could all just plod along as before, a happy, care-free little foursome . . . There was no point even finishing that train of thought because it was never going to work. The truth was out there and another glass of Merlot wasn't going to make it go away. But, reaching for the bottle, she decided she'd give it a try anyway.

The phone rang again, making her jump and spill a few drops of wine on the chunky, solid oak table. She imme-diately reached for a wipe to remove it. It was the neat-freak in her. For Suze to ignore spills in her minimalist home, overlook cushions that were out of place or forget to take her make-up off, she'd have to be sedated with a stun gun.

Housekeeping disaster averted, she slumped back down in the chair, her stare fixed now on the ringing telephone. It had to be Mel. It *had* to be. She should answer it and say that she needed to speak to her and meet up and get the whole business of destroying her life over and done with.

Stop ringing. Please stop ringing. I've changed my mind and I no longer have the nerve to speak to you. She let her head fall on to her arms on the table. This was not a good place to be. Shitsville. Turn right at Cheating Bastard Boulevard, straight into Temptation Street, left through Devastation Alley, turn left at the Horrific Truth Highway and *voila* – Shitsville Central.

This couldn't go on. If she was going to tell Mel tonight, then she had to do it right now.

She pressed the green button to open the message that had just arrived.

MEL MB.
HEY BABE, HOPE ALL OK. BEEN TRYING TO CALL BUT NO REPLY. ON WAY HOME, WILL BUZZ YOU AGAIN WHEN I GET THERE. WORRIED ABOUT YOU. LUV YA, MX

Head back down, another groan. This couldn't go on. She couldn't deal with this in such an immature, pathetic way. Getting pished was not a responsible adult reaction to a crisis of this magnitude. It was time to deal with this, to meet it head on and face the consequences of her attempt to set up her husband and Joe's betrayal.

Back ram-rod straight now, she inhaled deeply and shook her head to clear it.

Time to call Mel. There was no point in putting it off

until tomorrow and, besides, the next day was Sunday and as always they'd all arranged to meet for brunch at their favourite bar.

There was no way she could face that with both a hangover and a life-changing secret in her head.

Time to . . .

Her hand had been only inches from her phone when it had burst into life again, the shock making her snap her limb back like an elastic band.

Mel's number flashed on the screen.

'Are you going to answer that?'

It was difficult to know if the yelp of surprise or the expression of guilt came first, but she followed them both up with a weak, hesitant smile. 'Hey, you, I didn't even hear you coming in.' She was looking directly at her husband's face, yet, in the light of recent events (i.e. drama and vino overloads), all she could see was Joe's.

'Are you OK? You look —' he was staring at her quizzically now '— either upset or wellied.'

'Wellied. Long day at the office, empty stomach.'

His sigh was long and lasted all the way from the doorway until he pulled out a chair and sat down across from her, looking all businesslike in his smart grey suit and his shiny shoes.

'Suze, it's probably not a good time, but I think we need to talk.'

Her eyes flickered heavenwards as she had a private conversation with whoever lived up there along the lines of 'Dear God, you have got to be fucking kidding me!' For months she'd been trying to talk to him, trying to make him open up to her and now, now that she'd set him up, and discovered things she could have happily lived her whole life without knowing, *now* he wanted to talk to her?

'Suze, we have to sort out what's been going on. I know

55

I've been distant lately and I'm sorry, Suze, but, you know, work, the whole kids thing . . .'

'Don't even mention that just now, Karl, because I swear my heart couldn't take it.'

The tears were flowing now, coursing down her face, such an unusual development for his wife that it seemed to flip an internal switch that moved him from pragmatic and measured to genuinely concerned. She couldn't remember ever having cried in front of him before. But then, at that precise moment, she couldn't remember what she had for breakfast that morning either.

In a split second, he was round the table, crouching down next to her, wrapping his beautiful, big builder's arms around her and pulling her head on to ten inches of rock-hard shoulder. 'Sssshhhh, baby, it's OK.'

It had been months since she'd heard him speak to her like this: caring, tender. The sobs were racking her chest now, huge big thunderous gasps that made every inch of her shake violently.

'Suze, it's OK. I'm so sorry. But it'll be OK. We'll fix it.'

Fix it? This one was definitely, completely un-bloody-fixable.

Why now? Why did he have to do this *now*? Why couldn't he have said this last week, before the call, before the set-up, before she'd even heard of Gloria whatsername?

'Karl, I . . . I . . .' It was no use, she couldn't get the words out. It was time for honesty and full disclosure but her mouth was refusing to co-operate. 'I . . .'

'Ssssssh, Suze, it doesn't matter. Baby, it's going to be fine. Come on, let's go upstairs. You need to lie down and then we can talk later.'

He stood up, taking her with him and then gently swept his arm under her and lifted her in the air. It was like the closing scene from *An Officer and a Gentleman* only without the white suit and with the very real possibility that the heroine would throw up all over her hero's back.

A minute later, they were upstairs and she was lying on top of the duvet when Karl disappeared into the en suite then returned with the chrome waste bin and placed it on the floor beside her. He climbed on to his side of the bed, wiped away the tears that were still rolling down her face and kissed her gently. 'I love you, Suze. And I know it's been rough, but we'll get through it. We'll get through anything.'

The sound of the phone punctuated the end of his sentence and he reached back to grab the receiver at his side of the bed.

Suze shot her arm out to stop him. 'Leave it, it's just Mel.'

'Don't you want to talk to her?' he asked, puzzled. This was a new one. In the eight years that his wife had known his sister-in-law, she'd never, ever avoided her calls. In fact, on two occasions his wife had even broken off in the middle of having sex to talk to Mel.

'Not right now. Tomorrow . . . Tomorrow will be soon enough.'

Nine

There was nowhere else Mel would rather be on a Sunday morning than Princess Square, the upmarket mall on Glasgow's Buchanan Street that hosted a cornucopia of designer shops, bars and restaurants, all topped with a glorious atrium that let the sun streak through, shooting rays of light off the brass banisters that bordered all four floors.

'No Suze and Karl yet,' she observed as they weaved their way through to the corner table in the top-floor restaurant that, for two hours every week, belonged to them. It was the one golden rule: Sunday was always, always her day off. They'd been coming here for years now and knew the waiting staff so well that without even asking a large pot of coffee materialised in front of them.

'Thanks, Jason – how was uni this week?'

Jason, the waiter, was in his third year studying political science and Mel loved him for his . . .

'Sucked.'

. . . blunt, straight-talking ways.

'How was the knicker world?' he replied, equally mono-tone.

'Ups and downs.'

Joe shook his head woefully at her shockingly bad pun as Jason headed off to collect their brunch. Mel's eyes followed him. 'Wait for it . . . Wait for it . . .'

Jason was twenty feet away when he suddenly emitted a loud guffaw and turned back to Mel.

'Good one. Ups and downs.'

'And there he goes. Should it scare us that he'll probably end up running the country?'

'There's always emigration,' Joe replied, liberating a piece of bread from the basket on the thick walnut table and dipping it in a tiny ramekin of olive oil.

'Soooo . . . What do you think he'll look like?' Mel's eyes lit up as she asked.

'Pretty much the way he does now, only with a suit and ten bodyguards.'

Her brow furrowed. 'Who are you talking about?'

'Sorry, I thought we were still on Jason for Prime Minister. Who are you talking about?'

'Joe junior! Or Josephine junior, depending on what way the chromosomes go.'

'Ah, we're back on that then,' he replied with a conspiratorial grin.

After waking early and indulging in an hour of leisurely sexual activities, they'd lain in bed for two hours, daydreaming aloud about what they hoped would be imminent parenthood. It was only their second month of trying, but Mel already had her hopes up that they'd be in Mothercare before the year was out.

'I think black hair like me, green eyes like you, and with any luck he'll get my height because otherwise we can rule out any possibility of a career in basketball.'

She couldn't help but smile as the image formed in her head of a little guy in bright-red Converse boots picking a basketball out of the newly smashed hole in the green-house. Greenhouse. They definitely had to get one of those – although an actual house might be a bonus too. A two-bedroom flat in the middle of Glasgow city centre probably wasn't the most family-friendly place to raise a child.

'And if it's a girl . . . Change the subject, quickly, here they come.'

Telling her brother- and sister-in-law about their plans to start a family were on the To Do List, but languishing somewhere near the bottom in between 'clear out linen cupboard' and 'hose down wheelie bin'. Yes, she realised it made her a big fat coward, but she preferred to think of it as pain and drama avoidance. The subject of children was the one topic of conversation that everyone knew never, ever to raise in Suze and Karl's company, because for them it was a raw wound, a mutual source of conflict that showed no signs of resolution. For Mel to break the news about their plans just seemed, well, tactless. Like rubbing their noses in it. There would be plenty of time to find a way to break the news gently after it became a reality and there was an actual baby on the way.

But, in the meantime, back to more pressing issues – how did Suze look? Whoa – rough. Three words: sunglasses, indoors, January. Suze normally took the piss out of people who wore shades indoors no matter what the month, so there was clearly a serious problem here. But . . . it didn't seem to be with Karl, because they were definitely holding hands and, had the meeting at the Honeytrap Agency had a negative outcome, Mel had no doubt that Suze would have handled it in her typically measured, constructive way – by making him wear a sand-wich board declaring 'I'm A Cheating Bastard' and nudging him across the restaurant using the encouragement of an electric cattle prod.

Yay, so she'd been right all along – Karl was innocent of all charges. Despite her faith in her brother-in-law's monogamy, she'd been worried the night before. After half a dozen unanswered calls, she'd been ready to put her coat on and head over to Suze's when Karl finally answered and said she was sleeping. That, combined with the current hand-holding (and overlooking Suze's impersonation of an American rap star), proved that all had turned out well and life was back to normal.

She stood up and leaned over to give Kanye West a hug.

'Hi, hon, sore head?'

'Too much of the red grape juice last night. There are things vibrating inside my skull that I definitely don't think should be there.'

'But apart from that everything is . . . ?'

Mel left the question hanging, knowing that Suze would pick up on the hidden meaning and run with it.

'Everything is –' was it just Mel's imagination or did a teardrop just squeeze out from under Suze's Ray-Bans? Imagination – Suze *never* cried '– fine.'

Another two coffee cups materialised into the space in front of them.

'Morning, Jason,' Karl said chirpily. 'So did you finally get it together with Latisha?'

'Naw, man, she's still playing hard to get.'

Mel marvelled again at her brother-in-law's inherent ability to get into the lives of everyone he met. Obviously Karl ransacked the womb of the extrovert, joking and volatile genes, leaving Joe with the more caring, quiet, steady ones.

'I'm telling you, Jase, you're just going to have to go for it – ask her straight out.'

'But it'll be a beamer if she knocks me back, man. That'd be seriously uncool.'

'Yeah, mate, but sometimes you just have to take a risk in life – it adds a bit of excitement and drama.'

Mel felt Joe's hand grab hers under the table and smiled. Not for the first time, and much as she adored Karl, she reflected that she was glad she was with the decidedly non-risky, grounded brother. There was a lot to be said for trust, predictability and a man you could always depend on.

Ten

'Will you sack me if I tell you that you look like shit this morning?'

'Yes, Avril.'

'OK, then – loving your look today, boss. Great how you managed to get your eyes to match your dress.'

Suze glanced down at her scarlet cheongsam and resolved to fire her second-in-command. And she would, just as soon as she could find another fully trained beauty therapist who was an absolute genius on make-up and nails, a thorough professional on lasers and wax and who – in Suze's absence – ran the place like clockwork while maintaining a great rapport with all the regular customers. Oh, and who also happened to be the daughter of Josie from La Femme, Le Homme and therefore extra-loyal to the company because of her family connections. On second thoughts, it would probably just be easier to develop a thick skin to Avril's brutal honesty. After all, it was clearly a genetic flaw in her blood line.

'Anything you want to talk about?' Avril asked tenderly.

Suze shook her head.

'Thank fuck for that, you know I hate all that sharing stuff. Stay in here, you'll scare the customers and I'll get one of the girls to bring you a coffee as soon as we get organised. I'll take your clients this morning – I think they like me better anyway.' Avril realised that her attempt to lighten the mood was failing miserably, so she did an about-turn and headed out of the staff room and back on to the shop floor.

Suze slumped back in her chair. She knew that she should have argued, taken charge, done that whole 'show must go on' bollocks, but she just didn't have the energy. It was now Monday morning, ten o'clock and she'd had exactly forty-five minutes' sleep since the day before. Brunch had been excruciating. She'd kept the sunglasses on all the way through, as much to disguise her swollen eyes as to mask the fact that she couldn't bear to look at Joe. Devious bastard. It was a miracle she hadn't gone across that table and slapped him. And Mel . . . Mel had been so full of joy, so smiley and happy. Urgh, this was a living, breathing fucking nightmare.

Last night, she'd lain in bed staring at the ceiling all night, desperately trying to decide what to do. Karl had tried to talk to her but she'd claimed a hangover-induced migraine and put him off, ignoring him until he gave up and went out for a run. The situation between them could wait. First, she had to tell Mel, but how? She would never believe her. She'd be destroyed. Ill. Broken. How could she do that to her?

Avril burst back in, looking wide-eyed and flustered. 'Er, we've got a bit of a situation out there.'

'What's up?'

'You might want to buzz Cammy next door and give him a heads-up because some idiot has booked Anna and Anneka in at the same time and they're circling each other like hyenas. I think there could be blood.'

Suze shook her head. 'Don't worry, it'll be fine – they know all about each other and it's cool with them.'

'You're kidding me.'

'No, seriously. I think they're both seeing other guys too. It's a whole "consenting adults" thing.'

'Eeeeew – more like a whole STD-certainty thing. That's so messed up.'

She turned and strutted off allowing Suze to slip back into a catatonic state of woe. The truth was that there was no way of breaking this gently. At one point last night, she'd been convinced that the best course of action was to corner Joe and tell him to confess all, but ultimately she decided that was giving him too much of an opportunity to laugh it off or spin Mel some line that made the whole episode look like just one big misunderstanding.

No, there was only one way to deal with it and sitting there moping wasn't going to get it over with.

The phone was answered on the third ring. 'Good morning, La Femme, Le Homme, the delectable Josie speaking.'

'Hi, Josie, it's Suze.'

'Are your legs broken?'

'No.'

'Then why are you phoning and not walking ten feet from your door to ours.'

Dear God, she didn't need this. Sometimes the company policy of hiring bolshy staff with bags of personality was a real pain in the arse.

'Aren't you supposed to be halfway to Italy?'

'On my way to the airport. Left my purse here on Saturday so popped in to collect it in the hope that someone would have come up with a catastrophic event that will prevent me from spending four weeks eating pasta while listening to my daughter-in-law point out my son's failings.'

Suze immediately realised that she had just the kind of catastrophic event that Josie required, but she decided not to make her day.

'Can I speak to Mel please?'

There was an episode of fumbling before Mel's breezy voice came on the line. 'Hey, you, you must be psychic – I was just about to call you for a catch-up. I'm guessing since you didn't push Karl over the balcony at Princess Square yesterday that he passed the test. See! I told you it'd be fine. It was all just in your ima—'

'Mel, I need to go somewhere this morning and I need you to come with me – can you get away?'

'Sure, hon, no problem at all. Are you OK?'

Suze's stomach lurched as she heard Mel's voice flick from sunny relief to concern. It was classic Mel – she worried about everyone else, nurtured all around her, and yet she was the one who was about to get crapped on from a great height. This was way, way beyond unfair.

'I'm OK; I just need to do something. Meet you outside in ten minutes. We'll need a couple of hours.'

Typical of Glasgow in January, the rain was torrential and the wind was gale-force. You could tell the residents from the tourists – the tourists left their hotels with those instruments of optimism, the umbrella, unaware that at the first gust the brolly would turn inside out, take off and they'd end up chasing it all the way down George Street.

Glasgow residents went for the less attractive but more practical option: the hooded jacket. It was warmer, more reliable, but made conversation more difficult, so they'd already made their way to a coffee house fifteen minutes from their shops before any form of cohesive communication was possible. They pulled out two white curvy chairs from a cream Formica table, and ordered two lattes from a bloke with a bored expression and several facial piercings.

'OK, what's going on, Suze? Start from the beginning.'

So Suze did – she burst into tears. Again. Shit, this wasn't going according to plan. She was supposed to be the strong one, the one that was going to hold it together for her friend, right up until the point where she trampled all over her happiness. Mel grabbed a napkin from the chrome dispenser in the middle of the table and handed it over.

'Thanks.' Calm down. Focus. You have to do this. Stop being pathetic and deal with this. Pull yourself together because Mel is going to need you. Focus. Focus.

Two elderly ladies in matching beige felt hats at a nearby table both snapped their heads round in irritation as the noise of Suze blowing her nose thundered over Il Divo crooning in the background.

'Mel, I went to the agency on Saturday.'

'And everything was OK, right? I mean you and Karl were fine yesterday and –'

'The girl they sent didn't find Karl.'

Mel groaned. 'Oh no, so that's why you're still upset. Look, honey, maybe it's a blessing in disguise. I mean, perhaps this is the universe's way of telling you not to go ahead with this. Honestly, I know Karl would never do anything to hurt you. We married good men, Suze. So can't you just forget the whole thing? Maybe a holiday would help. Yeah, I'll have a look on Expedia when I get back and . . .'

'She met Joe.'

'. . . see if there's anything that . . .'

'Mel, she met *Joe*.'

'What?'

'The girl they sent to meet up with Karl – she met Joe instead.'

Suze watched as the emotional equivalent of a fifty-pound mallet slammed into Mel's forehead.

'But . . . but . . . that's impossible. Joe was at circuits on Friday night as usual. And then he caught up with Karl for a quick beer at Club 80 afterwards like he always does, and came home about eleven. It was a bit later than usual but . . .'

Suze reached over and put her hand over Mel's. 'I don't know if he went to circuits, Mel, and he did go to Club 80, only he wasn't with Karl there. He was on his own, until the girl from the agency met him and –'

'And he ignored her right? Didn't he?'

The felt hats were craning their necks again now, alerted to gossip by the shrill escalation in volume coming from the redhead.

If desperation could be captured in an image, Suze thought, then it would be the one in front of her: Mel, wide-eyed in incomprehension, silently begging her for a happy outcome to a story that didn't have one.

'Mel, he didn't ignore her – he . . . he asked her out, Mel. And I'm sorry. I'm so, so sorry.'

The felt hats gasped as the redhead jumped up, sending the chair underneath flying backwards.

'He didn't. You're making this up. Come on, Suze, you know he wouldn't. It's a mistake.'

Suze shook her head. 'It wasn't a mistake, Mel, he asked her to –'

'*No!* Why are you doing this? Why did you have to do this whole fucking thing in the first place? Joe would never do that, you've got it wrong! She must have asked him. *She* must have done it, not Joe. Not Joe, Suze, how could you even think that?'

She was screaming now, giving the felt hats enough gossip to keep them and their Monday-afternoon knitting group going for weeks.

'Mel, he –'

'No! Enough, Suze! Enough!'

Suze lurched to grab her but it was too late – Mel had sprinted across the café and was out of the front door, no jacket, no bag. She raced to catch up with her and only managed it because Mel stopped to apologise to an elderly *Big Issue* seller that she'd bumped into. Suze threw her arms around her from the back.

'Mel, stop,' she spat, trying to speak through the sheeting rain that was assaulting her face. Mel violently pushed her off. 'Leave me alone! Just because your marriage is messed up doesn't mean –'

'I'll show you, Mel. I'll show you the tape! Gloria's office is right there. Just watch it, and then you can decide. Please, Mel.'

Passers-by were giving them a wide berth – the blonde in the red silk dress and the redhead in the green fitted pencil skirt suit, neither of them wearing coats, both of them hysterical, both of them drenched.

As Suze pulled a stunned, reluctant Mel back into the shelter of the café, one disgusted felt hat leaned over to the other. 'Aye, I read it in the *Daily Record*. Even these middle-class lassies are all taking drugs now.'

Suze put ten pounds on the table and grabbed their coats and bags, then eased Mel's coat around her trembling shoulders and gave her a squeeze. 'C'mon, Mel, let's go.'

Eleven

She'd read once that people could die of shock. Literally keel over there and then, heart stopped, journey ended. She and Joe had talked about dying once. Cremation not burial. Ashes scattered over Loch Lomond. It was where he'd proposed to her. He'd borrowed a speedboat from a client (ten-storey office block with landscaping and car park), taken her out into the middle of the still loch on a perfect summer's day and told her that he would love her forever. Only her.

Her surroundings permeated her thoughts and gave her a quick kick of a reality check. What was she doing here? This was stupid, crazy, surreal.

'Melissa, I'll just put the tape on now. Are you sure you're OK?'

OK? No. Nothing about this was OK. There was a squeeze on her right hand and she turned to meet Suze's concerned gaze. This was all wrong. Mel was the one who should be supporting her friend, helping *her* through a hard time, giving her a shoulder to cry on. This morning she'd woken up perfectly normal, her life in order and happy, her husband wonderful, yet now she was sitting in a private-investigator's office in the centre of town, looking like she'd showered with her clothes on, receiving comforting gestures from her best friend and sympathetic expressions from a woman she'd never met before in her life. What was going on?

The shivering was getting worse, so she pulled Gloria's cardigan tighter around her shoulders and watched as a grainy image filled the TV screen on the wall.

Suddenly, her diaphragm spasmed and a wave of light-headedness over took her. 'Suze, I don't want to do this.'

Gloria hit the pause button. 'Melissa, I can put it off. You can come back later. Tomorrow. Whenever you feel ready.'

But Mel barely heard her because her eyes had been drawn back to the screen, to the image that had cleared now, and there it was – that face that she knew every single contour and crevice of, the one that was as familiar to her as her own.

Trancelike, she shook her head, taking no comfort from the arm that was around her now, nor Suze's whispers telling her that it was going to be OK.

This was definitely not going to be OK.

Nothing about this situation could ever be OK.

'Go on,' she told Gloria in a voice she didn't even recognise as her own.

Hours later, sitting in her darkened living room, she could barely remember what Gloria looked like, what colour the office walls were, how she'd got home or what she'd said to make Suze leave her alone.

But, for the rest of her life, she'd always remember hearing her husband say, '*I'm separated. Have been for a long time. We've both moved on and put it behind us, but I haven't met anyone else yet. Until now . . .*'

71

'Hey, gorgeous, why are you sitting in the dark?'

She hadn't even heard him come in, and now her hands shot to cover her eyes as he flicked a switch and light seared through her swollen lids.

'Mel! Oh my God, what's wrong? You look terrible.'

She sniffed loudly, desperate to stop the dam of fluid that was building up behind her eyes and threatening to burst.

'Sounds like flu. Did you call the doctor? Or get something from the chemist?' He was kneeling in front of her now, pushing her hair back from her face and checking her forehead temperature at the same time. 'Wow, you're really warm – have you taken your temperature?'

How could he? How could this man kneel there looking so concerned, so loving, so sweet, yet on the other hand be capable of taking her trust and drop-kicking it right into the cleavage of some female he met in a bar?

Did she really know him? Had she ever? Had he been having affairs since they met – a whole train of women parading behind her back like some kind of fucked-up mistress pageant?

How? How could this be happening? Only a few days ago, they'd been planning the names of their children. *Their* children – the ones he'd been so desperate to have, the ones that they'd planned and dreamed of and imagined as they grew up. Joe. Josephine. Fucking greenhouses! And all the time he'd been out trawling the bars, telling other females he was single and trying to pick them up. How? How could that even happen? Did she really not know him at all? How could she have been so stupid? What was wrong with her? She'd thought she had the perfect marriage and now ... now her husband was kneeling in front of her, looking like the same guy when, in fact, she realised that she didn't recognise him. This wasn't the person she planned to spend the rest of her life with, to raise a family with, to grow old with. She had absolutely no idea who this man in front of her was at all.

'I'll go get you some tea and some Nurofen and then you should head off to bed, love. Do you want me to stay with you? I was going to head out to meet Karl at the gym but I could give it a miss.'

The hand that shot out and cracked across his face surprised her as much as it did him.

'Shit, Mel – what was that about? *What?*'

'Get away from me, Joe,' she hissed, her tone weary but absolutely resolute.

'Why? What's going on?' He'd fallen backwards and was sitting on the floor now, rubbing his face as if trying to erase both the irritation and confusion. 'I don't . . .'

'Where were you last Friday, Joe?'

'I was . . . I was . . .'

That's when she saw it – a tiny little flicker of under-standing flitted through his eyes and made his aching jaw clench just a little tighter. He opened his mouth to speak but she cut him off.

'Don't, Joe. If you're even thinking about lying to me, then stop right now because this is about as bad as it gets and lying to me again will only make it worse.'

The silence stretched on for what seemed like hours, all the while he stared at the floor. The inherently caring Mel wanted to reach out to him, to hold him, to kiss this whole mess away and tell him it was going to be fine. But the newly devastated Mel wanted to tie him down and kick him until his ribs cracked through his traitorous fucking heart.

She compromised by doing nothing. Just sitting perfectly, silently still.

73

'I was in Club 80 all night. Karl and I both had a shit day at work so we decided not to go to circuits and just arranged to meet there instead. Then he called off.'

There was a momentary pause as he searched her face for any sign that he'd disclosed enough but she answered by staring him down.

'So I stayed there and had a few drinks.'

Another pause. One that didn't show any signs of ending.

'With?'

The muscles across her chest tightened as he choked, the palpable misery all over his face making it obvious that any hope he had of finding some way out of this was most definitely gone.

'Don't, Mel, please don't do this.'

Her head was shaking slowly from side to side now, her tears dropping like pennies into a wishing well. '*I'm* not doing anything, Joe. I think *you've* already got the "doing stuff" all sewn up. Who were you with, Joe?'

'I met someone, a woman.' He was choking again. 'And I . . . Mel, I'm so sorry. I'm so, so sorry. But nothing happened, I swear.'

The crack didn't particularly surprise either of them this time. Mel had never hit anyone in her life, wouldn't have thought she was capable, and definitely would never have believed that she could ever want to physically hurt her husband. Now, she was just grateful that she didn't own a gun.

'Nothing happened? Apart from asking her out, apart from telling her you weren't married any more, apart from breaking my fucking heart?'

'Mel, I . . .'

'How many? How many others, Joe? How many women have you chatted up, asked out, screwed behind my back?'

'None, Mel, I –'

74

'DO NOT LIE TO ME! Get out, Joe. I don't even know who you are any more.'

He swung back round on to his knees and grabbed both her hands – she wasn't sure if it was a conciliatory gesture or a defensive move to stop her hitting him again.

'I'm not going, babe, we need to sort this out,' he begged. 'Nothing happened, Mel, I promise you nothing happened.'

'But it would have if she'd allowed it to, if she'd stayed. What would you have done, Joe? Gone back to her flat? To a hotel? Then come back to me, all steady, reliable bloody Joe?'

'Wait a minute – how do you know all this? How did you –'

'It doesn't matter,' she screamed. 'Joe, it's over. Get out. And take your stuff with you because I don't want you to come back. Please, Joe – I can't even stand to be near you.'

'Mel, no . . .'

'Go! Now!'

With another choked sob, he stood up and headed through the door, then thudded into their bedroom. The banging of the wardrobe doors told her that he was packing a bag, then he thudded back towards the living room again. Although she felt his presence in the doorway, she didn't turn around.

'Mel, please . . . I don't want to leave you.'

'You did that last Friday night when you told some female that we were already separated. Remember that bit, Joe? Now get out.'

With a slam of the door, he was gone and she buckled over in two, her breath strangled by the pain. She had no idea how long she sat like that. Minutes. Hours.

'You are my sunshine, my only sunshine, you make me ha-peeee . . .'

She snatched her mobile phone off the table and checked

the screen. That message alert had seemed like a really funny idea at the time.

It was a message from Suze.

HON, SO WORRIED BOUT U. CAN I CM BACK OVER? LOVE U, SX.

There were only two options – ignore it and Suze would be over within the hour or reply and put her off. Her thumb raced across the screen as she answered.

THNKS, BUT JST WANT TO BE ON OWN. JOE GONE. PROB ON WAY 2 U.

'You are my sun . . '.
Mel snatched at the phone again.

OK, BUT IF U NEED ME I'M THERE. AND U R RIGHT. J JST PULLED UP OUTSIDE.

Twelve

As the doorbell rang, Suze weighed up the options. So far, the high likelihood that she would plummet to her death while trying to escape down the drainpipe outside her window seemed like the most preferable option. Fuck, what had she done? All she'd wanted to know was whether or not her husband was being unfaithful to her but she'd somehow managed to unleash the family crisis from hell and ruin her best friend's life in the process.

She pulled on a long, thick cream chunky-knit jumper over her black skinny jeans and shoved her thick honey hair into a messy ponytail at the nape of her neck.

Despite the warmth of the wool, she shuddered. Surely that wasn't game over for Mel and Joe? Hell, if *they* couldn't make it, there was no hope for anyone. They'd always been the happiest couple she knew, so in love, so compatible, so in sync with each other. She'd never managed that kind of unequivocal balance with Karl. Their relationship had always been based on love, passion, bloody-minded arguments and threats of desertion.

She contemplated heading for the drainpipe again, then

eventually gave in and went for the option that hopefully wouldn't involve flashing blue lights and traction. Although, given her plans to have it out with Karl tonight, that situation might change. If one good thing had come out of all the drama, it was that she'd decided to face him with her fears about their marriage and his fidelity – no more of this sneaking around, plotting subterfuge and duplicity. From now on she was sticking to a policy of brutal truth and honesty.

'You're not serious! Fucking hell, Joe, what happened?' Karl wrapped one arm around his brother and ushered him in from the front door and then as he turned he spotted her halfway down the stairs.

'Did you know about this, Suze? About Mel chucking him out?'

Brutal truth and honesty. Brutal truth and honesty.

'Er, no, of course not.' Aaargh! What should she do? Despite wanting to annihilate Joe for his stupidity, she knew that she had to stay out of it. This was between Joe and Mel and other people getting involved would just lead to chaos. And yes, she did realise the irony in that newly developed thread of emotional awareness.

Karl headed over to the huge fridge freezer and returned to his brother with two bottles of Miller lite.

'So what happened? Time of the –'

'Karl, if you finish that sentence with "month", I swear I'm going to deposit that bottle in a place that will chill you from the inside out,' Suze interjected.

Ignoring the exchange, Joe shook his head furiously. 'I fucked up, Karl. I really fucked up.'

'How? What did you do – shag someone else?' Karl laughed as if taken with the ridiculousness of the thought.

'She thinks I did.'

'That's nuts! I'll go talk to her, tell her it's a mistake. Look, mate, this can be fixed. We'll fix it.'

Opting to stay in the background for a moment, Suze perched on a seat over at the granite breakfast bar, flipped the top off another bottle of Miller and took a long drink. Typical Karl. Always being the big brother, the Alpha male, the fixer. If only he was so good at fixing his own marriage, then none of this would have happened. The cold fizz of the beer going down failed to head off the wave of anger that was sweeping upwards. She wasn't even sure any more who she was angriest with: herself, Karl or Joe.

'You can't, Karl, honestly, I *really* fucked up.' Joe's head was in his hands now. 'I'm such a stupid prick. So stupid. I can't believe I did this.'

'What? What did you do?' Karl seemed to be beginning to grasp the severity of the situation and threw Suze a searching look.

She blanked him.

'I met someone else.'

'YOU WHAT?'

'I met this other woman, last Friday night. We were supposed to go to circuits, remember? Then we decided not to bother?'

And there it was – the one, singular line that would change everything, reinforce Suze's doubts and in some small way vindicate her recent actions. From her bird's-eye view on her perch, Suze watched Karl's expression change from stunned to shifty, via confused, horrified and panicked, as his brain shuffled backwards and stopped at the relevant evening when, yes, they were supposed to go to circuits and, no, they didn't go. It was now clear that they hadn't hit the gym, but yet when Karl came home that night he told her that he'd done two hours of weight training and three sessions of cardio. If her swanky, high-gadget kitchen had a bullshit detector, it would be screeching like a smoke alarm in a bush fire.

But this wasn't the time to deal with that. This was Joe's

crisis and, although it was obvious that Karl realised he'd been caught out in a lie too, sense and sensitivity told her that her own marital situation should be dealt with later.

'Where were you, Karl?'

Or not.

'What?' His head whipped around like he'd been slapped. Which could either have been a reaction or a premonition.

'Where were you? You told me that you went to training, you clearly didn't. So where were you?'

'Look, Suze, can we talk about that later? Joe is –'

'Where were you?' Her voice was raised now, urgent.

'Not now, Suze! Just leave it! Let's deal with one thing at a time, eh? Let's worry about Joe and Mel just now and we'll talk about that later, OK?'

If she was a pressure cooker, her steam valve would have punctured a hole in the ceiling. How dare he? How bloody dare he tell her what to do when he was the one who had caused this whole situation? If he hadn't been acting so damn weird lately, she'd never have suspected him of having an affair, and there would have been absolutely no need to call in a honeytrap agency. Thus, whatever way you slice it, dice it or analyse it to bollocking death, this whole big sodding debacle was all Karl's fault in the first place!

And now – oh dear God – she could not believe what she was hearing him tell his brother.

'Look, mate, just deny it. So what, you were talking to some other bird – that means nothing. There's no way Mel could have proof that you've done anything wrong. Deny it again and again until she believes you.'

How. Dare. He.

How dare he lie. And cheat. And sit there telling his brother to do the same. No, this wasn't going to happen.

'She has proof.' Suze's voice was so calm and deadly that she almost didn't recognise it. 'She has proof because I sent someone to check what you were up to and they picked up Joe instead. Mistaken identity. But he fell for it. Should have been you. Mel has a tape of the whole thing.'

Silence. So quiet that you could hear a Miller bottle drop. Which is exactly what happened when reality dawned and Karl realised that *he* had been the intended victim of a set-up by his own wife.

His stunned astonishment left a gap for Joe to speak first.

'I can't believe you did that.'

'Yeah, well, I can't believe you let your dick take charge of a conversation that didn't involve your wife. You're hardly on the moral high ground there, Casanova.'

'Jesus, you're a complete bitch,' whistled Karl.

'No, no, no – don't you dare go trying to turn this on me, Karl Marshall. Where were you last Friday night?'

'You know what, Suze – I'm telling you nothing! You're a nasty, conniving cow and I can't believe you would stoop this low.'

'LOW? You haven't seen low yet! You know what, you two deserve each other. Obviously being a cheating, unfaithful bastard is in the genes.'

Karl's face was a picture of blind fury now as she strutted past him, pausing only to snatch her handbag and a set of keys from a hook at the door.

'I wish I'd never met your cheating arse!' she yelled as she wrenched open the door.

'Trust me, Suze, that feeling is . . .'

She didn't hear the rest but she was guessing that she could fill in the blanks with 'mutual'. The exhaust roared as she pressed down on the accelerator and headed down towards Giffnock, one of the suburbs that lay between Whitecraigs and the city centre. Taking his Mercedes had been a small victory. He might not care about her, but he loved that car more than life itself. Materialistic, show-off bastard.

She didn't even know where she was going. Maybe down to her dad's house in Helensburgh, but she hadn't spoken to him for weeks so she didn't even know if he was in the country or over at his flat in Alicante. He wasn't a wealthy man, but he'd brought Suze up single-handed after her mother had buggered off with the postman (yep, truly clichéd) when she was four, so now was his time for enjoying himself. And enjoy it, he did. A small house in Helensburgh where he lived during the summer months, a cosy apartment in Alicante where he lived in the winter, and at least three single/widowed/divorced lady companions in each place. Oh, and the discovery of Viagra – a fact that she would have probably preferred he'd kept to himself. There were worse ways to spend a retirement.

Giffnock disappeared behind her as the bright lights and crowds of Shawlands materialised. Even on a Monday night the streets were full of revellers bouncing from pub to club, big groups of twenty-somethings out on the . . .

Shit! She slammed on the brakes, just missing the drunk teenage girl who had wandered out on to the street right in front of her, crying her eyes out as she went. Suze was just about to get out of the car when another girl appeared and pulled her pal back on to the pavement, cuddling her tight and shushing away her tears.

At that moment, her brain realised what her internal sat nav already knew – she knew where she was going.

Ten minutes later, she parked the car directly outside their shops, and then dodged a Porsche, three cyclists and a busload of tourists on the Glasgow Cemeteries By Night Tour to dive across to the other side of the road.

The door was answered on the forty-seventh ring. She counted.

'Hi,' Suze said, trying not to flinch at the sight of Mel's ravaged face. It looked like it had been inflated, her bloodshot eyes oozing pain and devastation. 'Julia Roberts must be shitting herself,' she added.

Despite herself, Mel laughed. 'I thought I said not to come,' she pointed out.

'Nowhere else to go. Told Karl and Joe they were welcome to each other and stormed out. Forgot to think through the consequences first.'

Mel quietly harrumphed, but not unkindly. 'Now there's a surprise.'

'So can I stay here?'

The door opened wider as Mel stepped backwards. 'Of course you can. But I warn you, I still harbour a bit of resentment that your stupid bloody idea started this whole thing off.'

Suze nodded knowingly. 'I can understand that. But since my husband will never, ever forgive me and probably wants to have me bumped off right now, I'll take your resentment over going back home. At least here I'll be able to sleep with both eyes shut.'

Suze got the wine out of the fridge and Mel got the glasses. 'So, before we get into all this, just tell me – what did you do that Karl will never forgive you for?'

'The thing that I knew would hurt him more than anything,' Suze replied.

'Took his Mercedes?'

Suze held up the key with the famous crest and wiggled it.

And that's how, even on what had to be a front runner in 'The Worst Day Of Their Life' awards, two friends ended up laughing through the pain.

The weekend that made it
all even worse . . .

Thirteen

'Do you want to talk about this?'

He shook his head and turned to stare out of the car window. It was one of their favourite spots – the open-air top floor of a city-centre, multistorey car park that came with three definite bonuses: it was almost always deserted after 6 p.m., it had an incredible view of the city and there were no CCTV cameras.

'No. Do you?'

She mirrored his reaction and he was glad, because the last thing he needed was an in-depth analysis to add to excruciating embarrassment.

This was the first time it had ever happened to him. Sure, he'd seen it in movies, read about it in books, but never actually experienced it before.

They'd been in the throes of passion and he'd been in the moment, he really had, when all of a sudden an image came into his head and, before he knew it, the urge had disappeared. Gone. Vanished. Even worse, it took her a few moments to notice, during which time he was sure some physical damage had been done.

She reached over from the passenger side and stroked his arm. 'Look, it doesn't matter. It happens.' It seemed like the thing to say.

If she was being really honest, she'd have added, 'although it's never happened to me before,' but she didn't want to make a bad situation any worse.

She wondered how long she should wait before suggesting they call it a night. Damn, what was the etiquette on lost hard-ons? There was no way she was sitting here for much longer, watching him brood over his sudden crisis of macho-ness. This whole situation was difficult enough without adding drama and emotional turmoil into the equation.

Her touch snapped him back to the moment and he shrugged apologetically. 'Sorry, just got a lot on my mind right now.'

'You've been like this for weeks. Want to tell me why?'

He stroked her cheek, so beautiful and yet so . . . just not right. This wasn't part of their deal and he could tell that she was struggling with how to react. But there was no way he was going to get into this with her. They both knew why this started, what they needed out of this, and it wasn't shared confidences and cosy chat.

'Like I said, just got a lot on my mind.'

She sighed as she slumped back in her seat and lit a cigarette. 'Well, look, I haven't exactly been skipping through meadows lately either.' She exhaled with an irritated pout.

'I know, you're right. It's just that . . .' He caught himself. He was almost going to tell her what was going on but stopped – what was the point? He had to get a grip of himself, deal with what had happened and get on with it. It was too late to change anything and, even if he could, he would always be worried that these little tête-à-têtes would be discovered and he'd be back to square one.

It was hopeless.

Well, maybe not completely hopeless.

She was stroking the inside of his thigh now, running a long manicured nail from the tip of his possibly sprained penis to his knee and back up again and it was definitely having a stirring effect. In fact, there was markedly more than a stir . . .

'Let's get out of the car.'

'What? You have got to be joking? It's minus four out there.'

He pulled her fake-fur coat out of the back seat and handed it to her.

Her hesitation was brief. 'OK, but tell me you're coming with me because if you drive off I could lose my nipples to frostbite.'

Before she even finished the sentence, his door was opened and he – in all his perfectly formed, gym-honed, naked glory – was standing outside, in front of the car, in minus temperatures.

'Shoes,' he shouted to her. 'Put your shoes on.' He'd had an image of how he'd like to spend the next twenty minutes of his life and it wasn't sitting inside a car basking in self-pity.

Her grin gave way to uncontrollable giggles. This is why he'd been unable to resist her in the first place. God, she was so, so sexy, so comfortable in her own skin and willing to share it. This time, even the sub-zero temperatures couldn't put a dampener on the occasion.

Fourteen

'Right, I'm back, I know all about it and I'm armed. Where is the cheating dickless wonder?'

For the first time in almost a month, Mel shrieked with laughter as Josie barged into the office, dressed in her trademark black polo neck jumper and black trousers, and clutching the biggest baseball bat she'd ever seen. From the neck down, she was a Bond villainess; from the neck up she was a grey-haired Glasgow granny with a wild twinkle in her eye. Mel flew out of her chair and into Josie's arms.

'Oh, Josie, you've no idea how much I missed you.'

'And I've missed you, sweet girl. I'm so sorry about what happened. I was only home from the airport an hour last night when Cammy phoned and told me about it. I want you to know that I'm available for random tyre-slashing and episodes of prolonged violence.'

'Thank you. Are you sure that wouldn't interfere with your arthritis, though?'

'I'll take the pain, don't you worry, love. So. What's the situation now?'

Mel thought about it for a moment and realised that she

didn't know where to start. What exactly *was* the situation?

'Marriage fractured. Heart broken. Suze has moved in with me and the Marshall brothers are about as popular in our house as, say, fungus. But I'm managing to go stretches of an hour now without bursting into tears, so that's progress.'

Josie picked up a Ken doll from the desk, remarkable for both its nakedness and the fact that there were several large pins sticking out of it.

'It's Suze's stress toy. Says it gets her through the day.'

'So they're over too?'

Mel shrugged her shoulders. The truth was, it was difficult to know what was going on. Karl and Suze, both as singularly stubborn and indignant as each other, hadn't spoken a word to each other since the night she'd stormed out. The following morning, the car was gone from outside the shop, so either it had been stolen or he'd come in the middle of the night with the spare key and reclaimed the love of his life. The lack of police investigation suggested the latter. Suze had gone back to the house while he was at work the next day, collected her own car, filled three suitcases, all of which were now blocking the entrance to Mel's spare room. But as for grand, sweeping gestures towards reconciliation from either party? Nothing. Nada. Zip. Karl was obviously just getting on with his life and ignoring the Suze-shaped hole next to him.

Joe, on the other hand . . . well, he'd tried.

He'd called constantly that first week, appeared at the door three nights running and even came to the shop twice, but on every occasion Mel refused to speak to him. She just couldn't do it. And strangely, the more he tried, the angrier it made her. She'd seen what he did and said with her own eyes, and, just because he wanted to salve his conscience by speaking to her, how dare he assume that she was ready to reopen lines of communication with him? He'd betrayed her. She couldn't see any way forward from that and, until she did, she couldn't bring herself to see him. It just hurt too damn much. In the end, she'd finally answered a call from him, but only to tell him to give her some space and time. He'd reluctantly agreed.

There were only two options left open to her – bed/food/moping or work/denial/oblivion. She'd chosen the one that wouldn't make her gain ten pounds. Every morning, at 6 a.m., she'd climbed out of bed after a fitful sleep, showered and headed straight across the street to the shop. Every night she'd stayed there until Suze came and dragged her out, sometimes ten o'clock, sometimes eleven, sometimes even later.

The good news was that she'd lost almost a stone, surviving only on what Cammy brought in for her and cajoled her into eating, and takings were up by twenty per cent because the new opening hours meant she was catching a whole new market of late-night workers who headed in and out of the city after dark.

Oh, and the shop had never looked so beautiful. She'd reorganised the storeroom, updated and rejigged all the displays, redressed all the mannequins in the latest ranges and cleaned every inch of the interior until it gleamed. She'd also completely caught up with her annual inventory check, her VAT return, her book-keeping system and established new marketing plans for the rest of the year. Marital disaster might be playing havoc on her emotions, but at this rate it was going to make her entrepreneur of the year.

'How's Suze handling it?' Josie interrupted her thoughts.

'She's up to two Pilates classes a day and she's talking about getting a boob job.'

Josie roared with delight. 'That's my girl! Well, my second favourite one. Look, Mel, I know it doesn't seem like it just now, but maybe this will get easier over time and you'll be able to work things out.'

Mel felt her eyes fill up as she shook her head. 'I don't

think so, Josie. It's all gone. The Joe I thought I knew would never have done that, so obviously I never knew him at all. And if I didn't know him, then none of it was real.'

Josie, her hands on hips now, dispensed with tact. 'Good. I was only saying all that "work things out" nonsense because I felt I should. You're too good for him, Melissa. And he's a daft fucker if he let someone like you go. I wish I had a spare son I could set you up with. We could always bump off our Michael's wife and you could move in there – I've never liked the shallow cow anyway. I swear the last four weeks have permanently damaged my hearing.'

'Josie!' Mel roared through the giggles. 'Will you stop saying stuff like that.' She paused, and then giggled again. 'OK, say it once more, just the bit where I'm too good for him, not the bit where you whack your daughter-in-law.'

'Who's whacking who?' Cammy asked as he materialised clutching a cardboard tray with three Starbucks coffees, two cinnamon Danish pastries and a toffee and apple muffin for Josie. She always said the pastry played havoc with her false teeth.

He put them all down on the desk and then enveloped Josie in a massive bear hug. 'All right, you old tart – we've missed you.'

'Less of your cheek, boy,' she answered affectionately. 'So how is life with Tweedle dum and Tweedle dee?'

'Er, dum and dee are no longer.'

Mel's cinnamon Danish bulged out of her cheek like a ping-pong ball as she stopped chewing. 'They're not? Oh, crap, Cammy, I'm so sorry. I've been so wrapped up in my own bloody drama that I didn't realise you'd split up with them. What happened?'

He perched the arse of his black, straight-legged Replay jeans on her desk and motioned to Mel's open mouth full of semi-chewed food. 'Very attractive look there, boss.'

She snapped her jaw shut and he continued with a nonchalant shrug.

'It's honestly no big deal; I just figured that neither of the relationships was going anywhere so we'd be better off calling it a day. They were crushed, naturally,' he finished with an exaggerated head nod.

Josie threw one arm around his shoulders. 'Well, studly, if you ever fancy dabbling in antiques, I'm yer woman. And just to up the odds of that eventuality, we're going out tonight and we're going to get wellied.'

'Thanks, Josie, but . . .'

'Don't you dare object, Melissa-soon-to-be-de-Marshalled. We're going out and that's that!'

Resistance, they knew, was futile. Despite coming up with at least a dozen perfectly reasonable excuses not to go, all of which Josie batted out of the cage, at six o'clock the 'open' sign on the door was flicked over and a large box of some unpronounceable Italian white wine materialised.

Reluctantly going along with the coercion, Mel changed into another outfit that had been lying at the back of the storeroom cupboard ever since she brought it back from the dry cleaners weeks ago and emerged to a low whistle from both Josie and Cammy.

'Way-hey, you look gorgeous.'

'Do I?' She turned to check out her reflection in the freestanding mirror outside the changing rooms.

The dress was a black jersey halterneck, absolutely without adornment, gathered by a simple band under the bust and falling in sleek lines to just above her ankles. She'd teamed it with the high black strappy sandals that – until an hour ago – had been on the second mannequin from the left in the front window and pulled her hair back into a high pony-tail that left a cascade of curls trailing down her bare back.

'Overdressed? Too much?'

'Nope, just perfect,' Cammy countered. 'Now drink this cheap vino that Josie brought back from her holiday – at least, until your stomach lining falls out.'

The first sip burned, the second seared, but by the third her tongue was numb and she no longer cared.

'Did you ask Suze if she wanted to come with us?' Josie asked and was answered by Mel's nodding head.

'Yep, but she didn't – got another Pilates class tonight and apparently she'll wake up weighing sixteen stones tomorrow morning if she doesn't go. Anyway –' she raised her glass '– here's to Josie. Welcome home, my darling, we missed you.'

'Likewise. Let's go eat. I need something hugely fattening and I need it now. Anything but pasta.'

In the end they settled for steak at The City, an upmarket club on St Vincent Street, built over three floors with distinct areas for eating, drinking and private functions. They all skipped starters and went straight for main courses, thick rib-eyes of steak drenched in a whisky sauce, accompanied by champagne cocktails at Josie's insistence.

'I've been deprived of frivolous spending for nearly a month and I've got a new credit card that's burning a hole in my pocket, so let's go for it.'

Mel could see that Cammy was about to argue over who was paying, so she got in there first. 'Nonsense! Guys, we were so busy over Christmas and New Year that I think we should count this as our official festive company night out, so this one is on the shop. Just remind me to sleep with my accountant before telling him.'

Diners at the nearby tables smiled as the infectious giggles permeated outwards. They drank, they ate, and, for the first time in weeks, Mel managed a whole hour without thinking about Joe and a whole three hours without crying. In fact, she felt almost . . . normal. Not better, not healed, just temporarily, drunkenly normal.

'I feel like dancing,' Josie announced as the waiter took away the last remnants of their desserts: three mouth-watering toffee sponge cakes, washed down with yet more cocktails.

'There's nowhere to dance in here,' Cammy argued, managing to get the whole sentence out without slurring his words too badly. 'And, Mel, why are you looking at me like that?'

'Like what?' The surprise of his question made her elbow slide off the table, an unfortunate manoeuvre because until that moment it had been supporting her chin.

'I don't know, just . . . weirdly,' Cammy replied.

Mel was lost for words. She'd no idea she was staring, but, hey, every other female in the place, married or otherwise, had checked out Cammy at one point over the evening. He was pure oestrogen eye candy. Like fabulous shoes or posters of Brad Pitt with his top off.

'Excuse me, could you two please return your attention to actions in aid of Help The Aged. I'm extremely aged and I want to dance. Follow me.'

Taking Josie's lead, they headed out of the restaurant, proceeded up a flight of stairs to the private function suite, and over to a set of double doors that announced 'Scottish EAS Annual Dinner'. The sounds blaring from inside made it obvious that the event definitely featured the swinging of pants to music.

They barged through the doors and straight on over to the dancefloor, so exuberantly joyful that no one thought to question whether they belonged there. Even if they had, Josie would no doubt have talked them round. There were about sixty people on the sprung wooden square, all of them dancing. Actually, all of them dancing at the same time using incredibly similar movements.

Mel grabbed Cammy's arm in panic. 'Cam, I think I'm hearing things.'

'No, you're not.'

'So I really am concerned about someone stepping on my blue suede shoes?'

'The Elvis Appreciation Society. Dear God, I've died and gone to heaven – I always did fancy him,' Josie hollered as she started to shake her right knee in what – had they been sober – would have been a slightly disturbing fashion.

Josie gyrated over in the direction of the closest male. As soon as they spotted his sideburns, Mel and Cammy turned away to preserve her dignity.

Dancing alone now, they simultaneously twisted downwards and their knees were almost touching the floor, when Mel shrieked, 'Cammy, I don't think I can get up again. My legs aren't resplending.'

'You mean "responding"?'

'I mean, I'm stuck! Get me up please.'

In perfect sync with the music, he worked his way back up to a standing position and then heaved her up too, just as the song beat changed and a smooth, unmistakable voice uttered the first dramatic line of 'One Night With You'.

The assorted revellers immediately paired off and settled into the slow smoochy number. As Cammy held out both hands to her, Mel caught sight of Josie, burrowed deep in a worryingly hirsute face.

There was nothing else to do but acquiesce to Cammy's request and let the music dictate the pace. It was strange, though, how her head just fitted perfectly into the nook under his neck. And how he smelled so . . . well, good. And how they seemed to be moving in perfect time with each other, like the invisible force of too many champagne cocktails had slowed them to an identical pace. Mel gulped, as she realised that she felt . . . happy. Just happy. And drunk too, but mostly happy.

She felt Cammy's arms tighten around her and his breath

on her ear as he began to speak. 'Mel, can I ask you something really important?'

Ignoring the swelling crowd that was gently jostling around them, she lifted her head so that their eyes met as she nodded, a very strange feeling rising from the pit of her stomach. Hang on, was this . . .?

He looked at her earnestly, his tone suddenly serious. 'Promise me, if I get suffocated by this lot, you won't let them put "Death By Elvis" in my obituary.'

Now she was laughing again, a strange mixture of amusement and relief that a momentary pang of something had gone as quickly as it had come. It was back to her and Cammy, her employee and friend, the one who, even in her inebriated state, she knew she would never dream of crossing that line with. And she also knew, with absolute certainty, that he felt the same. They had been on a hundred drunken nights before, all of them ending in similar situations to this, all completely innocent. Obviously, all the stuff with Joe had put her emotions on some kind of heightened state and . . . Joe. Bloody hell, what had happened with her and Joe? How? She immediately blocked the subject, and then decided that it was probably time to get Josie and head off home before the temporary dam of self-preservation burst and the tears started again.

Her dance partner had something else on his mind. 'Mel, can I ask you something else?' She knew that look in his eyes, and had an inherent sense of what was coming.

'Yes, I'll remember that you want "Don't You Forget About Me" by Simple Minds played at your funeral. You tell me that every time you're drunk.'

He nodded sagely, cracking her up into cocktail-flavoured giggles.

How had Anna and Anneka ever let this one go? He was handsome, and funny, and like the adorable little brother that she'd never had. And again, he smelled so, so good.

'Mel?'

'Uh-huh?'

'Mel, do you know that you're sniffing my neck?'

Her head snapped up. 'Shit, I'm sorry! I was . . . Oh, Cammy, I don't know what I was . . . I was . . . bloody hell, I'm drunk . . .'

The words got lost in the music, in the atmosphere, but mostly in the mouth that was now attached to hers, the lips that were slowly, absolutely, utterly beautifully caressing his. And – oh, dear God – her tongue was now running slowly, teasingly across his, probing and devouring and tasting every crevice.

And, perhaps most surprisingly of all, he was doing it back. Receiving the signals from above, their hips seemed to press even more tightly together, their arms came up higher and hands found their way on to faces that they'd never touched in that way before.

Suddenly, her brain caught up with the train that her body and emotions were already riding and Mel felt something altogether new, something so strong that she broke off from the tongue-tickling and pulled back to face him again. 'Cammy, I . . .'

The shift seemed to have snapped him back to reality too and he looked seriously shocked and mortified. 'Shit, I'm sorry, Mel. I don't know how that happened. I swear I didn't mean to do that.'

'I have to go. I feel ill.'

A sea of Elvis Presleys from every decade parted to let the running redhead through.

Fifteen

Suze reached over to turn up the heating and realised that it was already on the highest setting. Bloody Glasgow in winter – you could wear electric knickers and you'd still be freezing to the core. She contemplated taking another slug of soup from the flask on the passenger seat and then decided against it as that would just make her want to pee and then she'd have to find a petrol station or a pub and . . . oh, it was just too much hassle. Charlie's Angels never had these problems when they were on stake-outs. In their world, when the bad guys showed up, they just flew out of the car looking like they'd stopped off at the salon for a quick mani/pedi and blow-dry.

Waiting. Just waiting. She shook back her long shards of honey highlights and pulled her black baseball cap down over her eyes. It was a miracle none of the neighbours had called the police yet because she'd been sitting there for hours. And this wasn't the first night either. So much for the neighbourhood-watch patrol that they were all forced to contribute to. She could have ram-raided every house on the street by now and got away scot-free.

Waiting. Just waiting. The clock on the dashboard clicked as it hit nine o'clock, and her exaggerated sigh caused a cloud of condensation to form on the side window. Suddenly, her heart thudded as a light in the lounge flicked on. Shit! How had he got in without passing her? She was about to roll out of the car in an SAS fashion and commando crawl to the front door when she remembered the automatic timer on the big lamp in the lounge.

Maybe a wee drink of soup would be a good idea, after all. At least it would break the monotony.

Perhaps she should have gone out with Mel and the crew from La Femme after all, but the truth was she just couldn't face it. The City was Karl's favourite place to go and they'd been there hundreds of times over the years, hundreds of happy times before their relationship fell into an express elevator and plummeted straight to marital hell.

Waiting. Just waiting. This was torture. Too much time to think. A quick flick of the CD system provided a momentary diversion until Celine Dion started wailing something about being all by herself. She really had to have a word with Avril about her taste in music.

Borrowing her assistant's car was supposed to be a masterstroke of subterfuge, not trauma for the ears. And yes, it was definitely best to avoid thinking about what Avril was doing right now in Suze's six-month-old Mazda convertible.

Where was he? She'd checked the gym car park and his Merc wasn't there, and if he was going out he would always come home after work, shower and change first. Karl was a creature of habit and after ten years together she knew every one of them. She knew he'd left the office at six o'clock, because no one had picked up when she called his direct business line from a payphone at five minutes past.

So where had he gone? Where was he? Was he with *her*? Whoever she was? A familiar knot of unadulterated anxiety started to twist in her stomach. Almost every night since abducting the Mercedes and storming out, she'd found herself drawn back here to look, to see if he'd brought the other woman back. It was becoming almost an obsession, borne as much of a need to know that she was right as to get some kind of closure. Nothing could be sorted out or tackled until she knew the truth and if he wasn't going to tell her then she'd bloody well find out for herself.

The only blessing about this whole pathetic situation was that Mel had been so absorbed in work that she had no idea where Suze had really been spending her time. However, the Pilates excuse was starting to wear thin, especially as she'd gained five pounds through munching down on junk food while trying to watch her former bedroom window through binoculars.

Where had her toes gone to? She couldn't feel her toes. She began a tapping motion against the pedals, causing the engine to break into an indignant roar when she touched the accelerator. Couldn't be helped. If she turned the engine off, she'd be hypothermic in seconds. She switched to ankle rolls to try to restart the circulation and then did some stretches up to the car ceiling to help the circulatory process along.

There was no way she was giving up, not until she had proof. It was absolutely astounding to her that Mel had retreated into some kind of protective shell that apparently prohibited any kind of pursuit of the truth. Didn't she want to hear Joe's side of the story? Didn't she want to know what other secrets he'd been keeping? Didn't she want to see him beg and grovel for forgiveness? Apparently not. Instead, she'd just gone in to some kind of life-avoidance strategy that involved doing nothing but sleeping and working.

Waiting. Just more waiting. And . . . oh, crap, next door's bloody great big dopey retriever was making a beeline for her car, followed at a distance by Mrs McNee, next door's bloody great big narky owner, the woman whose dulcet tones could crack windows at a hundred yards. A formidable woman (church elder, member of the community council, head bouncer for the local WI), they'd had a hate/hate relationship ever since Mrs McNee decided to practise her opera singing with a view to entering *Britain's Got Talent* and Suze called the police to report that someone was being strangled next door.

The retriever stopped right below the driver's window.

'Nooooo, don't you dare!' It was too much, just too, too much. She was cold, she was hungry, she'd been betrayed, duped, devastated, she was doing a bad impersonation of a bad private investigator and now some daft big bloody dog was about to pee just inches from where she sat. She rolled down the window. 'Go home! Don't you even think about pissing on my car, you inbred mutt.'

The frantic hand signals that were intended to shoo him away somehow got lost in translation and were interpreted by Rex as, 'Sure, carry on – it would be an absolute delight to have you urinate all over my hub caps.'

'How dare you abuse him in that manner?' And there was the screech. 'Don't you ever speak to my dog like that again!'

Any modicum of calm shrivelled quicker than Rex's bladder. 'Mrs McNee, I say this from a place of neighbourly friendship – please, please, take your mutt and waddle right back up that driveway before I go over there, right now, and give your hydrangeas the same treatment the bold Rex just gave my front spoiler.'

Mrs McNee spluttered in disgust, outraged and appalled at the audacity – then she cut the poor, bewildered Rex off mid-flow and marched him off in the direction of home.

After a few more minutes of quiet fizzing, Suze sat up as she came to her first sensible conclusion of the night. When you reach a low point of threatening to do unthinkable things to a neighbour's blooms, the cosmos was definitely telling you to go home.

Her numb foot was just about to hit the accelerator when she spotted headlights in the rear mirror. It had to be him! The most dignified, mature course of action came to her immediately – she threw herself down across the passenger seat and covered her head with her hands. There was no way she wanted to get caught out – the object of this exercise was most definitely the other way around. One. Two. Three. She started counting, reckoning that by the time she got to fifty he'd be past her, have pulled into their drive, and she could then peek and catch him, hopefully with whatever bit of cheap trash he was fooling around with.

Twenty-eight. Twenty-nine. It was difficult to concentrate on counting slowly when all she could hear were the beats of her heart, thundering like hooves across the roof of the Vauxhall Corsa.

Aaaaaaargh!!! She clapped her hands over her eyes as a searing light invaded the car interior. Temporarily blinded, she sat upright and responded to the knocking on the window. One fumble for the window lever later, she was face to face with two of Strathclyde's finest protectors of the law, one of them a broad, fifty-something, ram-rod-straight sergeant, the other a younger, narrow-featured apprentice.

'Good evening, ma'm. Can you tell me why you are sitting here in this vehicle?'

Oh, crap. There was no way she was going to fess up to stalking with intent to castrate. Her mind was racing. Why would she be sitting there? Why?

'I was just . . . just . . .' It came to her in a flash. 'Just stopping to use my mobile phone. I'd hate to break the law by using it while driving.'

OK, so the extra bit was perhaps overdoing it, but these were desperate times. At least she wasn't resorting to using her feminine charms to get on the policeman's good side. No, she'd never do that. It was just purely coincidence that she chose that very moment to pull off her baseball cap, run her fingers through her golden mane, give her long, luxurious eyelashes a quick up and down in the breeze and exercise her lip muscles by pouting.

'According to a report, you've been sitting here for over two hours.'

'It was a very long call, officer.'

While Batman was giving her the most cynical, disbelieving look she'd seen since she was sixteen and trying to convince her mother that the pot that had just been found in her bag was actually oregano for her pizzas, Robin was now circling the car like a buzzard round roadkill. Wasn't at least one of them meant to be 'good cop'?

Robin returned to the front and Suze knew by the expression on his face that this wasn't going to go well.

'Ma'am, do you know that one of your back lights is out?'

How would she know that? How? When the back lights were on, she was in the car. When she was in the car, she couldn't see the back lights. It was one of life's great big catch-22 situations and she should just bloody well tell them that. But the feminine wiles were still calling the shots.

'I'm sorry, officer, I didn't,' she purred, taking the opportunity to blow wisps of hair out of her eyes in what she was sure was a cute and lovable fashion.

Batman regained control of the mantle of justice. 'Can I see your driving licence, please?'

'I'm sorry; I don't have it with me.'

The last couple of words sounded just a little shaky, as she began to get the sense that this wasn't going to end any time soon.

'Can you tell me the registration number of this vehicle?'

'No, it er . . . belongs to a friend.'

'A friend?'

'A friend.'

Suze could swear she saw the younger one's face light up as he sensed the possibility of a cuff. Or a collar. Damn, what was it they called it in *The Bill*?

Meanwhile, Batman fished a small notebook out of his pocket. 'Name?'

'Suzanne Marshall.'

'Address?'

Bollocks. She was stuck between a rock and a husband who would think she was demented if he ever heard about this. But maybe she could just tell the truth, brush them off and get out of there before any more damage was done.

'I live in that house there.'

Batman turned to look at the beautiful large house with the manicured lawn and the ornate water feature on the front drive, and then looked back at the some-what dishevelled-looking blonde, sitting in a clapped-out Vauxhall Corsa with only one tail-light. He didn't need super-powers to tell him something was amiss. 'OK then, madam – perhaps we should just go inside and you could retrieve your driving licence and we'll get this whole situation sorted out.'

Suze closed her eyes and exhaled wearily. 'I can't.'

'You can't,' Batman replied in a matter-of-fact tone. 'And why would that be?'

'Because I don't have any keys with me.' She hadn't brought her bag, her keys, nothing – just a flask of soup and a healthy portion of bitter & twisted.

'So you're locked out?'

'Not exactly.'

This was going from bad to couldn't-get-much-worse. Until suddenly, a beacon of hope emitted from the most unlikely of places: Mrs McNee was marching back down her driveway.

Yay – whoever thought that old bat would come to the rescue.

'Ask her, ask her!' Suze blurted, jabbing her finger in the direction of her neighbour.

But her neighbour got in there first. 'Ah, officers, thank you for coming so quickly.'

Holy shit, what did she say? *She* called the police? The headlines flashed into the forefront of Suze's mind – 'Local woman arrested for plant peeing scandal!'

'As neighbourhood-watch president, I'm always suspicious of strange vehicles. The streets just aren't safe any more.'

'Mrs McNee, is it?' Batman asked.

'That's right, officer,' she replied, and Suze couldn't be sure, but she thought she saw a smug grin aimed in her direction. 'Perhaps you can help us here. This lady claims to live in that house there – can you confirm this?'

Mrs McNee peered into the car. 'Well, you know, I can't see too well without my glasses, and, to be honest, I've never actually spoken to the woman who lives in there. We keep ourselves to ourselves around here.'

Liar! Suze wanted to scream. You couldn't fart within a hundred yards of this street without Mrs McNee having something to say about it.

'But I don't think that's her. No. The man who lives there is a lovely fellow, but, nope, don't think that I've ever seen her before.'

This time the smug grin was unmistakable.

'Madam, would you like to step out of the car, please?'

'Why?'

'Because I think it's best we nip down to the station and get this all sorted out there, don't you?'

Suze didn't. She really, really didn't.

Two hours later, when Avril finally turned up at the station to claim her car and her boss, Suze realised that she might have been able to take on Karl, she might have been strong enough to cope with emotional devastation, but she was no match for Mrs McNee and that bloody daft big dog.

'So, good night, boss?' Avril chuckled as they headed down the stairs of the station.

'Say another word and I'm putting you on minimum wage,' Suze warned, before a weird mixture of hilarity and upset overtook her and she had to hang on to the banister until the tears and laughter had subsided.

'Oh, fuck, Avril, you couldn't make this up. And look at you – did I get you out of your bed?'

Avril cast her glance downwards at her baggy pink trousers, tucked into furry pink Ugg-style boots, topped off with a baby-pink T-shirt that had fallen off one shoulder and a white headband that was keeping her loo-brush of platinum spikes off her face. 'No, I was just on my way out.'

Suze was off again, buckling over as huge big guffaws racked her ribcage.

'Seriously, boss, I was on my way out.' Avril was starting to look miffed now and Suze suddenly realised that she'd misjudged the situation completely. Lord, what was wrong with her? Her emotional compass was about as reliable as Avril's bloody tail-light.

'I know, hon, I was just . . . kidding.'

Avril didn't look convinced, but she decided it would be career limiting to argue.

'So where are you off to then?'

'Cammy and the rest from next door are in The City – thought I'd go join them. D'you want to come?'

Suze shook her head. 'No thanks. Mel invited me, but I think I'll give it a miss. I'll drop you off there if you want, though . . . on one condition.'

'Which is?'

'You never, ever mention tonight to anyone.'

Avril punched the air, to the amusement of the entire staff of the soup van next to them. 'Ah, this is great.'

'What is?' Suze replied bewildered.

'I've finally got something on you, boss.' She nudged Suze playfully with her shoulder. 'First time you ask me to do something I don't like, I'll be reminding you about our new big secret.'

Suze's chin fell open – who'd have thought Avril could be so shallow, so manipulative, so devious. Ah, it was like looking in a mirror.

Laughing again, she put one arm around her employee's shoulders and kissed her on the cheek. 'Yeah, but I was once a black belt and I reckon I can still kill with my thumbs, so let's call it quits.'

The city-centre streets were packed, so it took them fifteen minutes to make a journey of less than two miles. Eventually, they pulled up outside The City and Avril jumped out.

'Sure you don't want to come? I don't even know if they're still in there so I could end up looking like a right twat on my own.'

'Oh, I'm sure you'll cope,' Suze said with a smile. Mental note, must give Avril pay rise, she decided, as the vision in pink disappeared through the huge stone pillars at the front door.

Bed. All she wanted to do was go home, climb into bed

and forget the whole cock-up of a day. A taxi cut in from her left, blocking her in while it stopped to discharge its passengers. There was nothing she could do but give the driver a two-fingered gesture, then sit and wait. And think. It was time to stop all this nonsense with Karl: the ignoring, the stalking, the pin-punctured effigies. Tonight proved that it was time to grow up and start dealing with this in a mature, responsible way, commensurate with the fact that she was a successful, dignified businesswoman with only one police caution for loitering.

This was going to be the start of a whole . . .

The rest of the sentence never made it out, stifled by the sight in front of her eyes. The man and woman who had climbed out of David Coulthard's taxi were crossing the pavement, heading for the door of the club. They made a striking couple: him, so tall and handsome in his beautifully cut black suit and open-neck bullet-grey shirt, her in a stunning red, satin, off-the-shoulder cocktail dress that clung to every one of her fabulously proportioned curves. No wonder he couldn't keep his hands off her arse. No wonder she was throwing her head back as she laughed. No wonder they'd stopped and stepped to the side, him resting against the wall and pulling her tightly into him. No wonder her arms were going around his neck as she kissed him deeply, passionately.

And no wonder Suze's heart stopped beating as she watched her husband devour a woman who was definitely, absolutely not her.

Sixteen

Please be in bed. Please be in bed. Please be in bed. After three attempts to get her key in the door, Mel finally liberated the lock and staggered down the hall and into the lounge. Please be in bed. Please be in . . . 'Oh hey, Suze, you still up?'

Suze was lying on the couch with a cloth over her face, wearing her standard pyjama outfit of black Juicy Couture trousers and a Rolling Stones T-shirt.

Mel's stomach gave another token lurch and she half walked, half limped to the kitchen. Milk. She needed milk. She wondered if she was physically able to commando crawl back through the lounge and make it to her bedroom without stopping for a post-mortem of the evening's activities. It wasn't that she didn't want to talk to Suze, but at that moment Johnny Depp could be standing in front of the fireplace naked and she'd still opt for the straight-to-bed route.

She peeked round the doorway. The cloth suggested a headache, so perhaps Suze didn't feel like talking either. Perhaps she could just sneak on . . .

'So how was the night? Tell me everything and then I'm going to bore your tits off until dawn on my specialised subject "Karl Marshall is a wanker".'

Mel momentarily considered the options, starting with the truth: I snogged my Director of Sack and Crack Support Services while pished at a party we gatecrashed.

She then ratified that to a white lie: it was fine, we all got on great and a merry time was had by all. And finally, after applying due thought and measured reason, all fuelled by a bloodstream that could have pickled vegetables, she shuffled back into the lounge, flopped down on her huge cream squishy armchair and decided to avoid personal disclosure by cutting straight to 'Why? What did he do?'

Suze reached up and slid the cloth off her face, revealing two puffy eyes and a frown line that had challenged her Botox and emerged victorious.

'I was right, Mel. I was right all along. He's seeing someone else.'

'No way! How do you know that? Oh, bloody bollocks, my hair is in my milk.'

If Suze was disconcerted by her state of distraction, she didn't show it. 'I saw him. I can't believe it. And not that it matters but she's stunning. Arse.'

'But . . . but how? When? Where was he?' This was way, way too much to absorb.

'I was thinking about joining you at The City on my way back from Pilates, but, when I pulled up outside, Karl was there, up against a wall, with his tongue stuck down the throat of a brunette in a posh frock.'

Mel tried to process the information but she got stuck on panic at Suze's mention of The City. Suze had been there? Karl had been there? Did that mean that they'd seen her? Seen her with Cammy?

'I didn't . . . didn't see you there.'

Exasperation sneaked into Suze's voice as she tried to steer back to the crux of the situation. 'No, the fact that I saw my husband pressing a hard-on against some tart in the middle of the street somehow made me change my mind about coming inside. I mean, how could he, Mel? Is he banging down our door begging me to come back? No. Is he flooding me with flowers and token bloody gestures of apology? No. He's already moved on to the next one. What a prick. Shit, I can't believe I married him.'

'Oh, come on, Suze, you know this isn't like Karl.' Mel wasn't sure if she was talking out of some remnant of loyalty to a man she'd thought of as a brother for the last eight years or from guilt that just a short time ago she too had inserted her tongue into the throat of a non-marital recipient. 'He loved you, Suze, and you loved him – you were great together. I'd never seen a better couple than you two. You had everything.'

'Mel, don't take this the wrong way, but thank fuck you don't work for the Samaritans or the suicide rate would rocket.'

'Sorry, but it's just so . . .' She didn't get the rest of the words out before her face crumpled into a mass explosion of puckers and tears. So much for her temporary reprieve from mourning her lost love. Right there, right then, she felt every bit as bad as the first day that Joe left.

Suze realised that she wasn't going to get any further in her specialised subject, and settled instead for easing a sobbing Mel out of the chair and ushering her through to her room.

Thankfully, the Gods of Drunk Women waited until Mel was directly in front of her bed before allowing her legs to buckle.

'I never asked you, Suze, who was it?'
'Who?'

'The woman with Karl. Who was she?'

'Dunno. I only saw her from the back. But I'll find out – not that it matters now that I've caught him.'

'Yep, that's all that matters, isn't it?'

The edge in Mel's voice, an unfamiliar note of annoyance, made Suze stop in mid-pillow-plump. Her shoulders slumped as a flash of realisation dawned. 'Sorry, Mel.' She pushed a long red curl off Mel's face. 'I'm being a complete dickhead. I get so wrapped up in this that I forget that I've inadvertently trashed your life too. I've absolutely no idea why you put up with me.'

One big fat tear squeezed out of Mel's left eye and left a coin-sized stain on the buttermilk taffeta duvet. Brushing the wet track off her cheek, she managed a wonky grin. 'It's that or bumping you off and I don't fancy doing jail time.'

Smiling, Suze pulled the duvet up around Mel's neck, leaned down, kissed her cheek. 'Goodnight, babe.'

''Night.' Mel just got the reply out as exhaustion won out over nausea and her lids began to close. She'd just about made it to sleep when a question broke through the befuddlement. 'Suze, do you wish that you hadn't done it now? The whole honeytrap thing?'

'Sometimes. I still think I had to know but I'm so sorry you got caught in the crossfire.'

'Me too. I want my life back,' she whispered, half sleeping now. 'But he's gone.'

Suze flicked out the light and wandered back into the lounge, slumped back down on the couch, took a slug of Jack Daniel's and coke from the tumbler beside her, flicked PLAY on the remote control to activate the Killers track on the iPod dock and then lay back down, returning the cold damp cloth to its soothing position on the top of her head.

Bollocks, what a mess. Karl was the incarnation of evil on earth. She was a neurotic nightmare who had somehow managed to act as an incendiary device to her relationship and – worse – to her best friend's marriage too. Joe had turned out to be a faithless git. And Mel . . . well, there was the real kick in the crotch. Mel didn't deserve any of this. Just a few weeks ago, Mel had been perfectly happy, totally content and excited about the life in front of her. Now everything had changed. And it was all her fault.

Suze turned her head to the side and let the towel slip to the floor. Opening one eye, she stared at the phone in front of her, an idea formatting in her brain. This was crazy. Yes, Joe had done something terrible and, yes, he deserved to be punished, but didn't Mel just say that she wanted him back? Well, if Mel wanted him back, surely he should know that and maybe then he'd stop being a prick and come fight for her. Yep, fight for her. Win her heart back. Make Mel smile again. That's exactly what had to happen and it had to happen right now. She stopped staring at the phone and snatched it from its cradle, then punched in Speed-dial 1.

It answered on the first ring.

'Mel?' Joe's voice was sleepy but with definite overtones of hope.

'No, it's Suze.'

'Oh.' As hope left the building, it passed urgency on the way in. 'Is something wrong? Is Mel OK?'

'She's fine. Listen. Here's the thing. I still think you're lower than pond life, but I think you should know that she misses you. I know it's none of my business –' she ignored the ironic snort that came right back at her '– but I think you should contact her and have another shot at grovelling.'

'But last time I tried she was really insistent that she wanted space.'

'Look, it's up to you, Joe, but she said tonight that she wants her old life back so I think it might be worth another shot.'

Awkward silence. The kind of silence that happens when both people have so much they want to ask each other, but neither can find a way to start.

Suze cracked first. 'So I have to go. I'll er . . . well . . . goodbye.' Her finger was just about to press the disconnect button when she heard him speak.

'Suze?'

'Yes?'

'Thanks.'

Seventeen

'Working on a Saturday? Business must be good.'

Karl glanced up, face passive, like there was absolutely nothing extraordinary whatsoever about his estranged wife standing in his office doorway.

'Well, well, well – my absent wife. Run out of marriages to break up or have you retired happy now that you managed to go for the double and wreck two in one weekend?'

Ouch. To think that his quick wit and bolshy attitude used to turn her on. She leaned against the doorframe and contemplated whether or not to give in to her sudden urge to take off one of her shoes and throw it at him. But how she handled this was important. She had to be calm. Collected. Play her cards close to her chest. She was a chic (legs shaved, hair pulled back into an elegant chignon and the fact that she was wearing his favourite black fitted skirt suit was purely coincidental of course), assertive woman who just wanted to gather the facts and move on.

He casually leaned back in his brown leather chair, the one that had been his dad's before him and, even from a position of unadulterated blind bloody fury, she had to admit he looked good. The sleeves were rolled up on his pale-blue shirt, top two buttons open, showing just a hint of the white gold chain she'd had made for his thirtieth birthday. The small dog-tag pendant on the end had his initials engraved on the back. He'd loved it. His face had lit up when he'd opened the box, and her thank-you kiss had lasted for the next four exceptionally orgasmic hours.

A gasp of sudden breathlessness told her that either there was no oxygen in the room or her lungs were on a go-slow. She went with the lungs, since he was still sitting there, staring at her, one eyebrow raised in expectation, showing absolutely no sign of needing breathing apparatus.

'So were you ever going to come to talk to me?' she asked. Great. Staying calm. Aloof.

'No.'

Hackles up, back teeth grinding. And the fleeting thought that she should have brought two pairs of shoes. Stay in control. Do not freak out. 'That says it all, doesn't it?'

The flash across his eyes told her that one had rattled his cage. 'Just exactly what does it say, Suze? Come on then, you're the expert. What does it say? Does it say that my wife loved and trusted me so much that she set me up? Does it say that she walked out and left? Does it say that she took down my brother's marriage? Does it say that she still, *still* thinks in her twisted, screwed-up mind that there is some kind of justification for all of this? What, Suze – go on tell me – what does it say?' Every word had been delivered with the ice-cold, menacing tone that she'd only ever heard him use on cold-callers and a boy racer who'd rear-ended his Mercedes with a souped-up Subaru.

'Don't you *dare* lay all this at my door, Karl,' she hissed, control slipping, freak-out looming. Ugh, why did nothing ever go to plan?

'First of all, what Joe did was entirely his own fault. He behaved like a bastard and he got caught. His problem, not mine. Mel deserved to know what he got up to behind her back.'

The vein on the side of his neck was throbbing now. 'Shit, Suze, you're priceless. Joe had never cheated on Mel. Ever. He just got carried away that night, said a couple of stupid things that he'd have regretted the next morning anyway. He'd never have gone through with it. But, thanks to you, what was a momentary lack of judgement by a bloke who was flattered by some attention turned into the biggest disaster of his life. Way to go there, Sherlock.'

Still ice cold, still menacing and now with an extra hint of disgust.

When she met him back in college, the first thing she realised about him was that he was the kind of guy who just had a presence. When Karl spoke, people listened . . . usually because he was being funny or fascinating or just injecting some energy into everyone around him. If there was a spontaneous game of football at lunchtime, Karl was invariably behind it. Saturday-night pub crawl? Karl's idea. En masse expedition down to the shores of Loch Lomond for an all-day barbecue that melted into great music and dancing through the night? Karl drove the bus and brought the boom box. And the flip side of his character, the one that never ran from a crisis, that faced problems and persevered until he'd sorted them out, the one that was just as bloody-minded and stubborn as she was, was as much of a turn-on as the lighter shades of his personality.

However, now that she was the problem, his measured control was fast losing its appeal.

'What was I supposed to do? Ignore what he'd done? Not tell Mel?'

119

'Yes!'

'How typically male – ignore the facts and go the subterfuge line,' she blurted, then immediately realised that she'd just put herself in a pot/kettle situation.

'That's pretty rich coming from a woman who brought in an undercover investigator to set up her husband.'

'KARL, YOU WERE HAVING AN AFFAIR!' If the windows hadn't been installed by master-craftsmen they'd be rattling by now.

'I wasn't.' Two words. Delivered completely deadpan and backed up with eyes that were blazing with rage.

Deep breath. Deep breath. She fought to regain control, knowing that going the screaming-banshee route was only going to add yet another layer of humiliation to the Mortification Kilimanjaro that was currently sitting on top of her.

'Come on, Karl, it's time for a bit of truth here. For months, you were detached, elusive, ignored me. You haven't been present in our marriage for a long time and it doesn't take an idiot to work out why. And, since my husband wouldn't talk to me, I just had to find another way to get confirmation of the facts.'

Back upright now, elbows on the desk, his head fell into his hands. Eventually, almost sadly, he spoke. 'I'm only going to say it one more time, Suze. I wasn't having an affair.'

Fuck, was he never going to stop lying? She pulled herself up to her full height, took a deep breath and fought to stay as cold and calm as he was. She had the smoking gun and right now she could think of a couple of really interesting places to shove it.

'Karl, I *saw* you.'

That one got his attention. Almost wearily, he glanced up at her. 'What did you see? Huh, Suze? Whatever it was, you were mistaken.'

'You. Her. Last night. Outside The City. I saw you. Right at the point where you kissed her in full view of half of Glasgow. The half that included your absent wife.' The pain was deeply physical as a tsunami of blood rushed to her head and threatened imminent explosion.

It was a killer blow that even made Mr Cool flinch. He rubbed his eyes, as if that would make this whole scenario vanish. But, no, when he opened them again, she was still there, facing up to him, expression furious, bitter, hurt. She resisted the urge to scream, to shout. Silence. Make him squirm. Let's see how he would lie his way out of this one.

'Suze, in all the years we were married, I swear I wasn't having an affair.'

AAAAAAAAARGH! Fuck silence, it was time for all-out verbal combat. She opened her mouth to scream, yell, castigate, but he got there first.

'But I am now.'

He didn't even see the Louboutin stiletto coming.

Eighteen

Josie, dressed in her finest Pussy Galore, stormed into the shop with her customary calm, conservative, refined elegance.

'Sixty-one years old and I finally slipped the tongue on a man with sideburns! Give this old slapper a coconut!' With that she took a deep bow of thanks to her audience, which – at that moment – consisted of six mannequins, the postman and Mel.

The postman fled, looking terrified, taking a circuitous route around a rack of Calvin Kleins so that he stayed at least four feet away from Josie at all times.

Despite the drums that were beating out a tribal warrior tune in her head, Mel had to laugh ... up until Josie weighed in with an enquiry into her state of wellbeing.

'What's with the dark shades? Migraine, hangover or are you practising for fame?'

'First one. And the second,' Mel replied. 'Actually, more the second.'

Josie tutted. 'I just don't know what has happened to the younger generations. It's bloody disgraceful. When I was your age, I could empty Oddbins and party for four days straight.'

'Josie, you can *still* empty Oddbins and party for four days straight.'

'Very true. But my arthritis doesn't half play up on day five.'

Mel gave up trying to negotiate a multi-way bra that seemed to require intelligence of MENSA proportions.

'So where did you two disappear to last night? One minute I was feeling up Elvis on the dancefloor and the next you were gone.'

Mel felt small beads of sweat pop out across her fore-head. She'd been dreading this. Her first thought when she'd woken up that morning was 'God, I feel ill,' followed by a horrified 'Please tell me I didn't kiss Cammy,' and a groaned, 'Oh, crap, I did.' She had just been about to go sob like a small toy-less child on Suze's shoulders when she heard the front door banging and realised she was alone and would just have to go the merciless self-recrimination route.

How could she? Really, just how? For the last eight years, she'd only kissed one man and now four weeks into a crisis and she was suddenly puckering up in a random fashion. How could she? And Cammy? How would she face him? He was one of her best friends, closest confidants, like the brother she never had and now she'd ambushed him with Dyson-like suction. What had she been thinking?

She'd castigated herself all through her shower (extra hot), her breakfast (two Paracetamol) and her wardrobe selection (purple skinny jeans, black basque, sheer chiffon psychedelic tunic with a chunky copper belt), and come to the conclusion that she was a terrible person and the only hope was that Cammy was so drunk last night that he'd have no recollection of it whatsoever.

'Bloody hell, it's like a secret-service convention in here today.'

Josie's running commentary was interrupted by the opening of the door and in walked Cammy, dark glasses firmly in place.

'Would you look at the state of you two? You're light-weights. Serious lightweights,' she announced.

Stomach flipping with anxiety, Mel went for the breeziest 'good morning' she could manage, underpinned with a desperate hope that Cammy's memory was a blank.

'Morning,' he replied. Hopes up. 'I er, I . . . I . . . doesn't matter.' Hopes dashed. Cammy never stuttered. Never blustered. He was the personification of smooth. Even Josie was left open-mouthed as she glanced from one to the other, eyebrows sitting somewhere close to her hairline. 'Oh, no. You two didn't . . .'

'No!' they both blurted simultaneously.

She stared at Mel, then Cammy, then Mel, obviously not convinced. 'Mmmm. I'm thinking there's been some form of scandalous behaviour here. Maybe there's hope for the younger generation after all. I'm going to make a cuppa – if you have a shag in the changing rooms while I'm gone, I'll be totally impressed.'

The silence lasted for several unbearable seconds.

Cammy broke it first. 'Do you want to talk about this?'

Mel shook her head. 'No. Do you?'

'No.'

'Can we forget about it and pretend it never happened? Seriously. Just wipe it out?'

There was a pensive pause before Cammy smiled and walked towards her, then wrapped his arms around her bear-hug style. 'Of course we can. I'm really sorry, it was just . . . madness. Drink. I don't know.'

'Exactly!' She reciprocated the squeeze. 'Thanks,

Cammy. And I'm sorry too. I'm such a mess just now and I've no idea what I'm doing half the time. So thanks. Thanks for being so sweet.'

'No problem. Now go brush your teeth again because you smell like a Jamaican rum shack.'

'Thank you. Not one of your most flattering lines, but appreciated nonetheless.'

She threw up a mental prayer of gratitude, spun round and headed off in the direction of the staff room, passing Josie on the way back.

'Well, madam, anything to confess?'

Cammy answered before she could even get her mouth open. 'Cubicle two and she made the earth move, Josie.'

Josie cackled into her Tetleys. 'Ah, I love my job.'

The smell of fresh coffee assaulted Mel's senses the minute she reached her office. God bless Josie. She'd left a fruit juice, a coffee and a banana muffin on Mel's desk, with a hastily scribbled smiley face on a post-it note stuck to the muffin.

Slumping in her chair, she weighed up the options: coffee would make her feel better, orange juice would give her an infusion of vitamin C, muffin would form a comfort-eating situation appropriate to her fragile, heart-sore state. The ringing of the phone stopped her as she was just about to take her first bite. It was a sad day when she couldn't even manage to console herself with stodge.

'La Femme, Le Homme, how can I help you?'

'Hi Mel, it's Avril next door. Have you seen Suze today? She hasn't shown up for work and I just want to check where she is before I shut up shop and blow the week's takings on a fortnight in the Bahamas.'

'I'm not sure, to be honest.'

'Dead? Missing? Sick? It's unlike her not to call so I'm thinking death or alien abduction.'

'You are so your mother's daughter. I think she's fine, though. I heard her going out this morning really early so maybe she just had something to do before she came in.'

'Bugger. I really fancied the Bahamas.'

'Yeah, well unpack that suitcase because I'm sure there's a very simple, harmless explanation.'

'Shame,' Avril tutted.

The phone was barely back in its cradle when the door swung open and, in a scene scarily reminiscent of the one that heralded the worst afternoon of her life only a few weeks before, Suze burst in, emanating pent-up fury like an emissary from the Consulate of Really Bad News.

The groan was out before Mel could stop it. What now?

'He admitted it, Mel – he *is* seeing someone. And you're never going to bloody believe who it is!'

Nineteen

Not for the first time, Suze cursed herself for moving out instead of kicking his lying arse through the door. True, she'd have to deal with the operatic overtures of that maniac old boot of a neighbour, but at least she'd get some kind of spiritual comfort from being able to cut up his clothes, melt his CD collection and donate his golf clubs to the local Scout group's bring-and-buy sale.

He'd done it. He'd met someone else. Ten years of their lives together had just been thrown away for what? Apparently it was great sex with a woman who had the body of a goddess. And she didn't believe for a single minute that it had only started after they parted ways. Karl's behaviour in the months leading up to that was so erratic that it had to have been going on then too. Guilt. Guilt makes people act very strangely and obviously he was feeling so guilty that he just withdrew from her completely. Although he wasn't quite guilty enough to call it off when he realised that she was suspicious. Nooooo. He'd decided that the other obvious strategy was the most sensible one: snog the face off his new tart in the middle of Glasgow city centre for the world and his voyeuristic bloody granny to see.

But then, if she was shagging a six-foot model called Anneka, she'd want the whole world to know too. Oh, the irony. Karl sleeping with Cammy's ex-girlfriend. They were only fifty years and a few introductions away from a hippy commune.

OK, plans. She needed plans. There was no way she was letting him get away with this. She'd done the whole hysteria thing in Mel's shop that morning, ending only when Josie had trapped her in a hug that was thinly disguised as a choke hold and held her until she'd finally stopped hyperventilating and regained the powers of non-supersonic speech. Mel had offered to come home with her but what was the point? Then the two of them would be sitting wailing about the unfairness of bloody life. So she'd refused, and, instead, Josie had walked her home, removed all sharp objects from the immediate vicinity and refused to leave until Suze promised not to make abusive phone calls to her soon-to-be ex.

Right now, the thought was still tempting. Nothing too crazy – just a few calls that sat somewhere between 'I hate you for this' and 'you might want to investigate the process for obtaining a restraining order'.

Instead, she snatched the remote control for the iPod dock, flicked on some classic Guns n' Roses and grabbed a pad from the kitchen worktop. List. She needed a list. There was no way she was going to be the victim in this and the only way she knew how to deal with it was to take back control, make a list, get going, move on . . . OK, so she needed to:

1. Get a lawyer. A ruthless one who would leave him with nothing but bruised bollocks.
2. Split all joint finances.
3. Have him removed as director of Pluckers.

4. Retrieve everything from home.
5. Put house on market.
6. Find somewhere flash-fucking-tastic to live. A city pad. Penthouse.
7. Take Josie up on offer to slash Mercedes tyres.
8. Drink. Lots.
9. Book a holiday. Need sun.
10. And . . . and . . . buy new Louboutin stilettos.

Apparently marital strife came with the side-effect of chronic attention deficit disorder because before she got any further she realised she wanted coffee. Tossing the pad aside, she went into the kitchen. For Mel's next birthday, she was buying her a decent coffee maker because this instant stuff was a disgrace to coffee beans. While the kettle boiled, she perched on one of the stools at the breakfast bar. This room was so Mel. Sunny-yellow shaker units, white oak flooring, with a collection of pots and jars and little trinket boxes strewn over every surface. The huge vase of sunflowers that usually sat in the middle of the old reclaimed-wood table was gone now as, unsurprisingly, the urge to replenish it had left Mel sometime around watching her husband disappear off into the sunset. She loved the huge hand-painted canvasses on two of the four walls, gorgeous abstracts that blended thick ridges of golds and coppers and creams. Mel had always been the more artistic of the two of them. While Suze could throw together a great outfit in ten minutes, or read a balance sheet upside down, the thought of spending an afternoon in a paint-covered smock filled her with horror: the mess, the unflattering shape – no one ever looked good draped in excess fabric.

The knock of the letterbox interrupted her thoughts and she yelled out as she reached the hallway.

'Josie, I've no intention of topping myself,' she shouted, 'so you can take me off suicide watch.'

As she wrenched open the door, the first thing she saw was the large Elastoplast that was stuck across his forehead.

'Nice fashion accessory – did your new girlfriend choose that?'

'We need to talk, Suze.'

'No, we don't.'

'We do.'

'We don't.'

'Suze, please, we . . .'

She didn't hear the rest over the noise of the door slamming in his face. Let his new girlfriend pick out a suitable fashion statement for a broken nose.

He knocked again, several times, then a draught reached her as he opened the letterbox and shouted through. 'Suze, I'm not leaving until we talk. You can kick me out afterwards if you want but there's stuff you should know. Either let me in or I'm just going to start telling you, and every neighbour in the block will hear.'

Her reply was succinct and far from the normal advice of a relationship-counselling service. 'Piss off.'

'OK, so we do it my way. Remember that time we were having sex and you were . . .'

Shit! A vision of the old couple next door flashed into her head in a whole shock, exploding-pacemaker, sudden-death scenario. She wrenched the door open, standing back to let him enter. 'You've got ten minutes. Maximum. I can't stand to be around you for any longer than that.'

For a moment their eyes made contact and for a split second Suze thought she saw the old Karl, the one that she had loved on sight. How had this happened to them? They'd been so great together, so tight. Sure, they'd always been fiery but, come on, who wasn't? Actually, she already knew the answer to that: Joe and Mel weren't. They'd had one of those harmonious, serene, sweet relationships that was pretty close to perfect – and would have bored Suze to fucking death. No, she always thought that, in marrying Karl, she had met her match. Her throat tightened as she wondered if they'd be so compatible when it came to divorce.

Like an obedient Labrador, he followed her into the lounge and sat on the edge of one of the armchairs, directly across from her position on the moral high ground of the sofa.

'So . . . ?' Her chin led the question, jutting out, demanding.

A couple of clearings of the throat punctuated Karl's long hesitation. 'You're not going to like anything I have to say, Suze.'

'Trust me, that's not exactly a newsflash. Let me save you the trouble. If it's about a divorce, you've got it. If you want me to move the rest of my stuff out, you've got that too.' She picked up the list from beside her and worked her way through the rest of the To Dos. 'I also plan to split the finances, find a new house, go on holiday . . .' She omitted the tyre-slashing, not wanting to incriminate Josie or make a return journey to the police station.

'I promise you I wasn't having an affair before you left, Suze.'

Her temperature went straight to volcanic lava. 'I don't want to hear it. We've had this conversation and I don't believe you. I DON'T BELIEVE YOU. Now if that frankly majestic attempt at talking shite was your reason for coming here, then go. Just go. Because . . .'

'The business was in trouble.'

'. . . I don't want to – what?' Mission aborted by large spanner suddenly clanging in works.

'The business was in trouble. *Is* in trouble.'

131

'Wha– Wha–' The mouth was moving but the powers of articulation were taking a few moments to catch up. 'What business? How can it be in trouble? I'm fully booked from morning until night, Mel has never been busier. Our businesses are fine. And, if things are a bit slow over on the construction side, then, hey, that's your problem, Donald Trump, isn't it?'

Hang on, was this a ploy? Was this some kind of pre-emptive strike to convince her that he was skint so that she would go easy on him financially? Of all the . . .

'I wish it was that easy, Suze. But . . .' A strangled noise caught in his throat, and if Suze didn't know with one-hundred-per-cent certainty that she'd married the man who would win the 'Least Likely To Get Emotional In Any Crisis' Award, she'd have been pretty sure it was a sob. Watching his face, ashen, suddenly crumpled and etched with deep frown lines across his forehead and between his eyebrows (why had she never noticed them before?), all doubts immediately dissipated. He *was* telling the truth. The grains of certainty that she had about the situation began to slowly slip through her manicured fingers.

OK, calm. Stay calm. She made a conscious effort to bring her pulse back down to something approaching normal.

After a few deep exhalations, she motioned at him to go ahead. 'Talk. Just talk,' she told him. For the first time that day she didn't sound homicidal. Crap, she would never admit it but she was almost starting to feel sorry for him.

'We took a big hit last year with the Foreman contract . . .'

OK, that much she vaguely knew already. The Foreman Group, a national chain of leisure centres that had planned to add another ten outlets to their portfolio and had contracted Marshall & Sons to build them. The first five venues were well into construction when the global financial system had gone into meltdown and the credit crunch had hit. The bank withdrew funding for further expansion, and the Foreman Group had crashed almost overnight, one of thousands of companies that met the same fate last year.

'It was too big to recover from. They owed us nearly a quarter of a million when they went down and we just didn't have the kind of resources to sustain that loss. We'd bought the supplies, paid the men. I swear, Suze, there was no way we could have seen that coming. Foreman has been solid for over thirty years and they . . . are you OK?'

The realisation that she was doing an impression of a puffa fish had just struck home. Her brain had stopped functioning at the very moment he'd said 'quarter of a million'. Holy shit! Quarter of a million what? How could they possibly run up a liability that came to a quarter of a million fricking pounds? It was obscene. Impossible.

'Breathe, Suze, just breathe.'

'I'm trying to fucking breathe,' she hissed. While holding her breath. 'Quarter. Of. A. Million. Pounds.'

Dear God, this couldn't be any worse. Acute self-awareness had several benefits, one of which was knowing and accepting without question that she was shallow. Materialistic. Held an exceptionally high appreciation for financial resources and the accruement of wealth. They both did. It was one of the core compatibilities of their relationship. And if she was feeling this bad, then . . .

Mist lifted. Situation cleared. It was suddenly all so obvious. Karl was the fixer, the doer, that Alpha male who was always in complete control. His company taking that kind of hit and crashing around him would have devastated every iota of his being. All this time she'd been blaming her reluctance to have children, other women, mid-life crisis, when all along the root of the problem had been something completely different.

'Why didn't you tell me? Karl, I could have helped, could have supported you, could have tracked down Mr Foreman and beat the crap out of him.'

He smiled, clearly unsure if that was an attempt to comfort him or a legitimate threat. 'I just couldn't. We've lost everything, Suze.'

'No, we haven't. We've still got the house and the shop and the salon and we can –'

Back in his seat now, the saddest expression she'd ever seen crossed his face and his head fell towards his chest.

'We don't have any of it, do we?'

Slowly, painfully, his head moved from side to side. 'It's all gone, Suze. Our businesses were all linked under one holding company. It was the only way to get the finance for you and Mel to set up and at the time we were doing great on the construction side, so, instead of taking out new-business loans, we just extended the overdraft and negotiated preferential repayment fees. Seemed like the best idea at the time. But now the bank wants the lot. We've got one month until they call in the overdraft and that will force all of us into bankruptcy.'

'Fucking hell! Does Joe know about this?'

'He knows we're in trouble but he doesn't know how bad it is. His job's always been to handle the workload, I handle the business side of things. It's the way it's always been. The nights when I told you I was at the gym, I was at the office, trying to find some kind of solution to this. I couldn't think about anything else, Suze. It's been constant, 24/7 for months, just the pressure and the desperation and trying, just trying to get us out of this big fucking black hole. And I know I was ignoring you but I just didn't want you to know. But now . . . now you do. Now you know

134

everything,' he finished, his voice so wracked with pain it was heartbreaking.

Suze took the only available course of action – she put her head between her knees until the urge to faint had passed. When she finally managed to retract it, she glanced up and realised that he was on his feet, staring at her, his face ravaged with pain, eyes red with unshed tears. She'd been right about the guilt, but wrong about the source. Of course he would have been destroyed by this, of course he would have been preoccupied and of course his West of bloody Scotland Alpha-male pride would have forced him to internalise it all and cut her out of the picture. And she was also self-aware enough to realise that in a small way she was complicit in this. Hadn't she always enjoyed the fact that he took care of things, didn't burden her with day-to-day stuff, just dealt with problems and issues without bothering her with the details? Wasn't she happy to know absolutely nothing about his business and leave that side of their lives completely to him? She'd never, she realised, asked him anything about work – just taken delight in cele-brating the new contracts and the perks, but shown absolutely no interest in the challenges and issues. And when things had started to crumble? She hadn't even known. What kind of a wife was she who thought her husband was having an affair when he'd actually been watching every-thing he'd built fall down around him?

'I've fucked up so badly, Suze, and I'm so, so sorry.' He turned and took a few steps towards the door.

'No! Don't you bloody dare.' Her voice, menacingly calm, stopped him in his tracks. 'Don't you dare come here and just tell me all that and think you can walk out and leave. Stand there and don't dare fucking move. I have questions.'

His eyebrows puckered into a line-enhancing perplexed frown as he muttered, 'Shoot.'

'Don't tempt me. OK, I need to know some things. Anneka – when did it start? And don't even think about lying.'

'Bumped into her in a bar the week after you left. Company was gone, you were gone and it was a stupid, immature way to stop me thinking about all the ways my life had fallen apart.'

'Great,' she offered, sarcasm dripping from every letter. 'Couldn't you just have turned to drink and drugs like everyone else?'

The corners of his mouth lifted slightly for the first time since he arrived. She soon sent them in the other direction with: 'And now?'

'We're still seeing each other.'

'Got that loud and clear last night. Do you love her?'

'No!' It was the first time he'd raised his voice. 'Look, Suze, we've been out, we've had dinner, and, yes, I'm really, really sorry but I've been sleeping with her. But it's not been a relationship, it's been a tool for denial that let me block out the crap-storm of day-to-day life.'

Ouch, painful on so many levels. That should have been her. *She* should have been there for him, *she* should have been the one soothing and comforting him in his darkest hours. After she'd murdered him for losing all their money, that is.

'Finish it.'

He nodded. 'You don't even have to say that. It was over the minute you walked into my office this morning.'

'Before I hit you with my shoe?'

Another smile. 'Way before. Although that did seal the deal.'

It was hard to comprehend. She'd just been given devastating news, her life had just been torn to shreds, yet for the first time in weeks she felt a glimmer of something approaching normality. Even relief. At least now she knew the truth, knew what she was dealing with, and that – at long last – pushed the fear and the insecurity-fuelled craziness to one side.

'Listen, Suze, I've been a complete prick.'

'Yeah, well, I haven't exactly been Einstein lately either.'

There was a moment of silence as they accepted the reality of both statements.

'You were supposed to argue with me there,' she informed him.

He shook his head and let out a low whistle. 'Sorry, but come on – the whole trap thing? Even for you, that one was nuts. Did not see that coming at all.'

'That's the whole point.'

His scent assailed her senses as he kneeled down in front of her and took both her hands in his. 'Suze, I don't expect you to trust me. I don't expect anything from you. But I love you. And, if there's any way back from this for us, you have to tell me because I'll do it.'

She shook her head dolefully. 'There's no way back, Karl, not now that you're poor.'

His eyes widened, then immediately creased as he realised that she wasn't serious. They sat there for a few moments, just staring at each other, both assimilating this new shaky truce, both unsure as to the next move. The first snap decision came from Suze.

'I've no idea if there's any way back.' Surprising even herself, she ran a hand through his hair as she spoke. The anger was gone. The fear was gone. And left behind was something entirely different. The real, simple, honest truth was that she loved him – flaws and all. 'But we could remain open-minded to the possibility.'

'Open-minded?'

'Open-minded. Oh, and I reserve the right to succumb

to paranoia at a later date and interrogate you at length as to whether she was better than me in bed, had thinner thighs, a nicer arse . . .'

Unexpectedly, the sound of his laughter made tears prickle up underneath her eyes. She blinked to beat them back into submission.

'No to all of that. Fuck, I've been such a prick.'

'You've said that already but you have my permission to repeat it hourly from now until the end of time.'

His mood suddenly turned sombre again. 'You do understand all this, don't you? We're broke. Wiped out. Everything's gone.'

'Stop, I get it. But, look, we'll cope.'

'How?'

She leaned down, picked up her pad and pen, and crossed out what was already written there. Then she flicked over the page. 'We need a list. There must be things we can do, options we can explore, people we can speak to. If there's any way at all to sort this out, then we have to put together a cohesive plan and get it done. We're not the first business to get into trouble, Karl, shit happens. But we need to try to find a way of coming out of the other end.'

'You're amazing, you know that?'

'I do. Now go to that kitchen and don't come back until you're in possession of wine. OK, so number one. Number one. What's number one? Oh, shit, Karl, I've just realised what the first thing we have to do is.'

'What's that?' his voice echoed from the depths of the fridge.

Suze put pen to paper, a feeling of dread rising from the pit of her stomach.

1. Tell Mel.

Twenty

'Mel. Mel. MEL!'

Mel didn't understand. Why was Josie there? Why was she shouting at her? Why was she disturbing her Sunday-morning lie-in with a voice that could act as a PA system for a large football stadium? This was so unfair. Just a few minutes longer. She'd ignore her for a few minutes longer. That way she could snuggle up to Joe and maybe even have a bit of a fumble. Mmm, that would be nice. And then they could go for brunch with Suze and Karl and . . .

'MELISSA!!'

She jerked up so violently every muscle in her lower back spasmed.

'Aaaw! What? Where is it? What?'

'Sorry to wake you, hon, but it's bedlam out there and Cammy and I just aren't enough to go around. He's feeling about as good as you and he's been rushed off his feet all day so I've told him to take a break. Hope that was OK.'

Panic rising, Mel quickly checked her watch. 2 p.m. Shit, she'd been splayed across her desk, sound asleep for nearly four hours – no wonder she felt like she'd been drop-kicked from one end of George Square to another. And she'd left Josie and Cammy to deal with the busiest day of the week on their own. That's it; she was never going out again. Ever. She was obviously far too past it to deal with the combination of late nights and the entire cocktail menu of a city-centre club.

'Sorry, Josie, I'll be right there, just give me a few minutes to sort myself.'

'No problem, pet. Oh, and much as it's an unusual look, you might want to scrape the banana muffin off the side of your face. And take my advice and down a couple of painkillers because you'll need it to deal with the zoo out there.'

'Why, who's in?'

'New customers – let's just call them the Paisley Six.' Right on cue, a massive roar of hilarity reached her from next door. 'Better go, they've probably got Cammy tied up and are using him as their own personal sex toy.'

It took less than five minutes for her to nip into the loo, brush her teeth and her hair, slap some foundation on her gleaming complexion, dab on a bit of lippy, a quick squirt of Thierry Mugler's Angel and have a ten-second pang of something resembling hurt about Joe. He'd have thought her fragile condition was amusing, would have teased her about it, dropped in a few comments about twelve-step programmes and then insisted she come home early. There he'd have run her a coconut bath, then called out for Chinese food and they'd have eaten it in bed, not giving a second thought to whether chicken-chow-mein stains would ever come out of the duvet. She missed . . .

Urgh, she shook off the melancholy and strode purposefully towards the shop floor. It was only when she got there and stepped, blinking, into the daylight that she realised that she could have spent two hours preparing herself and she'd still be woefully under-equipped for the scene in front of her. Three fifty-ish women, all in various items from her 'Femme Dangereux' collection, parading up and down in front of three other fifty-ish women who were parked in her overstuffed bergère armchairs, clutching glasses of assorted beverages, all giving a rousing rendition of 'You Can Keep Your Hat On'. And, no, shaking her head furiously didn't change the scene in front of her in any way whatsoever – it definitely wasn't another dream.

'Mel! Smashing to see you again, love. Our Stacey says to say hello and tell you it wasn't a porno flick after all. It was a condom advert, so she's rare chuffed.'

It took a minute for the whole bag of pennies to drop. Stacey. Now in LA. Mother. Senga – a 40DD that was actually a 44FF. And, apparently, she'd come complete with her own posse, all of whom – both dressed and undressed – were now grinning directly at her.

'And this is Ida, Ina, Agnes, Jean and Montana – her mother shagged an American serviceman in the war and Montana has been paying the price her whole life.'

The raucous laughter of the women filled the room and the urge to join in was irresistible. God, she loved this shop. It was everything she'd ever dreamed of. Exciting, friendly, crazy, unpredictable and endlessly entertaining. No matter what other crap life was throwing at her, at least she still had this.

'Great to meet you all, ladies.'

Senga spoke up again. 'We won five hundred quid on the bingo last night and decided, bugger it! There's no point telling the menfolk because they'll just piss it away on the drink and the horses, so we've come in to spend it on us instead. My Fred will never notice; he hasn't been near my knickers for years.'

'Aye, quite right, Senga. You don't know where he's

been!' concurred a baby-dolled Ida – or was it Agnes – to mass hilarity.

Oh. My. God. This was brilliant, Mel decided. It was like a bizarre cross between a Menopause Support Group and the Pussycat Dolls.

Hangover banished, she scanned the room. 'OK, ladies, we need to get things sorted here. First of all, let me bring out another couple of chairs from the office, then let's get some music on and food. Have you all eaten yet?'

There were a couple of shakes of the head. 'Right then. Josie, would you mind phoning round to the sandwich shop and asking them to bring round rolls and crisps and . . . oh, chips. Definitely in the mood for chips.'

That one earned her a collective cheer and a Mexican Wave that exposed more of Montana's barely clad bosom than Mel would necessarily have chosen to see.

'But, ladies, there's one condition!'

Six expectant looks.

'You have to tell me what you've done with Cammy.'

The chorus of laughter was barely over when something flickered to the right of Mel's eyeline and she turned to see a mannequin's arm materialise from behind the stock-cupboard door in the gents section, dangling a pair of white boxers in what was obviously a surrender situation. It was immediately followed by a bashful Cammy and a delighted chorus of 'ooohs' from the ladies.

'I sent him in there for medical reasons – didn't think his fragile constitution could take the strain of this lot,' Josie explained.

Mel giggled and gave Josie a hug. 'I think you're absolutely right, my darling.'

Three hours, a dozen bags of chips, two rounds of sandwiches, and the collective works of Lionel Richie, Abba and *Now That's What I Call A Party 54*, Josie flipped the sign on the door to 'closed' and slumped against it.

'I've now realised I'm a mere lightweight party animal compared to that lot.'

'You'll never be a lightweight, Josie – not with that arse.'

A tuna and sweetcorn sarnie went flying in Cammy's direction, over the head of Mel who was propped against the base of a now naked mannequin stand.

'Well, that one wins the medal for the most bizarre day of all time. And I have to say – Councillor McBride and Montana? Would never have seen that one coming.'

The whole afternoon had descended into party central, with every customer coming in the door being immediately immersed into the festivities by the Paisley Six, no one more so than Councillor McBride, who'd popped over from working a little overtime in the nearby civic buildings to replenish his Y-fronts stock. He'd been forced into doing the Locomotion with Jean, Ida and Montana, and ending up leaving with the latter, two pairs of Prada pants, a red all-in-one cami and a huge smile on his face.

Coat on, bag over her arm, Josie was making the quickest of exits.

'Where are you off to, Josie? Don't you want to stay for a drink? You've worked your pop socks off today.'

'Don't you be bloody cheeky, madam,' she bantered. 'I'm much more of a hold-ups kind of chick. And no, I'll pass on the drink. I'm meeting the Paisley lot in the wine bar round the corner and I've got some serious catching up to do. Told Councillor McBride to phone Councillor Davidson and get him over there too. Always had a bit of a thing for him – looks like the sexy brooding type in those posters they put up on the lamp-posts.'

And with that she was gone, leaving a slipstream of incredulity in her wake.

'That's our Josie,' Cammy said with a whistle. 'Elvis fans and politicians in one weekend. Shit, look at the state of this place. I'll come in early in the morning and get it cleared up.' He wandered over to where Mel was sitting on the floor and slid down beside her.

'I'll come in and help,' she replied.

'No, no. It's Sunday – you take it easy and chill out and I don't want to see you all day. Understand.'

'Yes, boss,' she said with a smile.

Much to Mel's relief, they sat there for a few moments in blissful, comfortable silence. Thank goodness last night's antics hadn't made things awkward between them.

'Listen, about last night . . .' Cammy blurted. 'I'm glad you kissed me.' Cue a whole lot of awkward.

'You are?'

'Yup.'

'Why?'

'Because in the mood you were in you were always going to kiss someone and I'm just glad you didn't slip the tongue on a bloke singing "Heartbreak Hotel". That could have scarred you for life.'

Phew. Bullet. Dodged. She'd thought for one horrible moment there that he was going to get all deep and meaningful. She should have known better – banter was the mainstay of all the relationships in this shop. When she'd first moved up to Glasgow, it had taken her a while to get used to the relentless cheek and the raw humour, but now she wouldn't have it any other way.

'You're right . . . any more of that Elvis stuff and I could have pulled a muscle.'

Ouch! The painkillers were wearing off and laughing had rewarded her with a shooting pain in the left temple that caused her to flinch.

'What's wrong?'

144

'Nothing, just a bit of a headache.'

He tugged at her hair. 'Put your head in my lap and I'll give you one of my famous Indian head massages.'

'Cammy, the closest you've been to an Indian anything is an onion bhaji over at The Taj Mahal Bhoona Bar.'

'C'mon, I promise I'm really good at it.'

Rolling her eyes, she succumbed, flipping her legs around and letting her head fall on to his thighs and, yes, there was a tiny voice inside her that realised that after the night before this might not be entirely appropriate. However, she chose to press the mute button. Over the years, they'd always been hugely tactile. He'd seen her in her knickers. They had at least a couple of hugs every day. They'd even once shared a bed on a camping weekend that had given her a lifelong aversion to tarpaulin. It would be churlish and petty to change their behaviour now because of one drunken moment that they both accepted meant nothing.

The rotation of his fingertips – sod inappropriate, it felt amazing – twanged another little nugget of memory in Mel's consciousness. She thought about ignoring it but she realised that as a friend it was better if it came from her.

'Listen, I think you'd better know that Suze saw Anneka last night. And she was with . . . someone.' There was no point in pouring out the details. Probably best if she left out the rest.

'Who?'

She bit her lip. 'Karl.'

'Bloody hell. Did Suze have a meltdown? Are they still both in possession of their teeth?'

'Yes and yes. I think she's getting soft in her old age.'

He nodded pensively. 'I wondered what all the drama was about this morning, but with Suze . . .' He trailed off, leaving the rest to her.

'I know, it could be anything. Bad eyebrow wax. PMT. Queue at the post office. So. You don't mind about Anneka?'

He shrugged casually. 'We're not together any more so she can do what she wants. In fact, even when we were together, she could do what she wanted. I've never been one for the whole ties and chains thing, you know that. Feel sorry for Suze, though. That must have been rough.'

Just like that. How liberating must that be? No ties, no chains, no jealousy or resentments. If she'd had Cammy's attitude, then she'd just have shrugged off Joe's behaviour as harmless and not given it a second thought. But . . . that just wasn't how she worked. She liked all those unfashion- able, meddlesome values like trust and fidelity and loyalty.

'Why, Cammy? Why are you like that?' All the years that she'd known him she'd just accepted him for who he was and never thought to delve underneath the actions, but now curiosity had the better of her.

'No idea. It's a cliché, but sometimes I think I just didn't meet the right person.'

'And how will you know when you do?'

He smiled. 'Maybe I already have.'

'What? You've met someone?' She forced herself not to add, 'and didn't tell me!!!'

'Yep, but Josie won't have me – says I'm too old for her.'

Phew. Joke. She elbowed him just a little bit harder than necessary.

'Suppose I should really get up and go cash up the till. Wouldn't surprise me if this was our best day's business since Christmas.'

'I'll stay and help.'

'No, don't be daft. I still feel bad for my four-hour power nap today. You go home. Or go out on the town. Or what- ever it is you do. I'd avoid the wine bar round the corner, though – you'd never make it out intact.'

146

Cammy got to his feet first, held out his hand and pulled her up – a good idea until she swayed and he had to lurch to catch her.

'Wow, blood rush. Think there's still some alcohol surging about in there. Thanks, Cammy, you can put me down now.'

Slowly, gently, he released her, but strangely, didn't move for a few seconds. 'Mel . . . nothing. OK, I'm off.'

He'd taken a single step backwards, smiled that adorable crooked grin, when a bang on the front door startled them both.

For the umpteenth time that day, Mel felt her legs turn to jelly, but this time it wasn't because of the alcohol. Joe. Staring at them through the glass. Goosebumps immediately sprung up on every limb. What was he doing there? More importantly, how *long* had he been there?

Cammy opened the door and was met with a fixed stare and an 'All right, Cammy?' that, in the ancient language of man-talk, would have been translated as 'Could you step outside so I can beat you to death with a club.'

Apparently, Joe had been there for quite a while.

It was such classically unfortunate timing that had Mel not been in a state of abject horror/apprehension/nervous frenzy she would have laughed. But, for the moment, she stuck with abject horror/apprehension/nervous frenzy. What must he be thinking? The shop looked like it had been ransacked, she looked like she'd been tumble-dried, he'd just witnessed an easily misinterpreted situation and her ability to formulate speech appeared to have momentarily escaped her. A problem that was apparently mutual. He closed the door behind him and took a couple of steps towards her. Instinctively, she stepped back, her reaction jolting him to a stop.

'I, er . . . like what you've done with the place,' he said

147

in what might just have been the coldest voice she had ever heard him use.

'Today turned into a bit of a party. Bingo win. Long story.'

Another long pause, and not of the comfortable version she'd experienced with Cammy just a little while before. Thankfully, shivers joined the goosebumps in an attempt to divert her attention from the tension in the air. She had never felt this uncomfortable with Joe before. But then he'd never propositioned a pneumatic stranger in a bar and purported to be single before. Nor had he gone on to spend four weeks in the relationship equivalent of solitary confinement then reappeared to see his wife with her head in another man's crotch in what could very well be perceived as a blow-job situation.

However, he was here now and maybe it was time she dealt with it. The whole denial/avoidance route couldn't go on indefinitely. It was immature. Cowardly. And absolutely indicative of her lifelong avoidance of confrontation.

'I don't know what to say to you, Joe.' Get out. Stay. How could you? Why? What did I do wrong? Aargh, she wasn't prepared for this yet. Not today. So she settled for: 'And I can't do this here.'

'Why? Something else you were busy with?'

His disdainful expression went from her, to Cammy, who had just reappeared from the back office with his jacket in hand.

'No, it's not that. I just can't do this standing in the middle of a shop, surrounded by mess, while the smell of chips makes my stomach turn. Rough night last night.'

Joe's stare went to Cammy for a second time.

Catching the gist of the conversation and the undertones that were coming through loud and clear, Cammy shrugged his jacket back off again. 'Look, you two go on and I'll cash up and take care of things here.'

'No, no, I couldn't . . .' Mel began to object.

'Honestly, go – I really don't mind. I don't think you should be trusted with a calculator and cash in your condition anyway.'

She nipped into the office, grabbed her coat and bag, switched the computer off, wiped the muffin crumbs from the top of her desk, popped a Wrigley's Spearmint in her mouth and wrote 'Thank you' on a post-it note and stuck it to the safe where Cammy was sure to see it. Walking back into the gothic knicker equivalent of Antarctica, she realised the atmosphere could still comfortably sustain polar bears and penguins. Joe sat on one of the chairs previously occupied by one of the Paisley Six, pretending to be immersed in the underwear supplement of a bridal magazine, while Cammy was counting the notes out of the till. A swift departure was obviously best for all concerned and given her fragile state there was an obvious destination.

'Joe, er, so why don't you come home with me. If you fancy taking your chances with Suze, that is. I have to say that the Marshall brothers are not top of her Christmas list at the moment.'

Wrong thing to say. Cammy now laughing. Joe not. What she'd give for Senga and her chums to storm back in that very moment and whisk her away from all this.

Miming a surreptitious 'sorry' to Cammy as she left, she followed Joe out of the door. They trudged up the stairs, every step depleting more and more of what little was left of her energy reserves. If there was one night she could have chosen not to do this, it would be tonight. Tonight all she wanted was to climb under a blanket on the sofa, put on a chick-flick and block out the world. But then, hadn't she been doing enough blocking for the last few weeks? Maybe it was time to face up to this situation

149

and find a way to deal with it. And anyway, if she watched any more movies featuring Kate Hudson, she was going to get serious gold locks/gleaming teeth/house in Malibu envy.

Weirdly, so far, it wasn't as bad as she'd anticipated. Now that her initial reaction had calmed, she didn't feel anxious or stressed, she just felt ... detached. Perhaps she'd gone through the stages of grief and he'd reappeared just as she got to acceptance and recovery. Or maybe she was still drunk.

There was complete silence when she opened the door. Suze must be out. On the one hand, that could be a bad thing, because who knew what she was up to? But, on the other, at least they weren't risking her taking her considerable ire out on Joe. It would be a whole big Jeremy Kyle show that she was frankly too tired to participate in. He closed the door behind him and followed her along the hall and into the ...

'Suze! I thought you were out. Listen, don't freak out but Joe is with me.'

That's when it happened – bizarre event of the day number, *oooh*, 164? Suze spotted Joe, smiled and said, 'Hey, how're you doing?'

Uh-huh.

Mel scanned the room for signs of crack use. Or a fall. Maybe that was it, maybe Suze was concussed.

'I've, er, got company too.'

Bizarre event number 165. Karl appeared from the direction of the kitchen clutching a bottle of wine and two glasses and – bizarre event number 166 – sporting a large Elastoplast on his forehead.

Mel turned to Joe. 'Am I hallucinating?'

'No, he's really there.'

'Excellent. Hi, Karl.'

'Hey, Mel. I'm really sorry but we've decimated your wine supplies. I'll go out and get some more.'

'Trust me, the last thing I want to do is drink wine,' she replied with a smile.

None of this was filtering through to the parts of the brain involved in comprehension. Why was Karl here? Why was Suze not freaking out? The tension and dread in the air was almost palpable but – and it may have been her imagination – they actually seemed to be OK in each other's company.

Considering that only a few hours before Suze would have happily amputated his balls, this was bizarre event number 167.

'Karl, get another two glasses. Trust me, Mel, you're going to need it.'

'Why what's wrong?' She glanced at Joe but he shrugged his shoulders.

Karl interjected as he headed back to the kitchen. 'Actually, Joe, it's good that you're here because this involves all of us.'

'What does?'

Once again, Mel felt an urgent pang for a blanket and a chick-flick and, bugger it, she'd just have to learn to deal with Kate Hudson envy.

She plumped down on one armchair, Joe on the other, took the drinks from Karl and then listened in stunned silence as he and Suze alternately delivered blow after blow. Business. Crashed. Linked. Everything. Gone. Overdraft. Bank. Deadline.

Later, all Mel would remember was that her whole life was delivered yet another thunderous blow in the space of just five minutes.

Sensing the rising horror in her husband's demeanour and watching it portrayed in his expression, she realised that he was completely unaware of the gravity of the situation. Other men (including, it had to be said, Karl) would have shouted, screamed and demanded thorough explanations, but not Joe. It just wasn't in his nature. And besides, he loved and respected Karl too much to ever lose his temper or become confrontational with him.

Looking at his brother with pained incredulity, he did, however, venture, 'Why? Why didn't you tell me it was this bad?'

It was exactly how she would have anticipated that he'd act. Calm. Seeking to find reason. Prepared to listen.

Karl shrugged apologetically. 'I'm sorry, Joe, but I didn't know how to. I really thought I could find a way out of it before everyone had to worry.'

'Karl, I'm not a kid! For fuck's sake, our business was going down the tubes and you didn't think to tell me?' Joe yelled.

Mel put her head in her hands. So much for calm and un-confrontational. Who was this guy and what had happened to the one that she married? Did she know him at all? And – oh fricking hell – he was on his feet now, in Karl's face and there was definite prodding of the chest area.

Karl's expression was aghast but he didn't fight back, too consumed by a combination of sorrow and surprise.

Suze sprang to her feet. 'That's enough, Joe – no more! Look, I know it's a shock but it is what it is and we just need to handle it.'

Mel reached over and pulled on the back of his T-shirt. 'She's right. Come on, sit down.'

Reluctantly, he did what she said, his face still contorted by fury.

Mel leaned over and placed her hand firmly on his arm as she offered her contribution to proceedings, all the while

152

fighting a wave of nausea that could be the result of either the lingering hangover or the news.

'OK. So, where are we at now? Just tell me the facts, that's it. No arguing, no drama or I swear I might throw up and that'll add a whole new shade of ugly to this.'

Suze picked up a pen and pad from the floor, pulled her hair back from her face, cleared her throat and began to read.

'All the businesses are under one holding company, total liabilities £250,000.' There was a simultaneous sharp intake of breath from both Mel and Joe before Suze plodded on. 'Our house is only mortgaged up to eighty per cent . . .'

'Eighty per cent? I thought you only had a twenty per cent mortgage on your house,' Mel interrupted.

Karl had the decency to look shamefaced as Suze batted that one back. 'Yes, but apparently our hero here increased the mortgage to put Marshall & Sons in a financial cash-flow position to take on the Foreman contract. And, yes, I'll be torturing him at a later date. Anyway . . . If the ruthless bastards at the bank will give us another ten per cent and we sell the cars, cash in our insurance and endowment policies and put Karl on the game, we reckon we can raise about £80,000.'

Mel mulled it over. She and Joe had about twenty per cent equity in the flat, but they wouldn't get much for the cars and she had nothing else of value to sell. Suze had taken a large salary from Pluckers right from the start – her lavish wardrobe and extravagant gadget habit had demanded it. Mel, on the other hand, had taken nothing, figuring that she really didn't need it. She was much happier just to put all profit straight back into building up La Femme, Le Homme. As a result, the shop was doing great, but she and Joe had no savings and a fairly asset-free lifestyle.

'Joe? What do you think?'

Joe flopped back in the chair and absentmindedly rubbed his face with his hands. 'I don't know. The flat. My car. Maybe seventy grand, tops? We'll never get a buyer for the flat in this market so the most we can hope for is that they'll let us take it up to ninety per cent too.' He finished his analysis of the situation with an evil look directed in Karl's direction.

'OK, so that's £150,000,' Suze said. 'More than halfway there.'

'And if we don't scrape together the rest? What does that mean?' Mel asked, the realities of this situation becoming clear in a way that she didn't even want to begin to accept. This was too much. Twice in the last hour she'd been ambushed and playing dead was starting to look like the best option.

'Everything closes. The bank calls in our overdraft, we won't have enough to pay it, which will leave us with no money to pay the rents, the wages, the bills, nothing. We have to file for bankruptcy, Mel. Everything goes.'

Mel closed her eyes, put both index fingers on her temples and started to rub in a circular motion. No. This could not be happening. Her shop was her life. And Josie and Cammy – what would happen to them? Who was going to take on a sixty-one-year-old woman who had a mouth that belonged in the gutter and dressed like the last of the Ninja warriors? She felt the weight of fluid building up behind her sinuses and realised that any minute now she was going to cry.

Joe obviously spotted it too as he leaned over and put his hand on her shoulder. She didn't have the energy or the inclination to push it away.

'Is there any other way? Anything else we can do?' Joe asked desperately.

154

Karl and Suze looked at each other, but Karl was the first to speak. 'We're not sure yet. To be honest, I've been so stressed out trying to find new contracts and trying to pull in every penny that's owed to us that I don't know what other options are out there, but Suze is going to get on to it on Monday morning – financial advisers, government help, banks, maybe even venture capitalists, if any of them have any money left these days. If there's any way we can salvage this, we will.'

'Forget it.' Joe's reply was as adamant as it was brief.

'What . . . ?' Suze replied expectantly, waiting for more.

'This isn't up to you two to fix, it's up to all of us. Mel and I are not the dependent couple in this family and we're perfectly capable of getting involved here too. I know we've all had a rough time over the last month –' he looked pointedly at Suze '– but this is as much our problem as it is yours and there has to be a four-way effort to find a solution.'

He glanced at Mel for some kind of affirmative gesture. Her nod was enough.

'First thing Monday morning, we all go to the bank, then we split up the other tasks and we all attack this from every angle. Anyone have a problem with that?'

There was more furious rubbing of temples as Mel continued to ponder the transformation in Joe. Karl shook his head and Suze raised her palms in an agreement gesture. 'Absolutely not – we need all the help we can get here. Mel, you're very quiet – what do you think?'

Mel suddenly realised that everyone was looking at her in anticipation. What did she think? She thought that when she woke up this morning she was in no way prepared for what this day would bring. She thought that she wanted to pretend that none of this was happening. But her inherent personality rose to the surface and claimed the situation as its own.

'I think I realise how bad this is but let's not give up until we really have to because we might somehow be able to fix it.'

Bizarrely, both Suze and Karl gave her identical grins. 'What? What did I say?'

Suze flew across the room and enveloped her in a massive bear-hug that sent her flying backwards in the chair. 'You, my love, said exactly what I told Karl you would say. If there was a Minister for Optimism, you would be it.'

'Erm, Suze?' came the muffled reply. 'Could I optimistically ask you to get off of me because you're suffocating me.'

With another affectionate squeeze, Suze disentangled herself, brushed down her skirt and reached for her bag.

'So what's happening with you two, have you sorted stuff out?' Mel asked, hoping she wasn't reading the signals wrong.

'We're, em, trying. Maybe,' Suze replied, stopping short when Karl gave her an indignant glance. 'Oh, OK, yes. We're going to see if we can work it out even though he doesn't deserve it. So I hope you don't mind but I'm going to go back home tonight. Unless of course there's a catwalk model in a bright-red dress sitting at my kitchen table in which case I reserve the right to resort to violence and then come right back.'

Karl had the decency to blush.

Mel didn't notice. Awkward alert. Awkward alert. Suze and Karl clearly wanted to be on their own so were they expecting Joe to stay here?

'If it's OK with you, I'll hang back here. In the spare room. Just for tonight?' Joe suggested, reading the same signals.

Mel nodded, too exhausted to argue. Frankly, she just wanted the day to be over before any more drama had a

156

chance to develop. She checked out the wall-clock: 7.30 p.m. Time for . . .

A phone started ringing and every one of them automatically reached for their mobiles. Joe was the lucky winner.

'It's Mum,' he mouthed, immediately striking fear and trepidation into all of them.

They could handle marital strife. They could handle the prospect of bankruptcy and potential poverty. But Joe and Karl's mother – a terrifying hybrid of Joan Rivers, Attila the Hun and a Rottweiler – took trepidation to a whole new level.

Joe flicked the call on to loud speaker. 'Hi, Mum.'

'Hello, darling. Listen, I'm just calling to check that you won't be late. You know how your father's blood pressure rises when he has to wait for things.'

In the background, they could hear their dad arguing that last point and being told to shush. It was the standard dynamic in their relationship, one that was little to do with mutual love and affection and lots to do with the governing strategies of a third-world dictatorship.

Suze was the first to catch on and started frantically flailing her arms. 'Date? What's the date?' she hissed to Karl.

He checked his watch. 'The fifteenth.'

'Oh fuck me gently! I don't believe this.'

Joe's hand flew to cover the receiver.

'Was that Suzanne I heard in the background there?' his mother asked in a tone that could crack glass. She'd never quite approved of her impetuous, strong-willed daughter-in-law. Rich coming from a woman who had the temperament of a Scud missile.

'Yes, Mother!' Suze shouted back. 'And Happy Anniversary!'

157

Three heads went into three sets of hands. Their parents' anniversary. It had been planned for months. Normally, the girls could be relied on to remember and make sure they all got to where they should be appropriately dressed and on time.

Not this year.

'Yes, well, thank you, dear. Anyway, we'll see you when we get there. We've just set off so we'll be there slightly after eight. Now don't be late – you know how your father's blood pressure plays up when he gets impatient.'

And that, Mel thought, as she finally succumbed to the lump in her throat, was why optimism was so important in life. Because, when a big black cloud was hanging in front of you, you had to feel confident that you'd get through it.

But when that big black cloud was called Virginia and came with hot and cold running bitchiness, maybe it was time to let a little well-founded pessimism into your life. Pessimism that would turn out to be more of a prediction of what was to come.

Twenty-one

8.45 p.m. The Grill Room, the elegant restaurant on the second floor of 29, the exclusive private members club housed in a stunning nineteenth-century blonde-sandstone building in Glasgow's Royal Exchange Square.

Mr and Mrs Willow-Jones of Newton Mearns were celebrating Mrs Willow's fiftieth birthday and both thoroughly enjoying their Roast Castle of Mey Lamb Chump with creamed potatoes and Provençal vegetable sauce.

At a long table by the window, the cast of *The Clyde*, BBC Scotland's new drama series, were thrilled that the producers were celebrating their BAFTA nomination by treating them to an all-expenses-paid dinner consisting of thick mouth-watering slabs of Chateaubriand.

To their right, Mr George Robertson was panicking into his 14oz Kansas City-Style Strip Sirloin Steak, because a woman who looked suspiciously like his wife's aunt had just sat down at a nearby table and was bound to spot that George was entertaining Claudie, his new twenty-three-year-old French secretary, instead of Gilda, his fifty-six-year-old wife from Greenock.

Meanwhile, the younger generation of the Marshall dynasty were grouped around a table in the family-celebration equivalent of the seventh circle of hell.

Suze had already excused herself to go to the loo twice, and on the second occasion had secured a steady flow of mother-in-law anaesthetic by collaring a startled waiter, slipping him £50, and telling him to make sure that her glass didn't fall below half-empty at any point all night. Hell, they were almost bankrupt – it was the least she deserved.

She wondered if there was a Guinness Book of World Records Category for maintaining a fixed smile on one's face in the midst of sustained torture. If so, she was a shoe-in. Although, looking across at poor Mel, she probably faced stiff competition. Mel's complexion had started to blend with the pallor of Joe's grey jacket and she had the glassy-eyed look of someone who could quite easily commit hara-kiri by bread knife at any moment.

Calling off or cancelling just hadn't been an option, not since the year that Suze had attempted to get out of Mr Marshall Snr's birthday party by claiming acute period pain and Mrs Marshall Snr had banged on their door at seven p.m. on the night of the gathering, clutching a box of Tampax and a packet of Nurofen and informed her that it was the role of women to 'triumph over such trifling things'. She then selected an outfit from Suze's wardrobe, handed it to her and told her she'd wait in the car until Suze was ready.

That's why, the instant that Joe had disconnected the call, there had been a mad, frantic dash by all parties to get dressed, made up, perfumed and transported to the venue before the grand arrival of the parents. With no time to go home, Karl had borrowed one of Joe's suits and Suze had slipped her size-8–10 body into one of Mel's size-14 black jersey cleavage dresses, added a ten-inch-wide, black leather corset belt around the waist, and hoped that no one would notice that the resulting excess of fabric in the hip area gave the impression of abdominal bloating.

So of course it was no surprise that the first thing Virginia Marshall said to her after one shrill 'Darling, how lovely to see you', two exaggerated air kisses and a head-to-toe judgemental scan that got stuck on her stomach area was: 'Suzanne, darling, I must ask you – do we have a little announcement to make?'

The woman should come with a warning from the Government Toxic Waste Management department.

Now, halfway through her starter of Bang Bang Chicken (and right now she knew exactly how that chicken felt), she pondered whether or not she should contact the Vatican and enquire as to the procedure for having Mr Marshall deified as a living saint. How he lived with her was truly a miracle exceeded only by the fact that two such cool, easy-going guys as Karl and Joe could have been expelled from her womb. Thank goodness the guys were keeping the conversation going and leaving Suze and Mel to use false smiles and consumption of bread rolls to mask their internal suffering.

Karl caught her eye and winked, and to her giddy surprise she experienced a momentary surge of happiness. If anyone had told her that she'd have found out her husband was doing the naked hokey-cokey with another woman, discovered they'd lost all their money and be sitting down with her mother-in-law for dinner all in the one day, she'd have told them they were insane then locked herself in a darkened room. Yet that's exactly what had happened and it just felt . . . well, *right*. In fact, in a strange way, she really felt that in the long term their relationship would be better for this. The months of worrying, stressing, of living in her own imagination, conjuring up scenes of Karl out shagging everything with a pulse had all melted away and the reality was that the truth was far easier to bear. Now she just had to get on with repairing the damage, and finding some stability again, this time based on full disclosure and honesty. Oh, and winning the lottery, robbing a bank and spreading malicious rumours about that cow Anneka who really should have known bloody better. She didn't fancy the tart's chances next time she came in for a Brazilian.

A sliver of guilt cut across the titillating prospect of retribution. If there was one thing that she would go back and change about all this, it would be that Mel got caught in the crossfire. Looking at her now, fake smile, trying so hard to be her sunny self, Joe beside her, nervous and uncomfortable; maybe they'd come out of this stronger too. And yes, she did realise that was a pathetic attempt to make herself feel better about what she'd done but it was the best she could manage on short notice and approximately a bottle and a half of wine.

It was time to move on. And Karl would be with her. And if that meant enduring yet another night with Virginia, then it was a small price to pay and she'd just have to put her head down and get on with it.

'So Suzanne, you didn't answer my question earlier, darling. Any news on the grandchildren front?'

Er, head right back up.

Sweet smile. Sweet smile. Do not throw knife in the manner of Jackie Chan movie.

'Not yet, Virginia, but I promise you'll be the first to know.'

Sweet smile. To her right she could sense Karl tensing, while Mel and Joe were looking at her with a mixture of pity and apprehension. Argh, why did it always have to come up? Why was her reproductive system anyone else's business? Wasn't there enough conflict between her and Karl on the subject already? Add to 'To Do' list – discuss future fertilisation with Karl. Maybe now they'd recommitted to their future, they could at least try to come to some kind of agreement when it came to children. A sudden under-table squeeze of her thigh hinted that he was thinking the same thing.

'Well, dear, you can't be leaving it too long, not at your age. I blame this modern-day obsession young women seem to have with careers, you know. All that running around trying to be Anita Roddick. What was it called? Body Shop. Cheap tat. Couldn't hold a candle to Clarins. Look at me – sixty-two, two strapping sons and barely a wrinkle.'

And there we have it. One of the most significant female businesswomen of the twentieth century maligned and her revolutionary company dismissed by Mrs Virginia Marshall (sixty-two, barely a wrinkle) as 'cheap tat'.

Sweet smile. Shoot to injure, not kill.

'I promise you, Virginia, my ovaries are fairly de-stressed at the moment and as soon as we've got something to report you'll be the first to know.'

The hand tightened on her thigh again and she endeavoured to summon a paradigm shift to a state of serene contentment. Hadn't she learned over the last ten years that Virginia just wasn't worth getting worked up about? The bare facts were that no one would have been good enough for her sons (although Mel was, apparently, slightly further up the daughter-in-law-acceptability scale than she was as a result of child-bearing hips, many years of thoughtful gifts and a reluctance to argue). It was nothing personal. Mothers-in-law had been disapproving of their sons' choice of wife since the beginning of time.

163

The waiter who was refilling her glass with another few inches of endurance juice was rewarded with a wink.

Another couple of hours and then she would be free. She could take her husband back to their home and get on with jump-starting their relationship, beginning with the tasks that had to be taken care of immediately: moving her clothes back in, giving Karl the shag of his life so that he would realise what he'd been missing, then waiting until he was asleep and rifling the house for any traces of that skinny, traitorous slapper. Then, tomorrow morning they would wake up and it would be a new dawn. She was well aware that her own behaviour hadn't exactly been without fault either, so together they'd draw a line under all their problems, and both of them would do everything necessary to clear away the baggage that had been piling up. Reaching under the table, she took Karl's hand from her thigh and squeezed it, feeling connected to him for the first time in months.

The cool green leather of the semi-circular booth soothed her neck she stretched back against it, feeling the months of tension dissipate with every second. She repeated her affirmation that, now that she knew what she was dealing with, she could handle the crap that life was throwing at her. In fact, she realised as her confidence surged, now that she and Karl were back on the same side, nothing seemed insurmountable. Except . . .

Three things happened at once. Karl suddenly clenched her hand so tightly that she had to bite her tongue to suppress a yelp; she retuned into the conversation to realise that it had stopped; and the entire younger generation of the Marshall clan was now staring at her with wide fearful eyes.

'What? Sorry, my mind wandered off there for a second, just, er, thinking how nice it was to be all together like this.'

'Well, dear, isn't that just lovely and long may it continue.'

Continue? What was the old bat saying now?

'You never were one for concentrating on the matter at hand, Suzanne, now, were you? Still I don't mind repeating myself.'

Urgh, maybe that hara-kiri by bread knife had something going for it after all.

'I was just saying that George had some investigations done on his heart problems . . .'

'There's sod all wrong with his heart! It's just lost the will to keep on beating because he lives with you, you fascist old git.' Thankfully, Suze managed to keep her mouth glued shut and her furious rebuke was only heard by the demons inside her head.

'. . . and they've discovered that there's a faulty valve. Lucky really that they caught it before it was too late.'

Looking over at Saint Donald Marshall, Suze felt a pang of shame that she'd underestimated his health woes. He was a sweet man. Quiet. Thoughtful. Although obviously he must have been a serial killer in a past life for the gods of karma to have doled out Virginia as a punishment in this one.

'Donald will be admitted to Rosshall Hospital on Monday morning for surgery, it's expected that he will be in there for some time, and we realise that travelling up and down from Ayr every day would be horrifically exhausting for me.'

Typical. That poor man was about to get his chest cracked open (albeit in the comfort of one of Glasgow's private hospitals) and undergo life-threatening surgery and she was worried about being knackered. Ugh, her self-absorption knew no bounds. Really. Self. Self. Self. That's all she ever thought about. Self. And . . . hang on, why was everyone *still* staring at her? What was she missing?

'So we've decided that it makes much more sense for me to base myself in the city for the duration of Donald's stay.'

For the second time in recent history, either the oxygen supply to the room had been cut off or Suze's cardiovascular system had just gone into panic-induced shutdown.

Her mother-in-law in Glasgow? Oh no, not again. It was bad enough right at the start of her marriage when Virginia and Donald had lived here and made it mandatory to meet every week for Sunday lunch. That was on top of all the occasions that she would guilt her into helping her with shopping, or party planning or decorating, or any one of a hundred other jobs that Suze, her personal slave, had been allocated. When they'd finally retired and moved to Ayr, Suze had splashed a tenner on bunting from eBay and hung it all the way around the house.

There was no way she could go through that again. Never. The only small mercy was that this time Virginia would be in a hotel so she'd have an army of staff to humiliate and dictate to.

'And since I can't abide hotels . . .' Virginia was still droning on.

Where was that waiter for another refill? And what was that she just said about hotels?

'We thought that it made much more sense for me to stay with family.'

Gulp. Family? Suze frantically cast her mind across the genealogical tree looking for an obvious answer. Virginia's sisters – one in Edinburgh, the other emigrated to New York in her twenties. Came back once, announced that Virginia was still 'fucking unbearable' and had never been seen again. No brothers. Donald? Only child. Neither of them had parents still alive so that left . . . where the hell was that waiter?

At least she now understood why horrified psychic messages were darting like bullets between the younger members of the family.

Finally, Joe took up the mantle of fear.

'That's a good idea, Mum, and, er, so have you already had a think about where that would be?'

Joe and Mel's flat. Of course it would be them. There was no way Virginia would want to stay with her and Karl.

Virginia reached over and patted Joe's hand. 'Oh, you sweet boy. I know I'd be more than welcome in your home . . .'

'You would!' Suze's subconscious survival instinct screamed silently. Go to their flat! They'd love to have you. Really! A barely discernible whimper came from Mel's direction and Suze realised that her sister-in-law looked like she might faint at any moment.

'But it's not really big enough, now, is it?' Virginia added.

It is! It definitely is! It's cosy. Great for family together-ness. Suze's internal fight or flight mechanism was using lies, manipulation in the bid to repel the imminent attack.

'So –' she grinned sweetly at Suze and Karl '– I thought I'd come and stay with you two. After all you've got all those bedrooms and plenty of space and you're only fifteen minutes away from the hospital. I'll be able to visit Donald at least twice a day.'

If one hundred members of the public were asked whether Karl, Suze or Donald looked more depressed at that last statement, there would be a three-way split on the answer.

And just when Suze thought the elevator of horror could plummet no further . . .

'After all, if I'm there to help with running the house, then you'll have so much time for other things. Like making those grandchildren that we're all patiently waiting for.'

After a very, very pregnant pause (one of life's little ironies), Suze realised that the fixed grin and the lack of response were about to veer into the rude and uncomfortable. This was one of those defining moments in life, the ones that can shape family relations for years to come. The bottom line was that Karl loved his father. He even, as a result of some deeply twisted genetic programming, harboured a form of love for his mother. And since only a few hours ago they'd turned over a new leaf of rebuilding and mutual support there was no way that she was going to create a whole new big powder keg of family disharmony.

Speak. Speak. She cleared her throat of a blockage that was apparently called 'You must be fucking joking,' and went with: 'Lovely. That would be lovely, Virginia. Karl and I would love to have you. We'll make up the guest suite for you as soon as we get home tonight. Oh, and Mel?'

Was it her imagination or did Mel's expression of relief come tinged with just a little smidgen of amusement?

'Could you pass the bread knife, please?'

The weekend that things got a little better . . . then plummeted to new depths

Twenty-two

'You're late.'

It wasn't a reprimand. Not even a complaint. Just an observation of fact.

'Yeah, I'm sorry. It was difficult to get away,' he explained. He was relieved that she didn't follow through with recriminations and complaints because that would have led to the danger that he would blurt out what he needed to tell her and he didn't want it to end that way. He owed her more than that. She was a decent person who had come into this with her own agenda and at the time it had matched his. Full disclosure of the facts, no expectations and the thrill of knowing that they were pushing life to the limits. All that and fan-fucking-tastic sex. It had seemed like a win-win situation. But that was then. Now . . .

She folded her arms as she wondered what he was thinking. There was a time when his tardiness would have kicked off a game of seduction and she would have teased him with faux petulance until he coaxed her round with wandering hands and orgasmic promise. Not any more. They were past that stage now. In fact, they were past all the stages of whatever this thing was that they were doing. An affair? An emotion-less shag? A sexual adventure? Whatever it was it was over. She knew

171

it. And she knew that he felt it too. She could tell by the way he touched her, the way he looked at her. No longer eager, desperate to be with her. A detachment had crept in, a reluctance. And it suited her fine because she knew she wanted this to be over too and had come here tonight to tell him that. Looking at his face, so torn, so blatantly unhappy, she decided that she had to get it over with. 'Listen, we need . . .'

'I know. But not right now.'

So she was going to call it off first, he realised. Brave. Bold. Looking at her with her pouting lips, hair falling in waves around her face, he realised that she had never looked more sexy.

As he reached for her, her gasp was involuntary, and she silently chided herself. This definitely wasn't going to plan. She rolled her eyes heavenwards, acknowledging that someone up there was probably commenting that she'd been behind the door when God was giving out all that 'resistance to temptation' stuff. But . . . he still just turned her on. Always had. And she'd be lying if she denied that there had been the occasional moment when she'd thought that maybe . . .

He watched as she closed her eyes and wondered what was going through that gorgeous head of hers. It wasn't playing out the way he'd expected tonight but, hey, he was only human. And so, he realised as she put up no resistance to the tongue that was now tracing a line from her collarbone to her ear, was she. As he inched her T-shirt up, she shuddered under his touch but didn't break the silence until he pulled it over her head, when she let out a low groan of pleasure. It was almost as if the fact that she might tell him to stop at any moment was adding to the excitement, giving it that element of intrigue and thrill that they'd had at the very start.

Despite the physical pleasure, she couldn't stop a little slice of self-irritation sneaking in. She'd had no intention of letting it get this far tonight. Although given that she was now standing in nothing but high heels, stockings and knickers that were so small they could be used for straining tea, maybe she'd – rrrrrrip, there went the knickers – had a hunch that it would turn out this way. No. Absolutely not. This wasn't what she'd planned. She'd thought that . . .

172

He'd known this would happen. The sexual attraction between them had been instant and irresistible and, other than a slight blip on their last encounter (he avoided using the word 'flop' so as not to relive the shame), he found it difficult to be near her without peeling her clothes from her skin and . . . no longer enough blood supply going to his brain for coherent thought, given that it was all being diverted to his significant erection, one that was leading where the rest of him could only follow. He nudged her backwards towards the window, sending a tray with two cups, two saucers and two packets of shortbread flying off the top of the mini bar.

Yes, it was definitely over . . . but there was more than one way to say goodbye.

Twenty-three

Josie had arrived in the shop approximately ninety seconds before, yet she'd just thrown out her fourth disapproving look of the morning in her boss's direction.

Eventually, Mel put the stock sheet back down on her desk and, with an admirable show of strength, pushed back her chair with her feet, sending it careering across the office, twisting as it went, so that the end result was one sixty-something woman cornered between a safe, a mini-fridge and an irate boss.

'OK, frosty-tits, it has to stop. You can't keep giving me the cold treatment like this. I'm almost thirty years old and I have to make my own decisions.'

Josie harrumphed. 'Even if they're the wrong ones and surefire steps on the road to Loser Town?'

Mel pushed off again, sending the chair skidding back over to her desk. 'Yeah, well, maybe I'll like Loser Town – let's face it, happy ever after didn't exactly live up to its promises, did it?'

'That's my point! He's not making you happy so why have you let him come back?'

'It's . . . it's . . .' The flush of discomfort rose up her neck and face so that, by the time she got to 'complicated', she looked like a tie-dyed T-shirt.

'Yeah, well, you're too good for the cheating twat. Even Cammy is an improvement on that one.'

'Josie, I promise you there is absolutely nothing going on between me and Cammy.'

'Well, there bloody should be. My spider senses tingle every time you two are in a room together.'

Mel was just about to object when, like the worst timing in the worst sitcom, Cammy materialised in front of her, hair still wet, Levi loose-fit vintage-wash jeans, black T-shirt that clung to . . . oh dear God, give her strength. She considered bluffing her way out of it, then realised that the one and only time she played poker she ended up naked and minus a CD collection. And yes, she was just grateful that, when she was a student, camera phones and YouTube had yet to be conceived. Bluff plan abolished, she went for squirm-inducing honesty instead.

'Mother Superior here is still giving me the stare of death because Joe has moved back in. She insists I kick him out and suggests that even you would be an adequate substitution. Feel free to sue her for inappropriate conduct and sexual harassment in the workplace.'

'It's all right. To be honest, I could do with some sexual harassment in the workplace.' He laughed as he threw his black suit jacket on to the coat rack, then disappeared back on to the shop floor, aware from experience that there are many dangerous locations in the world, but none more so than the space between two women who are having a disagreement.

'Melissa, you know I love you and that's why what I'm about to say comes from a place of concern.'

'Why are you talking in the voice and manner of Oprah Winfrey?' Mel asked, bemused.

'Just to give it added effect. Is it working?'

'No. But it's quite funny so carry on.'

This was the only way to handle Josie in a strop – humour and deflation. Because the thing was, Mel knew that the only reason Josie was being so vehement about the situation was that she really did care.

'He's just not making you happy. Look at you, Mel – he's been back two weeks and you're as miserable now as you were when he was gone. Don't think for a minute you can fool me with the cheery smiles and the forced joviality because I know you, my girl, and I know that you are faking it,' she ranted, before finally stopping, victorious, her piece said. 'Now I'll be out there serving customers so, if Oprah's producers call to ask me to stand in when she's on her holidays, just shout.'

And then she was gone, leaving Mel, her sinking stomach and her limited disclosure behind. Josie was right, she *was* miserable. It was a totally unfamiliar state to her but she was definitely miserable about Joe, she was miserable about their dire business situation but most of all she was beyond bloody miserable at the thought of having to tell Josie and Cammy that they might soon be out of a job. At the very thought of it, the recurring queasiness rose again, going in the opposite direction from her spirits.

Developments on the financial front had gone pretty much as anticipated. They'd all visited their banks, remortgaged their homes, sold everything of value and they were still roughly a hundred grand short to get the company back out of hock. A hundred grand. How did anyone even come up with that kind of money? Suze and Karl were trying to be positive, out talking to anyone they knew with a bit of dosh in the blind pursuit of a miracle, but even her general disposition of sunny positivity realised that it didn't look likely. The initial injection of cash had persuaded the bank to give them a bit more time, but it was more of a stay of execution. And, cowardly though she realised it was, she was hanging off breaking the news to Josie and Cammy for as long as possible. In the meantime, if Josie wanted to carry on thinking that Mel's woes were the result of stormy times with Joe, then that was just fine. It was actually preferable to the truth, which was that she was in a bizarre state of limbo. Or should that be purgatory? Neither climbing back up to relationship heaven, nor sliding downwards to the asbestos suits of separation hell.

Joe was still staying at home, he was still in the spare room and they'd resolved the sum total of nothing. They were polite. Amicable.

She took a hit of espresso, large, thicker than tar, but still the little black cloud of listlessness didn't lift.

The morning after Mr Marshall's excruciating party, Joe had tentatively knocked on the bedroom door and come in brandishing tea, croissants, Resolve sachets and a sheepish expression.

Rubbing the previous night's make-up further into her pores with one hand, she pushed herself up to a seated position with the other. 'Thanks,' she murmured with a half smile.

He sat on the edge of the bed, looking far more together than a man with his current palate of crises should look. 'Mel, I . . .'

All she could think was, Oh dear God, don't let him want to do this now. Her head hurt. Her pores hurt. Even her eyelashes hurt.

'I don't know if I can talk to you yet, Joe.' Translation: please go away, because I prefer to put off the awkward situation until I at least have full function of my faculties.

But apparently he didn't speak the ancient language of the tender heads.

'I think that's the problem – you won't let us talk about this and get past it. Mel, I can't tell you how sorry I am that you saw what you did and I promise you, on my life, it was just a stupid aberration and the first time I've ever, ever done something so crazy . . .'

She waited for the very obviously imminent 'but'.

'But . . .'

There it was.

'I've been thinking a lot about why I did it and I think . . .' He paused, struggling for the words. 'I think that we were in a rut, Mel.'

Her head bumped the headboard as she recoiled at his words.

'A rut? Joe, we were happy. We were planning a family. We talked. We had great sex. We laughed. We never fought.'

She left it dangling in the air, unable to argue any further when she had no comprehension whatsoever of his point of view.

He latched on to her last sentence. 'That's what I mean, Mel. I'm really sorry if this hurts, babe, but I want to be honest with you. We've been together since we were twenty-two, and where's the excitement? Where's the thrill? We don't even argue. It's just all so . . . Same. It's the same every day. I'm thirty years old and I've realised that hour in that bar was the first time in years that I'd actually felt something resembling excitement.'

For the first time in her life, Mel had felt something resembling a wish that she was Suze – then she could have taken this guy out with one right hook, stepped over him and got on with her day, instead of just sitting there, devastated, feeling like her heart was being ripped out via the lump in her throat.

Instead, she'd summoned every ounce of strength she had to get her motor skills working again and blurted, 'So, let me get this right – you're complaining because we've been *happy* for eight years? Because we don't fight. Because I love you. Because I want to make you happy?'

'I know it sounds crazy but . . . well, yeah. But I promise you, Mel, I would never have done anything with her. It was a moment. Just a whole big blip of stupid.'

She didn't argue. How was she supposed to absorb this? What kind of man complains about being too happy? It was just . . . just . . . wrong.

'So, what now, Joe? What do you want to do because, I have to be honest, I'm struggling with this one. I can't believe I didn't realise that we had a problem. We sat in Princess Square only a few weeks ago naming our children! Didn't you think of throwing in the little nugget about lack of bloody excitement then?' Right on cue, two fat tears broke through the storm barriers and trickled down her face. How could she not have seen this? How could she have been so blissfully unaware that he felt like this? There she'd been, so content, so sure of their relationship, a little smug even . . . Well, she wasn't feeling very bloody smug now. Two more tears joined the trailblazers.

His face crumbled with concern as he leaned over and wiped them away, then enveloped her in his arms. 'I know, honey, and I'm so sorry. I promise it was never my intention to lie to you. I do want all those things, Mel, I really do – I just think maybe I was having a minor mid-life crisis.'

He laughed at that last bit, but unsurprisingly she didn't join him. Didn't that just bloody top it all off? Only a couple of months ago she'd been telling Suze that perhaps Karl was having a mid-life crisis when all along it had been the guy lying next to her every night.

And now? Now she still didn't know what to do. The pragmatic side of her, the one that managed to run a business, a home and accept that her lifelong crush on Brad Pitt would never be reciprocated told her to let it go. Technically, and yes, it was all about perception, he hadn't been unfaithful to her. He hadn't snogged the face off the honeytrap girl. He hadn't been caught shagging someone else. And just look at Suze – Karl had admitted his fling with Anneka and yet they'd managed to put it all behind them, repair their marriage and it seemed to be working for them.

So was she just being an emotional drama queen who should just get over herself and patch things up? She was. She knew it. Yet . . . aargh, she couldn't let it go. There might not have been the exchange of body fluids – in fact, her little tonsil stunt with Cammy had gone further along the infidelity stakes than Joe had – but it still felt like he'd betrayed her, broken something that she didn't know how to fix.

Joe Marshall had always been the one person in her world that she trusted implicitly, knew for absolute certain would never let her down or break a promise. But that had shifted now (all the way to the spare room) and she just couldn't bring herself to accept it and get back to business as usual.

'Just let me know when you're ready and I promise, I *promise* that I'll never be such an arse again,' he vowed.

That's why, two weeks down the line, they were still in separate beds. Because if she ignored that pragmatic side, then what was left was the emotional side of her, the one that cried at *101 Dalmatians*, that never knowingly passed a *Big Issue* seller and that was never happier than when she was seated around a table with everyone she loved having brunch on a Sunday morning. And that fundamental part of her being just couldn't let it go. Although, since she'd promised to love him for better or for worse, she knew that she would have to. Was this it? Was this their 'tough times' that every marriage went through? Had she just been too pathetically naïve to think that they'd go through their lives together without a problem? Perhaps that wasn't confidence and contentment, perhaps it was complacency. She'd been so consumed with building her business that perhaps she'd just taken him for granted and stopped checking in, *really* checking in with what was going on with him. Did she want to be married to Joe Marshall? Yes, she did. Did she want to have his children? Absolutely. Had she ever wanted anyone else? Nope. So there was her answer. It was time to deal with their problems and move on . . . and eventually the little gnawing pain that chewed at her heart every time she thought back to that man on that tape would go away. Eventually.

She'd been staring at the stock sheets for twenty minutes now and she realised that she still had no idea what was on them. Tossing them to one side, she stretched, determined to shift this bloody depressing state of mind. She couldn't go on like this. It was time move on. Life would be good again. For all of them. The worst was past and now it was all about recovery and getting back to the good times. Karl, Suze, Joe, her – they were all going to get through this and get back to something approaching normality.

'Mel, sorry to interrupt you but can I ask you a favour?'

She snapped out of her contemplative state and turned to see her visitor. 'Avril, hey, you look great.'

It wasn't a lie. Avril had inherited Josie's tall, skinny frame and killer cheekbones and, with her newly dyed peacock-blue hair clashing against the red cheongsam, she looked like she worshipped at the Church of the Latter Day Punk.

'Thanks.'

'So what do you need?'

'Can you take Suze out somewhere this morning because her negative energy is seriously causing us pain next door.

And money. She just kicked a hole in the storeroom cupboard wall.'

Josie appeared at Avril's back. 'Tell her she should re-dump that twat she's married to,' she commanded her daughter.

'You should re-dump that twat you're married to,' Avril dead-panned.

Mel grinned as she rolled her eyes. 'Do you always do what your mother tells you?' she asked Avril tartly.

'Nope, I draw the line at drug smuggling and shoplifting.'

A roar of laughter came from the direction of a retreating Josie.

'I'll make you a deal – you get your mother off my case and I'll help you out with Suze.'

'You overestimate my powers. It would take more than me to call off my mother. I'm thinking weapons, great big weapons.'

'Sad but true. So what's up with Suze this morning? Why's she having a berzy?'

'Dunno. Something to do with the mother-in-law from hell, a vibrator and a visit from a priest. I didn't stay for the details.'

'Whatever it is, she'll get over it. Just give her an hour or two to calm down.'

'But that's the problem . . .'

'What?'

'Anneka's booked in for an eyelash tint in ten minutes.'

Mel sighed and shoved her feet into the Top Shop wedges that had been abandoned under her desk. 'OK, I'm coming. But I warn you, I'm not good with blood.'

Suze was on the verge of a freaky, Mel was going to the rescue, Joe and Karl were nowhere in sight . . . yep, the Marshalls were just about getting back to normal.

Twenty-four

'Did you hear? Anneka's in, my mother-in-law is driving me to the brink of insanity and I'll never be able to look Father Thomas in the eye again.'

'You won't have to if you end up doing a life sentence for murder. Put the mop down and come into the staff room with me. I'll rub your feet until she goes away.'

Suze reluctantly acquiesced as Mel prised her fingers off the wooden stick, then took her hand and pulled her from the store cupboard into the salon staff area.

'Can you believe she has the cheek to come in here? Fuck, she's brazen. She was only shagging my husband a fortnight ago! The cow should be in hiding in an under-ground bunker for fear of reprisals, not in getting a mani-pedi and a fucking eyelash tint!'

'Look, I know, darling, you're right, but, remember, that crowd don't think that way. Cammy had that three-way thing going with her and Anna for months and none of them minded. It's a generation thing.'

'Great. So now you're saying I'm bitter *and* old.'

'Exactly.' Mel steered Suze to the couch, pushed her

down and then pulled Suze's feet up on to her lap. 'So tell me about the priest and vibrator. Is it just me, or would that be a great name for a pub?'

'It's just you,' Suze replied, squeezing her eyes shut to halt the memory.

Oh, God (literally), the embarrassment. Not only had she been subjected to living under the scrutiny of Virginia for the last fortnight, but she'd had to listen to her moaning and bitching hour after hour after endless hour. The house was too cold. The house was too hot. The water tasted funny. All those trips back and forward to hospital were exhausting her. The bed was too hard. The pillows were too soft. And the combination of the two had given her chronic neck pain which was of course all Suze's fault. When she then went on to moan about her chiropractor refusing to do a house visit to administer deep-tissue massage (Suze suspected that he was dealing with Virginia's cancellation of her standard weekly appointment by cracking open champagne, phoning in two high-class hookers and employing a marching band to strut up and down outside his surgery playing tunes of jubilation), Suze had experienced a flash of inspiration. In a box in the garage, there were a few old sample vibrators from years before when they'd first opened the shop . . .

'Oh, no you didn't,' Mel gasped.

'I had to shut her up – you don't understand. If the CIA employed Virginia as a torture tool, they'd crack terrorists in minutes.'

'Didn't she realise what it was?'

'No. I told her it was a massager that I picked up from the bargain bucket in Boots the Chemist. And anyway, I don't think sex is Virginia's specialised subject. Can you imagine?' The thought made her shudder. 'I've no idea how Karl and Joe were conceived. I'm thinking Virginia just put on that voice of hers and terrified some poor people into parting with their offspring.

'Anyway, so I picked a straight, white one, no adornment, no suggestion of ribs, bubbles or bollocks, then set about massaging Virginia's shoulders with it. All was going wonderfully until the door went and Karl let in Father Thomas whose eyes near popped out of his head when he spotted me accosting my mother-in-law with a sex aid.'

Mel was choking now. 'What did he say?' she spluttered.

'Nothing. He just went bright pink, thanked Virginia for inviting him over and then told her the whole congregation was praying for Donald's recovery. Then he asked us all to hold hands and pray for our eternal salvation. Think I'm too late for that. I need to get rid of her, Mel, she's driving me insane.'

Leaning her head back on the arm of the sofa, she closed her eyes and exhaled wearily. She'd tried begging Karl to send his mother to the Hilton but it wasn't working. (Yes, she was once again applying the logic that, bugger it, they were skint anyway – what did a trifling four-figure hotel bill matter?) The only little nugget of joy that was keeping her sane was that things with Karl were good. Really good.

'Ouch, you're digging your nails into my toes!'

'Sorry, your ladyship,' Mel mocked.

Where was she? Oh yes, her and Karl were good. It was almost as if the mission to pull the business back from the brink had brought them together, made them stronger. And even if it did all go tits up – and the way it was looking that seemed to be inevitable – well, at least she'd still have Karl and a marriage that was worth saving.

Now if only she could get rid of the mother-in-law. And that cow who was sitting out in her salon having Revlon Red applied to her nails.

'OK, I'm done. Come on, let's nip along to 29 for a

lunchtime cocktail. After the month we've had, we deserve it.'

'But I . . .'

'Don't you dare object!'

'Suze, I have to get back to work – it's a Saturday and it's busy in there.'

'Are you saying Josie and Cammy can't handle it?'

'Of course they can but . . .'

'Then let's go – just for an hour.'

Suze watched as Mel's expression went from exasperated to a flicker of sceptical understanding.

'Are you just doing this so you can waft out there, right past Anneka, and act like the big-shot boss who can afford to go swanning off for cocktails in the middle of the day?'

'Absolutely yes.' There was no point denying the truth, Mel knew her far too well.

'OK then, let's go. But only if you promise to be aloof and diva-esque and not tell her she's a trollop.'

'Urgh, you drive a hard bargain.'

Suze scrambled to her beautifully massaged feet and nipped to the loo, making her last-minute preparations for her strut of superiority while she was there.

Make-up? Flawless.

Hair? Brushed, now perfect.

Shoulders? Back.

Expression? Haughty condescension.

When she got back to the staff room, Mel was already on her way out of the door. 'Here's your bag,' she said, tossing a Fendi clutch (Patpong market, a tenner, brought back by British Airways flight crew in return for free leg wax) to her.

Suze caught it and took a deep breath, then followed Mel out, giving herself an internal pep talk the whole way down the length of the salon.

OK, baby, work those hips. That's it. Think Heidi Klum, think

186

Gisele, and strut, baby, strut. Don't look at her, just keep those hips going. Don't look. I said, DON'T LOOK. Oh, fuck, I have to look.

Anneka came into her eye line, sitting at the white leather mani-pedi chair next to the window. The staff had obviously placed her at the furthest point from the staff room in the hope that Suze's eyesight and aim would be off. But unfortunately the consequence of that was that she was right next to the door so Suze would have to walk past her and somehow resist the urge to give her a slap across the back of the head as she did so. It just might be a challenge too far. Suze tried surreptitiously to check her out – usual long brunette glossy mane, black skinny rib T-shirt, grey jeans tucked into Ugg Locarno boots. Missoni black leather slouch bag sitting on the floor beside her. Shallow as it was, this would be so much easier if Anneka was a howler.

'Avril, darling,' she announced in her most superior voice, 'I'm just off out for a meeting with Melissa. I'll be about an hour.'

Avril looked up from Anneka's manicure, took in the scene in front of her and for once in her life couldn't get any words out.

'Hey, Suze, how're you doing?'

It took Suze a moment to process the new development. Nope, not Avril. Oh, the sheer shameless audacity – the cheery, blasé greeting was coming from the gob attached to the glossy mane. In front of her, Suze spotted that even Mel stopped and visibly bristled.

'Mel, did you hear something there? The voice of stupidity, perhaps?'

Childish, yes, but she couldn't help herself.

Glossy mane laughed. 'Oh, come on, Suze, let's just put it to one side, shall we? Look, as far as I knew, you guys were over, he's a good-looking bloke, and it was just a bit of fun. No harm done.'

Keep calm. Breathe. Take the moral high ground. Be the bigger person.

'Anneka, believe me, I really couldn't care less about you.' Great. Well done. Said in a haughty tone that conveyed appropriate diffidence.

Glossy mane, however, didn't even have the decency to blush or cower. The tension in the air was now palpable and every eye in the salon was fixed on the two of them, with even the clients who didn't know the details able to put together a pretty good picture of what had happened.

'Great,' came the sunny reply. 'Because I was thinking . . .'

'Well, there's a new approach for you.'

Anneka didn't even react to the dig. 'I was thinking that we should all get together some time. You know, you, Karl, me, Cammy, and have some, erm, *fun*,' she said, her voice dripping bitchiness.

Oh. Dear. Lord. Everyone within earshot held their breath. Avril's head went into her hands, but it was hard to tell if she was praying for this to stop or adopting the brace position. Suze, meanwhile, eyes wide with incredulity, was teetering on the precipice of volcanic. Did she really just say that? And did she mean . . .? Surely not! Oh. Dear. Lord. Was she honestly suggesting that . . .

'Right, that's it! Get out!' The voice was low but deadly and clearly not to be argued with. But Anneka had a try anyway. 'Pardon? But I'm in the middle of my –'

The mouth moved downwards until it was only inches from Anneka's ear. 'I said get out, you gloating, insidious bint.'

Brace. Brace. Brace.

Even Suze was taken aback, not only by the vehemence and menace in the order, but by its source.

All eyes were now on Mel, bent double, with the most ferocious look on her face that Suze had ever seen. What was going on here? It was Suze's job to be menacing and bitchy – Mel was there to provide calm reason and a positive spin.

Realising that retreat was the best option, Anneka reached for her bag with her half-manicured hand, and then slowly, with as much dignity as she could muster, rose from the chair and drew herself up to her full five foot eleven inches of body-perfect glory. 'Ah, touched a nerve there, did I, Mel? You know, you and Cammy . . . always thought there was something going on there. Seems I was right.' She took a few steps towards the door then paused. 'Oh, and, Suze, your dress is tucked into your knickers, love. Not a look that you can carry off.' With a smug, satisfied grin, she flicked back the – groan – glossy mane and strutted, catwalk style, out of the salon, leaving astonished silence behind her.

Suze was the first to break it – after removing the back half of her cheongsam from the depths of her La Perla pants.

'Mel, my darling . . .'

'What?' Mel replied through teeth that were still clenched together.

Suze was gobsmacked. Eight years and it was the first time she had seen Mel react to anyone like that. But . . . hang on, had she been missing something? She'd been so wrapped up in the grand reunion between her and Karl that she'd taken Mel's sunny 'Everything's fine' comments at face value. Obviously things were very far from fine.

'Can I ask you something?' she added.

'What?'

'Is there something going on between you and Cammy?'

Twenty-five

Mel had never understood what people meant when they claimed that they'd had an 'out of body experience' but she was getting the gist of it now. What had just happened? It was like she'd been possessed by the ghost of . . . of . . . oh, shite, she had no idea who. Just some really bitchy, fierce old dead person.

The strangest thing was that she couldn't even explain it to herself. Sure, there was a modicum of defence of her sister-in-law in there, but, let's face it, Suze was more than capable of fighting her own battles. Maybe there was also a bit of indignation that Anneka would dare to come to the salon and breach all standards of common decency. And, yes, all the worry and the stresses of late had certainly put her on edge. Oh, and she had PMT so admittedly she was on the three bars of Dairy Milk and occasional teary outburst side of chipper. But to go on the offensive like that? That was definitely a case of someone in the spirit world using her body as a vessel to channel justice. Either that or she'd been hanging around with Josie, Queen of the Straight Talkers, for too long.

Everyone in the salon was now making the pretence of going back to what they were doing before the drama, with the exception of Avril, who no longer had nails in front of her to paint. 'You know, that was worth the loss of £25 in the till and a fiver tip, Mel,' she volunteered, grinning as she gathered up the bottles and equipment in front of her and slotted it all back into the gloss black portable trolley beside her.

Mel shrugged, mortification written all over her face. 'Suze, do you mind if we give that drink a miss? I, er, really need to be getting back to the shop.'

'No, not at all . . . it's fine. On you go, hon. And thank you.' She gave her shell-shocked sister-in-law a tight squeeze and kissed her on the cheek. 'You were incredible. Scary, but incredible.'

'Er, thanks. I think. Any time. I can't believe I just did that.' There was no pride in her voice, only stunned amazement.

'Nor me, but you should do it more often – it suits you,' Suze replied. 'Come on, I'll walk you next door.'

'Suze, it's only twenty feet away.'

'I know but there's no telling what you could do between here and there. Assault. Mugging. Vandalism. Grievous bodily harm. This is a whole new you we're dealing with here and who knows where it's going to lead?'

Mel capitulated. Much as she was now the knicker-selling version of Rambo, she knew her limitations and arguing with Suze still fell into the 'Not to be attempted without body armour' category.

OK, twenty feet and she was home free. She could just sneak into her office and recover from the drama. Fifteen feet. Not far now. Ten feet. Wow, it was cold – should have worn a jumper. Five feet. Almost there. Two feet . . .

'So are you going to answer my question?'

She could run, but there was no point – it wasn't as if there was anywhere to hide.

'What question?'

Mel's nonchalant tone belied the fact that she had a resting heartbeat that sounded like an amp at an Ozzy Osbourne concert.

'Is something happening between you and Cammy?'

Yes, I snogged the face off him when I was drunk one night and that event has occasionally crossed my mind since then. Thankfully, that message got stuck in the shame synapse of her brain and didn't therefore reach her vocal cords.

'No.'

'Would you tell me if there was?'

'Of course I would, but there's nothing. Joe and I are working things out. We'll be fine. Honestly.'

Suze nodded, appeased, and gave her another hug. 'I didn't think for a minute that there was, my sweet. And I know you and Joe will sort this. You belong together. Shit, I have to go lie down – all this emotional stuff has turned me into a Hallmark greeting card. I'll buzz you later. Now try to get through the afternoon without indulging in any more acts of deadly intimidation.' With an accompanying chuckle, she practically skipped back into the salon.

Hand on door, Mel paused for a minute and took a deep breath. Time to compose and gather. She was fine. She would just forget that the last hour ever happened, paint on a big smile and get on with the day. Normality, that was the key. Normality.

Unfortunately, no one had passed that message on to Cammy and Josie, who were standing directly inside the door, providing a wall of curiosity that there was no scaling.

'What just happened in there?' Josie blurted.

'Nothing. Why?'

'Nothing?'

'Nothing.'

'Mel, is there something you're not telling us?'

'No. Why?' Oh, good grief, it was like the Spanish Inquisition – the Glasgow version that came with cold weather and the promise of Irn Bru at half-time.

Josie shrugged and moved out of the way to let her past. 'No reason,' she answered in a tone that made it very clear that a very big reason was looming.

Mel didn't give her the chance to follow through. 'I'm just going to catch up with some paperwork. Give me a shout if we get busy.'

She barely made it to the seclusion of the office when her legs buckled and she leaned over the top of the safe for support – a move that wouldn't have been her first choice if she'd realised that Cammy was going to follow her and be faced with a bird's-eye view of her arse.

'Are you OK? Before you answer that, you have to know that Josie sent me in here to get more information and she'll beat the truth out of me so be careful what you say.'

Straightening up, she kicked off her shoes and adjusted the chain belt that sat across her hips on the black sheath dress: square neckline, calf-length, split at the back to avoid the necessity to walk like a penguin. Compose. Gather. Compose. And stick to denial.

'I'm fine, Cammy. Why wouldn't I be?'

'Because Anneka just popped her head in the door, announced that you'd had a berzy at her in the salon and said that she hoped you and I would be very happy together.'

'Oh.'

'So, you want to tell me what happened?'

The urge to lean over the safe returned but she fought it off.

'She was having a go at Suze, being all smug and smart-arsed and I lost it. Threw her out.'

'No way!'

'Way.'

'Bloody hell, I'd have bought tickets to see that.'

'Yeah, well, it was strictly a one-off performance.'

There was a couple of moments' silence in which it was very obvious that Cammy was working out how that would look in his head.

'So, are you going to tell me what's going on with you? Things still rocky with Joe? I'm not trying to intrude but I know something is on your mind and you know that if I can help –'

'I know, Cammy, thank you.'

She *should* tell him. Tell him the whole story. Tell him that her marriage was still not fixed, that the shop was on the verge of closing, that there were so many things confusing her that she just couldn't think straight. Was it possible to drown in your own life? For everything to change so quickly that you went under and had to struggle as every last drop of oxygen was squeezed out of the lungs?

With admittedly childish naivety, she just wanted every-thing to go back to the way it was, with no drama, no problems and no uncertainty as to where she belonged and what she was doing.

And no very handsome employee who had suddenly realised that she had burst into tears and reacted by putting his arms around her and shushing her as she cried.

Telling him to stop and disentangling herself from his arms should have been her next move but she decided it could wait. Instead, she just stood there, listening to his heartbeat as it gently thudded against her ear and acknowl-edging that it felt great. Peaceful.

'Sorry, Cammy – PMT,' she murmured into his shoulder.

He didn't respond, just held her, breathing into the space above her head. Another day, another meltdown. At this rate, she realised, she wouldn't have to tell him that he was out of a job, because her unbalanced antics of late would have him tearing down to the job centre in search of any position that didn't come with a hot and cold running boss.

But, even as that thought went through her head, she knew that it wasn't true. And maybe it was time for a few other home truths as well. Like, when was she going to admit to herself what everyone else was already thinking? When would she fess up that she was having feelings for her formerly platonic best friend (for the purposes of this exercise, Suze had been moved into the family section of the relationship chart).

When? A sudden shudder washed over her. OK, so it was true. But it was a crush. A harmless, stupid crush that was nothing but a longing for warmth and security in the face of Joe's betrayal. Cammy was, literally, a shoulder to cry on. It wasn't love or lust – she still planned to reserve those two emotions for Joe until the death do us part bit. But like comfy socks and the woolly shawl that she always sought out on winter nights, she was just feeling over-attached to the comfort that he offered.

Comfort. That was it. And it was manifesting itself in a bit of a crush that was adding to the emotional overload of everything else. Obviously the reason that she'd flipped at Anneka was because she'd had a violent reaction to that trollop insinuating that she and Cammy still had something going on. An over-reaction? Yes. Stupid? Most definitely. But the main thing was, no one knew, no one had to know in the future and Cammy had made it quite clear after the snogging debacle that he didn't harbour any romantic notions towards her. So this was just a trifling, momentary issue that would soon pass.

195

'Come out with me tonight.'

'What?' Only it came out as 'ggnnot' because her head was still buried in his shoulder. She came up for air as he repeated himself.

'Come out with me tonight.'

OK, that was fine. They often went out on a Saturday after work. No big deal.

'Maybe – we'll need to see if Josie has plans. I'm not sure if the bloke with the sideburns is in town this weekend.'

Josie and Elvis (her nickname for him – sounded better than Bert) had settled on a casual fling based on a love of music, old movies and hair that was fashioned into a quiff of such solid proportions that it could be used to ram-raid shop windows.

'I wasn't talking about Josie. I meant just you and me.'

Pulling back, she looked at him inquisitively. What did he say? And did he have a sore throat because his voice sounded a bit weird just then. 'But, we always take –'

'Mel, I want it to be just you and me.'

Oh. On balance, this wasn't wise. It would not be in any way smart to put herself in a position where she was down, stressed, had PMT and was within touching distance of a burgeoning big bloody crush. Nope, it would just be plain stupid.

'OK.'

'OK?'

He looked surprised – and so he should be as she couldn't quite believe it herself.

'I'm going to get back out there before Josie grounds us for keeping secrets.'

'Did I hear my name being mentioned there?'

A head of silver hair popped in through the space in the door and Mel breathed a sigh of relief that there was now at least a two-feet void between her and Cammy.

196

'I was just saying that you're lovingly concerned for Melissa's wellbeing,' he replied innocently.

'No, I'm not, I just want to know if you two are doing naked duvet stuff.'

Mel frowned indignantly. 'Josie, if I fire you, will you leave quietly?'

'Not a chance. You'll have to physically remove me and I warn you I'm trained to kill.'

The jocular rebuttal gave her just the slightest sense of foreboding, but Josie was too busy making her big announcement to notice. 'Anyway, I hate to break up the party, but I just thought you should know that your husband is on his way over here and was just about to cross the road outside when Anneka spotted him and stopped her car. They're now having a chat in the middle of the road.'

A noise made her look back into the shop. 'Cancel that, he's just walked in the door.'

There was a scramble as both Josie and Cammy made a rapid escape, passing Joe on the way. Pulse racing, Mel swiftly slid into her seat and picked up a pen in the hope that it made her look like she was, well, holding a pen. Bugger, she was losing the plot.

'Hey,' he said, his tone giving no indication as to his frame of mind.

'Hey,' she replied. Checkmate.

'Was talking to Anneka there.'

'Oh? What was she saying?' Nonchalance. Act casual. Don't panic.

He shrugged. 'Nothing much.'

She resisted the urge to ask – nothing much: been leading a quiet life lately or nothing much: by the way, I think your wife's having it away with my ex-boyfriend? Damn, he was giving nothing away. When the resultant pause grew to a length that was bordering on uncomfortable, he finally made his next move. He bent down, picked up her bag, took her coat off the rack and flicked the off switch on the computer. 'Come with me.'

Whoa, what was going on? 'Come with you where?'

'It doesn't matter. Just come with me.'

'But, Joe, I can't go anywhere. I'm working.'

'Mel, this is more important than work.' He held open the door expectantly.

There was nothing else she could do but go along with it. As she passed, she replied to Cammy's quizzical look with a surreptitious shrug. 'I, er, have to pop out for a while. But if I'm not back by closing time will you lock up for me please?'

He nodded. 'No problem, see you later.'

'Bye, Josie, see you Monday.'

She didn't get a reply, what with Josie unwilling to punctuate her evil looks at Joe with the mild fripperies of everyday life.

Outside the shop, she put out an arm to stop him going any further. 'What's going on?'

He took her hand and guided her towards his car. 'I just had to get you out of there because it's time I did something that I should have done a long time ago.'

Twenty-six

Sex. It had been on her mind for days and now Suze had decided that she wasn't waiting any bloody longer to have wild, abandoned, make-up sex.

Eyes flicking to the clock on the dashboard, she made a quick mental calculation of the logistics of this mission. Right about now, Karl should be getting home from the gym. However, Cruella De Vil would still be at the hospital as visiting wasn't over for another hour and a half. Add on to that at least twenty minutes for her to point out to the nurses all the ways in which they weren't doing their jobs properly, plus another five minutes giving lectures on hand washing to the other visitors who'd had the audacity to walk past the anti-bacterial gel containers that were posted at the ward doors, then there was a fifteen-minute drive home, so that came to a grand total of two hours and ten minutes in which she and Karl could act out their hitherto suppressed need to have wild, frantic 'shag me on the kitchen table' make-up sex.

Pressing a button on her Bluetooth headpiece, she dialled the house number. No answer. He obviously wasn't home yet. She speed-dialled his mobile. No answer there either. Must be in the bottom of his gym bag. Didn't matter – she'd see him soon and maybe it was better that he had no idea he was about to have an earth-moving encounter with the love of his life.

Much as they'd had their problems, sex was the one area in which they were both absolutely compatible. Both with high sex drives, both with a taste for the adventurous, both experienced in knowing exactly what the other one liked. Other than the few months leading up to the whole honey-trap debacle, they'd rarely gone a couple of days without passion and his loss of libido had been one of the strongest indicators to her that something was seriously messed up. But she didn't want to think about that now. She'd got it wrong, she'd made a mistake, he'd made an even bigger one, they'd sorted it out and come out of the whole thing better and stronger and that was all that mattered. Well, that and the case of the wild, frantic make-up sex that they'd been dying to have for the last two weeks but couldn't because the house now came with an inbuilt sexual deter-rent called the mother-in-law. It had been a long fortnight of muted, silent quickies on the floor, not even daring to use the bed in case the noise travelled and Virginia heard them and died of outrage. They hadn't even had the privacy and time to put the subject of children back on the table and come to a new agreement about when they should start trying for a family. This time they'd both want the same thing at the same time, she was sure of it.

A surge of excitement shot through her. This was going to be the best afternoon she'd had in a long, long time, espe-cially as she had every intention of being suspended from the chandelier with her husband's gorgeous face clenched between her thighs in approximately twelve minutes' time.

Turning into the street, she spotted Mrs McNee in her

front garden and slowed down. Surely it was time to let bygones be bygones. Weren't they all mature, civilised adults?

'Afternoon, Mrs McNee, lovely day!'

The chin that dropped a good two inches indicated that Mrs McNee was surprised and decidedly unimpressed by the conciliatory gesture. Suze absorbed the reaction and acted accordingly. 'Heading home to have sex with my rampant big shag of a husband. Just want to make sure you've got all the facts for the neighbourhood-watch log.'

Leaving a horrified face staring behind her, Suze screeched round into her driveway. Damn, Karl's car wasn't there so he must have got held up at the gym. Unless of course it was still in the garage, but, no, he had definitely said he was going out so he'd have taken it out first thing this morning.

Never mind, more time for her to prepare. She was thinking new black Agent Provocateur quarter-cup bra and matching thong, black hold-ups and skyscraper heels. Or boots. Maybe the over-the-knee leather boots with the five-inch spiked heels that were a bugger to get on but made her look – quite literally – like sex on legs. Or the new white mesh baby doll that managed the impossible and screamed both 'virgin' and 'slut' at the same time.

Or the . . . damn, why wouldn't the key go in the door? She tried again – nope, it was getting only so far then stopping. Perplexed, she checked both sides of her key. Nope, all looked fine – not bent or broken. So the only reason the key wouldn't work was if there was another key already in the other side of the door, and that wasn't possible because Karl was at the gym. That's what he told her so she absolutely knew it to be true. And because he was at the gym, she knew that she could try the handle on the door and it wouldn't open. Definitely not. Yet . . . shit, why was the door opening right in front of her eyes?

Tentatively, warily, she took the few steps that were required to get past the door and gain full view of the open-plan living space and . . . the gasp was out before she could stop it. Because right there, over at the very kitchen table that she'd been fantasising about only minutes before, was a sight that made every iota of her being shrivel up in horror.

Eyes met hers, challenging, blazing. 'So when were you going to tell me?'

The sentence screamed latent, unadulterated fury. And Suze's legs went weak when she realised that it was aimed squarely at her. She opened her mouth to reply, but didn't get the words out because at that very moment Karl came loping in behind her. At least, she hoped it was Karl because whoever it was had just accosted her from behind, slid his arms round to her front and was currently massaging her tits while whispering, 'You are so getting shagged,' in her right ear.

Until, that is, he caught up with the scene in front of him. That's when he, too, saw her, sitting at the kitchen table, her face contorted with rage. Lying open in front of Virginia Marshall were the accounting books for the company and the notepad on which Suze had detailed list upon list of actions, problems and strategies.

Virginia had obviously read them all.

Karl immediately dropped his hands from his wife's tits, felt his bollocks shoot back up inside him to a place of safety, and adopted the demeanour of a twelve-year-old boy caught with a packet of cigarettes, a case of beer and a year's supply of *Hustler*.

'I'd like an answer, if you don't mind. I'd like to know when you were going to tell me that you have taken the company that my husband and I took forty years to build and run it into the ground?'

Twenty-seven

As soon as she'd passed the signs for the Erskine Bridge, Mel realised where they were going. Mar Hall. Turning into the long, narrow road leading up to the hotel that was once the grand baronial pile of the 11th Lord of Blantyre, she felt weeks of tension finally slipping away. As they pulled into the car park, she smiled at the sight of the stunning building in front of her, Gothic in style and built from slabs of stone that had been quarried from the surrounding land. She just wished she'd dressed for the occasion, a thought reinforced when she teetered on her Top Shop wedges all the way through the ornate beauty of the Grand Hall, then turned right to take the elevator to their room.

Or, rather, their several hundred square feet of unabashed opulence and luxury. The one and only time they'd been there before they'd stayed in an admittedly very grand standard room but this was in an altogether different class. Against one wall of the suite was a huge, mahogany four-poster bed, the struts of the frame draped with the thickest brocades and silks, the base so tall that a foot step nestled at one side to help with leverage for the vertically challenged. On another wall was a stunning, marble fireplace with two richly upholstered gold armchairs in front of it. There was a sumptuous black sofa in the middle of the room, beautifully carved drawers, wardrobes and entertainment units around the perimeter, but even more breathtaking than the glorious furnishings was the view. Through four Georgian-style ten-pane windows was a stunning menagerie of green, russets and browns on the Kilpatrick Hills, rolling inclines that sat majestically above the flowing waters of the Clyde. She managed not to gasp until the porter had deposited her bright-pink trolley case (packed and hidden in the boot of the car by Joe) and left the room.

'Oh, Joe, it's so . . . so . . . have we won the lottery?'

'Nope, we're still poor.'

'So then why?'

'Because you love it here. And I needed to be with you, just us, to reconnect and to remind you how good we were. You deserve this, babe. Although don't be charging too much to room service or the credit card will max out and we'll have to do a runner.'

A heartstring tugged as she realised that his humour was his endearing way of deflecting attention from his nervousness. This was the Joe that she knew – not that flash guy chatting up a stranger in a Glasgow bar on a Friday night. This was her sweet, lovely Joe and for the first time in a long time she felt the urge to go to him and put her arms around him. So she did. She held her breath as he slowly peeled her dress off her shoulders, running a finger along her collarbone and then down between her breasts, before – in a swooping movement that could have resulted in the need for medical attention to the spinal area – he picked her up and carried her over to the bed.

'Joe?'

'What, darling?' he whispered, placing her down gently on the thick silky blanket.

'You realise that we're having a Mills & Boon moment, don't you?'

He grinned and licked the tip of her nose in response.

'And you realise that it makes me really cheap that my emotions can be bought by a flash night in a swanky hotel?'

'I do,' he said, his tongue now following the route from her neck downwards.

'OK, that's fine then. Carry on.'

A party of middle-aged, American golfers passing by the room at that very moment raised their eyebrows as the shrieks of hilarity wafted out into the corridor.

As the blanket of dark quickly dropped outside, turning day into night in less than an hour, Joe touched her, whispered to her, made love to her and every stroke and caress felt as Mills & Boon-esque as it could possibly be without a ripping bodice and a long-haired Casanova with a clearly defined six-pack and thighs like logs.

As she came for the second time (an event usually reserved for birthdays and bank holidays), she realised that it felt . . . good. Great. Her earth was definitely moving and not just in the physical sense. Joe had been so clever to do this and, as she watched him fall back on to the pillow, a wave of love consumed her. She pushed herself up on to her elbow and faced him, Stroking his hair back and tracing his eyebrows with her fingers, smiling as he sighed contentedly.

She watched him, watched his chest rise and fall with every breath, until he broke the silence. 'So have I got my wife back?' he asked, voice thick with earnest hope.

She nodded in reply. 'But we have to make sure this never happens to us again. I still find it tough to accept that I didn't realise that you weren't completely happy.'

'Don't, Mel.' He took her hand off his face and kissed her palm. 'There was no way you could have known when I didn't even realise it myself.'

'You've told me that already but it doesn't make it any easier to take.'

'I know, babe, I'm sorry. It just terrifies me that I could have lost you for the sake of a night with someone I didn't even know.'

Hang on – what had he just said? 'But didn't you say that you'd never have done anything anyway?'

His face definitely flushed and there was a distinct element of bluster to his reply. 'Never. Of course I wouldn't have.'

Her sigh was as sad as it was resolute. There was no point even going there because she would never know the truth of what might have happened. 'Let's just draw a line under everything and learn from it. You have to communicate with me, tell me what's going on and I need to realise that not everyone trundles along happily day after day. But . . .'

'What?'

The thought had just come to her and she instinctively knew it was the right thing to do. 'I think maybe we should hold off on starting a family just yet, Joe. Maybe we should go back to just being happy as a couple, just taking care of each other for a while.'

Clearly crest-fallen, he pushed up on to his elbow too, so that they were facing each other, noses only inches apart.

'No, babe, come on, don't say that. You were so excited about having a baby this year.'

Staring into his almond eyes she was just about to argue when . . . Wow, where did that come from? A flashing mental image of a girl in a skin-tight dress, sitting in a bar, staring across the table at this guy who was now in front of her.

Thrown off balance by the flashback, she tripped over her words. 'But I . . . I mean . . . I am . . . but . . .'

Wow, another one – his hand was over the girl's now and he was asking her if she would . . .

'Let's just wait for now, Joe. Let's get things sorted with the business first. If it goes under I'll have to get another job and then there's maternity-leave restrictions and . . .'

'I'm separated. Have been for a long time. We've both moved on and put it behind us, but I haven't met anyone else yet. Until now . . .'

Bloody hell, where did that come from? The pain hit her stomach so hard that she visibly flinched.

'Are you OK?'

'I'm fine, just . . . hungry.' And hurt. And traumatised. And unable to get the image of you with her out of my head.

He leaned over and kissed her and the urge to push him away was almost irresistible. This couldn't happen. She had to get over this and she would. It was just a matter of time and the important thing was that they were both committed to making it work. Both of them.

'I'm separated. Have been for a long time. We've both moved on and put it behind us, but I haven't met anyone else yet. Until now . . .'

Aaargh, she had to get that voice out of her head! Pushing up, she climbed down what felt like several metres from the bed. 'Do you mind if I have a bath?' she said as breezily as she could manage.

'Want some company?'

Shit, she should have known that he would say that. Deflect. Deflect.

'Maybe later – want to shave my legs and pamper myself a bit first,' she replied, leaning over to kiss him again. Deflection accomplished. 'I'll be back in a . . .'

The noise of her phone ringing cut through the conversation. She automatically reached for her bag and dug her LG Pebble out from the depths of all her worldly goods.

The word 'SHOP' flashed on the screen.

Heart suddenly pounding, she mouthed, 'Josie' in reply to Joe's inquisitive stare and opened the phone, taking herself off to one of the armchairs by the fire so that she was out of earshot.

'Hello.'

'Hi,' came the reply. It wasn't a surprise. 'So I take it we'll have to postpone that drink tonight.'

'We sold how much? That's great news! Well done you.' Please understand, please suss this out.

'Ah, Joe is near you and you can't talk just now?'

'Yep, those bras are gorgeous. And I love the matching thongs. Remind me to order more when I get back.'

Over on the bed, she saw that Joe had picked up the remote control for the TV and was now aimlessly flicking through the channels.

'So where are you?'

'Mar Hall.'

Joe smiled over in her direction.

'It's beautiful.'

There was a pause on the other end, then: 'It's one of my favourite places. When I was there last month I didn't want to leave.'

Of course, he'd been here with Anneka – she'd completely forgotten. Tension slowly spread back across the top of her shoulders as she digested that thought.

'We were in room eleven – overlooking –'

'The water.' She finished the sentence for him. Shit, what were the chances? Actually, they were fifty-three to one. Fifty-three rooms and she had to end up in the same one that Cammy had been in. Had someone put a curse on her at birth and it was only now coming to fruition?

'So . . .' he started, but was cut off when her nerves switched her gob on to 'Blurt' mode.

'No, I definitely won't be popping in tomorrow, Josie.

We'll probably just hang out here and then head home late in the day. Maybe stop off and do some shopping in town on the way.' Why was she rambling? Why? She never worked a Sunday so no one would expect her there anyway. Stop talking. Hang up. Go for bath and then return to reformed, sweet husband.

But the voice on the other end of the phone wasn't letting her off that lightly and returned to his previous question. 'So have you and Joe worked it out then?'

There was another pause. A long one. 'Blurt' mode would appear to have moved swiftly into 'deer in headlights' mode.

'We have.'

Joe looked over at her with raised eyebrows. 'Josie was just asking if we'd seen the Grand Hall yet.'

As he nodded and refocused on the football match he'd found on Sky Sports, she switched back to the telephone conversation.

'You know, when something has been around that long it's just so important that they preserve it.' Where the hell had that come from? It really should disturb her that she was showing such a talent for subterfuge. Who knew?

'You're right, it is. I'm happy for you. You know that, don't you?'

'Absolutely.'

'You know I care about you – like all good employees should – and if you're happy then that's all that matters.'

Was it her imagination or was there an undertone of relief in his voice? Or concern perhaps? It was difficult to tell with Hibernian v Dundee United blaring in the background.

'I am.'

'OK. Well, I'll see you Monday. Enjoy the rest of your weekend.'

In the couple of seconds between his goodbye and the line being disconnected, she could hear Josie in the background shouting, 'Was that Mel? Where is she? Tell me she's told that daft fecker of a husband to pack his bags.'

Even in the midst of the emotional maelstrom it was hard not to laugh.

A few moments later, she sank into the peppermint and rosehip bubbles of the Aveda bath concoction and realised that she knew, *absolutely* knew that she was doing the right thing. Her feelings for Cammy? True friendship that just happened to be enhanced at the moment by a crazy, frivolous crush. That couldn't in any way compete with eight years of previously blissful marriage to Joe. Joe was her soul mate, her happy ever after, and it was a good thing that she'd nipped whatever was fermenting between her and Cammy in the bud. After all, she had no idea why he even wanted to take her out tonight. Maybe he sensed that she was an emotional car crash and on the verge of using him as some kind of crutch and wanted to let her down gently. Maybe he was freaked out by all the speculation over whether or not there was something going on between them and wanted to ask her to set the record straight. Maybe he . . . you know what, it didn't matter.

What mattered now was that she and Joe were fine and they were here, in the hotel version of paradise, with one of them in a claw-foot bath, smelling of peppermint and letting all the stresses and strains just slip away.

Slip away.

Just slip away.

Gulp! She got a mouth full of bubbles as Joe strode in, interrupting her karmic calm as he lifted the lid up to pee in the toilet that was three feet away from her. Smashing.

In a bid to divert her attention from the obvious, she exorcised a little piece of curiosity that had been niggling at her.

'Erm, honey, I forgot to ask – what was Anneka saying to you earlier?'

He stopped, shook, tucked himself back into the white towelling robe, then hesitated for a few seconds before answering. 'Mmm, yeah, really weird. She stopped the car when I was crossing the road and rolled the window down to chat. Bit strange. I've only met her a couple of times so didn't really know what to say to her.'

Phew, relief. There had been a distinct worry that Anneka would seek some kind of retribution for Mel's outburst that morning.

'And to be honest, I didn't want to stand around talking to her for too long in case Suze saw me and battered me to a pulp,' he joked, heading towards the door.

'Always a danger,' Mel agreed. Worry over. Fear of reprisals quashed.

He paused, hand on the doorknob. 'Strange, though – I thought I heard you say that she'd split up with Cammy?'

Fear of reprisals resurfacing.

'She has. I mean, they have. Why?'

'Because she said something about us all getting together one night.'

Oh holy shit . . .

'But I was non-committal. Like I said, I've no desire to upset Suze and be put in a testicle/electric-probe situation.'

Mel did her best not to show any exterior indication of the outrage that was bubbling inside. What a twisted little cow! What was she playing at? Was this some messed-up attempt to cause mischief or did she just bloody go around all day inviting people to party? And no, she realised, it wasn't the type of party that came with balloons and streamers.

And – eeeeew – the filthy slapper had already shagged one of the Marshall brothers so was this an attempt to hit on the other? No, she was over-reacting. Anneka was

211

just relishing the thought of causing trouble, making mischief, throwing out suspicion. That was what she did and Mel refused to let it bug her happiness. She was here with Joe, and they were going to be fine and that was all that mattered.

'Want company in there yet?'

Her nose wrinkled as she smiled and shook her head. 'Not yet. Is that OK? I'm just really enjoying stretching out.'

'OK, well, shout if you change your mind.'

'Will do,' she said, sliding down under the bubbles.

When she resurfaced he was gone. She'd call him back after she'd had another twenty minutes or so of bliss. In the meantime, she'd just close her eyes and let her mind go blank. Blank. That was it, completely blank . . .

Shit, had Cammy and Anneka had sex in this bath?

Noooooo.

Oh hell, the mental picture and the very thought of it. She had to get out, go back next door, lie down with her husband and block that from her mind altogether. Cammy and Anneka having sex. Urgh.

Cammy. Naked. Having . . . Oh. Cammy, naked.

If they hadn't had sex in the bath then they were sure to have had sex on the bed next door. Oh, no – the same bed that she and Joe had just . . . Stop! Don't go there. Don't think about it, don't even let it take residence in your brain. Melissa Jane Marshall (she always used her full name when giving herself a serious reprimand), do not dare go there. It's just a four-week interval away from a swinger session and you're not that type of girl.

But. Cammy. Naked.

Melissa Jane Marshall! Enough! No more! Get a grip!

Sticking her head to one side so that she could peek through the gap in the door, she knew what she had to do.

'Joe, honey!'

'Go on, my son!'

She assumed that one was directed at one of the twenty-two men on the TV who were engaged in the overpaid pasttime of chasing a ball.

A 'Yes, babe?' was tagged on to the end.

'That offer to join me still stand?'

In less than a couple of seconds, he was in front of her, the robe was off and his erection was heading in the direction of the tub.

See! Cammy and Anneka didn't have the monopoly on wild antics and sexual adventure – those were both healthy components of a good marriage and she and Joe had them too.

They did.

Absolutely.

A gentle nudge propelled her forwards and he slid down behind her, his hands immediately coming around to the front as he scooped bubbles on to her nipples.

'I love you, Mel.'

'I love you too,' she replied. And she meant it. She did.

I'm separated. Have been for a long time. We've both moved on and put it behind us, but I haven't met anyone else yet. Until now . . .'

No, go away! Argh, when was this going to stop? Melissa Jane Marshall, forget the past, forget Cammy, forget everything except the erect, erotic bliss of here and now.

Don't think. Just don't think.

And definitely ignore the little voice that she'd been denying for the last hour. The one that said that sex with Joe had felt good. Felt great. Moved her earth.

But it hadn't felt right.

213

Twenty-eight

'I think she's trying to kill him. I do. She's hoping the shock bumps him off and then she can swan around like the merry widow giving vast sums of money to charities in return for small children worshipping at her feet everywhere she goes. I'm telling you, she's in it for the adulation.'

'Suze, I love you. I do. But if you don't stop talking I'm putting you out of the car.'

'But we're in the middle of the motorway.'

'Exactly.'

Suze pursed her lips really tightly to stop anything coming out. Jeez, wasn't a girl entitled to an opinion these days? She stared out of the window and in the far distance spotted an aeroplane taking off from Glasgow airport. 'We could just go to the airport and get on a plane to anywhere and that way your dad's death won't be on our conscience. Not that it will anyway, because it'll be all her fault. She's a –'

'SUZE!'

'OK, OK.' Pursing of the lips, take two. But she refused to believe that, given the current situation, ninety-nine per cent of the population wouldn't hold the same view as she

214

did – that telling a man who was recovering from heart surgery that the company he'd inherited from his father, then dedicated his life to until the day that he handed it down to his beloved sons was about to hit the skids. Why did he have to know that right now? The biggest challenge of his day should be whether to watch *Richard & Judy* and have custard or jelly from the hospital canteen for lunch.

But, no, Virginia of the Coven of the Black Widows had gone off to church that morning, and informed them that she would go on to the hospital at one o'clock and they should arrive at two, thus giving her precisely one hour to attempt to kill her husband by shock.

Glancing to her right, she caught sight of Karl's white knuckles on the steering wheel and the clenched tightness of his jaw and her heart hurt for him. This was his worst nightmare, the thing he'd been trying to avoid for months. His father's trust was so important to him and he was devastated that he'd ultimately failed him. That's why the previous afternoon, when Virginia had discovered what was going on, he'd asked, almost begged her to give him more time to raise funds.

'And how, exactly, do you plan to do that?' she'd sneered, her jaw set in the same tight, unbreakable clench that Karl now sported. Shit, she'd never realised it before but actually Karl bore a faint resemblance to his mother from the side. A thought that she resolved to dismiss for fear of never being able to have sex with him again.

'There are still some people I want to speak to – investors, other banks. Marshalls has a good name, Mum, and I just need to find someone in the financial position to come on board until we've recovered from this.'

The bang from the notepad hitting the worktop had made them both jump. 'We are not having an outsider come into our family business.'

215

'Then our family business is over, Mum.' It was said not out of anger, but deep, deep sorrow and Suze could see that even Virginia recognised that.

There was a brief respite while they collected their thoughts and Suze knew that, as a mother, as the woman who had allegedly given birth to this man, Virginia would now show Karl some compassion and understanding.

'You failed. You got greedy,' Virginia said, her voice the approximate temperature of a polar adventurer's backpack.

And that, Suze decided, just went to prove how much she knew about motherhood. Less than nothing. Virginia Marshall was the human equivalent of wild animals that ate their young.

Reacting to the violence of her outburst, Karl slumped down on the sofa, rubbing his eyes as if he could reopen them and this whole situation would have disappeared. 'You're right, I did fail. But it wasn't through greed, it was through ambition. And through not foreseeing a global economic meltdown that would have repercussions all the way down the line until they reached smaller companies like ours. I wasn't alone in that, Mum. This is a global recession, not just a case of mismanagement in one construction firm.'

Suze silently applauded his spirit, swelling with pride that he was refusing to kowtow to Cruella's inherent evil.

'I'll speak to your father tomorrow.'

'Mum, you can't! He's in the hospital, for God's sake! You can't land something like this on him when he's ill.'

'How long have the banks given you?'

Ouch, low blow.

Karl sighed wearily. 'Couple of weeks. Maybe a month.'

'Then let me reinforce my earlier sentiment. No one outside this family will ever be a part of Marshalls. So unless you're about to find religion –' her stare of death transferred directly to Suze '– and somehow be blessed with a

216

miracle, then we need to solve this situation now. The only person who knows how to do that is your father. Don't ever mistake his introverted nature for lack of gumption.'

With that, she rose from her seat, walked across the room and climbed the stairs, leaving two astonished spectators frozen to their spots.

It was difficult to pinpoint the most surprising element of the showdown. The fact that she had discovered the truth, that she'd decided to tell Donald, or that she'd said something complimentary about the man she'd been serially belittling for the last forty years. It was like discovering Satan liked to spend his spare time spreading happiness and doing good deeds.

That was the last they'd seen of her until this morning when she left for church after giving them their orders for the day. Karl had tried to argue, but it had been pointless. That was why, on a Sunday lunchtime when they wanted to be sitting in Princess Square, drinking cocktails without a care in the world, they were in fact en route to Rosshall Hospital to break the heart of a man who already had a heart condition. It didn't take a genius to foresee that this wouldn't end well.

Ten minutes later they pulled into the car park and he of the frozen jaw took a deep breath, as if trying to summon up the strength to face what was about to happen.

Suze leaned over and squeezed his hand. 'You know, it's not going to be easy, but at least after this there will be no more secrets, no more stress of trying to cover up what's going on. There has to be some relief in that, darling.'

This must be so hard for him, her Alpha male, the one who'd spent his whole life taking charge and meeting with nothing but success. Until now. But this didn't change who he was. This was just one sad chapter, one unforeseen ambush, but Suze knew that whatever happened he'd pick

217

himself up and make a success of his life. Bloody hell, why was she sounding like a Hallmark greeting card again? This whole past couple of months had seriously upset her emotional equilibrium and eroded her deep-rooted cynicism and jaded demeanour. She resolved to get them back pronto before it got even further out of control and she developed sinister traits like selflessness and optimism.

The automatic doors slid open and they made their way up to Donald's room on the second floor. When they arrived, Virginia was already there, sitting beside the bed, back ram-rod straight, her hand on top of her husband's. Holy crap, physical contact! The shocks just kept on coming.

Suze put a pile of golfing magazines and a box of chocolate éclairs on the bedside cabinet, then leaned over to hug her father-in-law. For a man who'd been through so much in the last few weeks, he actually looked fitter than he'd done for a long, long time. Other than the general surroundings and the Hickman line that was strapped to the back of his hand, there were no obvious signs that he had been ill. There was colour in his cheeks, his eyes were bright, he was sitting up tall in his navy-blue Marks and Spencer pyjamas and his hair was longer, neatly combed back in a Cary Grant kind of fashion. In fact, Suze decided, he actually looked quite dashing. The tension in the air, however, was palpable, so Suze stepped back after her greeting and resolved to treat the situation with all due sincerity and not give in to her natural inclination to deal with uncomfortable situations using glib attempts at humour. Definitely not.

'You're looking fine, Donald. I've brought you some mags – golf ones on the top, but I slipped a *Playboy* into the middle where the nurses will never find it.'

If Virginia's puce face and sharp inhalation of breath were anything to go by, they were going to have to get Donald out of the bed and call the crash team for his wife.

Despite the amused twinkle that appeared in Donald's eyes, Karl gave her a disapproving stare as he nudged her out of the way and moved in to hug his dad.

That done, they sat on the two seats on the opposite side of the bed from Virginia.

'Is Joe coming?' Donald asked.

Karl shook his head. 'No, Dad, he went away with Mel yesterday and they won't be back until tonight.'

Suze's eyes darted from Virginia's inscrutable expression to Donald's then back again. Had she told him? He didn't look crushed or devastated so perhaps she hadn't. Perhaps that had just been an empty threat intended to lash out at Karl and punish him for crashing the company.

'Right then, well, let's get on with it. Your mother told me what's happened.'

Bugger! Why did she never get anything right when it came to this family?

'Dad, I'm really sorry. I just . . .'

The Hickman line flew up in the air as Donald raised his hand to stop Karl speaking.

Oh, this wasn't going to be pretty. Suze turned her most menacing stare on Virginia. If Donald got overwrought and pegged out right there and then, it would all be her fault and she would never, ever tire of reminding her of that.

'Son, it happens.'

What?

It. Happens.

Was that it? Donald was acting like they'd just told him the hospital shop had run out of grapes. And Karl looked just as surprised as she was.

'But, Dad, I –'

'Son, stop there. You don't have to explain. I handed the company over to you and Joe because I trusted you boys and I still do. This could have happened to anyone.'

219

Drugs. He must be on drugs. Suze leaned over to check if there was any other way that mind-altering drugs could be pumping into his body. Virginia rewarded her inquisitive search with her customary icy stare, and Suze decided that when she located the drugs some of them were definitely going to be earmarked for Virginia's tea.

'It didn't happen to you.'

'Oh, but it did. The year you were born. Overextended myself, too much on my mind, too busy trying to build some fast financial security for my family – same thing happened. Built a beautiful big house in the West End, owners went bust and I'm still waiting for the money.' Donald smiled and shrugged almost casually. 'Taught me a lesson.'

'I wish you'd taught *me* that one, Dad.'

'Nope, that's one you have to learn for yourself. Your granddad knew that too – that's why he gave me the money to get by, because he knew it was a mistake I wouldn't make twice. And neither will you.'

Karl's eyes looked suspiciously moist as he reached over and squeezed his dad's shoulder. 'Thanks.'

'For what?' Donald replied.

'For not criticising.'

If Virginia took that as a dig she didn't show it.

'There's nothing to criticise. The building trade is a precarious one – good times and bad. We know that. Like I said, it happens. Your mother said you need a hundred thousand to get back in the black.'

The realisation of what Donald was about to do elicited two very different reactions. Karl blurted out, 'Yeah, but, Dad, I'm not taking your money!' While Suze had to summon every ounce of self-discipline she had not to jump up, screaming and clapping before doing a lap of honour of the bed.

'Karl, that's enough. Listen to your father,' Virginia ordered.

Yes, Karl, listen to your father, Suze echoed silently. Dear Lord, she was agreeing with Virginia now – time to opt for voluntary committal.

'Being in here and going through this operation already had your mother and I thinking about putting our affairs in order.'

'But . . .' Horrified, Karl began to interrupt but was silenced by a Virginia stare.

'When we die, which incidentally I hope isn't for a long time, we'll get hammered in inheritance tax, so we've decided to offload some of your inheritance now. As long as I manage to keep this ticker going for another seven years, then the Government won't make you pay tax on it. Our company did well for me in the end, Karl. There's a hundred and fifty grand for each of you and that still leaves your mother and I plenty to live on from here on in.'

Forget the bed, Suze was about to go for a lap of honour of the entire hospital! But, to her eternal mortification, she burst into tears instead. Virginia rolled her eyes and tutted, so Suze dived around the room and gave her a huge, heart-felt hug.

A hundred and fifty grand! Somehow they'd managed to emerge from a bankruptcy situation with more money than they'd ever had. It was incredible! It was . . . it was a bloody miracle! The tears, the stress, the anguish of the last few months was finally over and they'd emerged from it stronger, wiser and richer. That was it! The good times were back and this time they were smart enough to know how to keep them.

For at least a few hours . . .

Twenty-nine

'I spy, with my little eye, something beginning with c.'

'Joe, if this is "cars" again I'm not playing any more, you've already done that one twice.'

'But we've been on a motorway for the last fifteen minutes – my choices are limited.' He laughed.

She was glad of the daft games and light-hearted banter – kept them away from the more serious stuff and that could only be a good thing. A phrase had been stuck in her head all morning; one she'd heard on *Oprah*. Or was it *Dr Phil*? Or maybe it was a poster on a bus shelter. Anyway, 'fake it till you make it' was going to be her new mantra.

It made perfect sense. OK, so she was still feeling just a few degrees out of sync with Joe and wasn't quite back to her previous levels of confidence in their relationship, but that would come in time. It would. All she had to do in the meantime was act like she was absolutely fine and in no time at all the emotions would be genuine. Perfect sense.

'I spy, with my little eye, something beginning with t.'

'Trucks.'

It wasn't exactly a stretch.

She was glad of the interruption when her phone rang and Josie's name flashed on the screen.

'Hello, my sweet, are you missing me?' Mel teased.

'Definitely. Cammy and I have spent all day pining for your return. But we coped with the loss by shutting up shop, turning the music up and sinking Pina Coladas until the pain subsided.'

'Excellent! I like that kind of devotion in my team,' she declared, her laughter definitely not of the fake variety. 'So what else has been happening? You've sold the entire stock on eBay? Repainted the shop? Or the office? Or Cammy?'

'All of the above, but you'll love it – insipid apricot is very in these days. Anyway, my love, I've got a huge favour to ask.'

'Uh-huh.'

Josie's favours usually involved long-lasting repercussions or the potential for police involvement.

'I know I'm not long back from holiday, but can I have a couple of days off?'

Oh, bollocks, this was the last thing she needed. There was the whole financial situation to deal with this week – there were meetings with lawyers, with accountants, orders to cancel, apologies to be made. It was going to be almost impossible to do everything without Josie there. But then, it was her beloved Josie and she needed a favour – Mel would only stop short at major organ donation and anything involving group nudity.

'Of course you can. Is something wrong?'

There was a long sigh at the other end of the phone. 'I have to go to Italy. Michael discovered this morning that his missus had been having it off with the baker down the road. Never bloody liked that woman. Anyway, she wants

223

to go riding off into the sunset with the pieman so I'm going over to help with the kids until they get everything sorted out. Can't have him out there surrounded by all her family without back-up. Although, from what he says, they're as disgusted with her as we are.'

'Oh the poor thing.' In some kind of bizarre kindredship-by-osmosis, Mel experienced pangs of understanding and affection despite never having met him. 'Of course you have to go. Take as long as you want and don't worry, we'll be absolutely fine.'

'Thanks, Mel, you're a honey and I'll repay the favour, I promise.'

'No need.'

'So where are you now?'

'Just driving home.'

'Tell me you left the dim one behind.'

'Josie! Of course not. Look, everything's fine, now go. And when you get there, just try not to lose the head – I'm sure there's an extradition policy between here and Italy.'

'I'll do my best, but I'm not promising.'

She rang off just as they pulled on to the slip road that led to the city centre. 'Josie – she has to go back to Italy. Family drama,' she explained to Joe.

'So it's not just us then?'

'It's not just us.'

He leaned over and took her hand and held it, steering with his other hand. Mid-afternoon on a Sunday, only a few shops were open so the streets were quiet, allowing them to make their way through the Merchant City in just a few minutes. Mel glanced over at the shop, gratified to see that it wasn't in fact a lovely shade of insipid apricot.

For a split second she considered going in but changed her mind. If she popped in she'd get stuck there and no, this was her day with Joe. Hadn't she been inadvertently prioritising her work over her husband for long enough? And besides, she realised with a sinking heart, the shop would soon be gone . . . but she and Joe would still be there to pick up the pieces. Joe grabbed her trolley case from the boot and climbed the stairs. The door was barely closed behind them when he smiled cheekily, grabbed her round the waist and pulled her to him.

'I spy, with my little eye, something beginning with h.'

'Husband with the horn.'

'How do you do that?'

'It's just a God-given talent.'

OK, so here was the thing. If she was entirely honest, she just wanted to go curl up on the couch and have a lazy day – just her, a family bag of hula hoops and her friend, Sky+ – so an afternoon of rampant shagging wasn't top of her wish list of things to do.

Fake it till you make it. Fake it till you make it. She could do this.

'I, er, just need to give Suze a quick buzz.'

'Can't it wait?'

'No, it's, er . . . I'll just be one minute.' It was lame, but all she could manage at short notice. What was wrong with her? Why couldn't she just suck it up and get back to normal?

Suze's phone started ringing and she was suddenly struck with the realisation that Joe was within earshot so she was going to have to invent a semi-important reason for the call.

Shit, shit, shit. Second ring. Third ring. Crap, what was she going to say?

Just as she was about to hang up a voice came booming down the line. 'You must be psychic, I was just about to phone you!'

225

'Why? And why are you whispering?'

'Because I'm at the hospital and one of the nurses gives me evils every time she sees me with my mobile phone out. She's obviously got no friends and no social life.'

Mel just caught the first part and her blood ran cold. 'Suze, why are you at the hospital? What's going on? Is Donald OK? Is there a problem? What's happening?' Her words were falling over each other now as panic began to rise.

'No, no, don't worry, he's absolutely fine. In fact, he's great. Mel, he gave us the money.'

'What money?'

'The money to save the company! He's decided to give the boys their inheritance early and it's enough to sort out the company with a huge big bloody wedge left over.'

Mel obviously couldn't see Suze, but she just knew that she was grinning like a maniac and the chances of her punching the air were high.

'Suze, that's amazing!'

'What's amazing?' Joe was on his way past with a bottle of beer from the fridge when she got to that bit.

'Your dad has just told Karl that he's giving you and him the money to bail out the company.'

Confusion and incredulity fought for control of his features, pipped at the last minute by utter delight. Just as Mel thought he was actually going to jump up and down with glee, Suze butted back into the conversation.

'Listen, I'm heading home now and Karl's waiting for another half-hour or so then heading off to the gym. Tell Joe to get his arse over here so they can fill him in on what's going on.'

As she hung up, Mel reached over and took the bottle of beer out of Joe's hand. 'You've to go to the hospital.'

Propelled into action by relief and wonderment, he

didn't need any persuasion. 'You don't mind?' he asked as he snatched up his jacket.

'Of course not! Your dad just saved our lives! Listen, I won't come up with you – sounds like a bit of a boys' thing going on.'

Translation: day off, couch, hula hoops, space, Sky+.

'But tell your dad I'll be up to see him tomorrow.'

He threw his arms around her, hugging her while moving in a pendulum motion from side to side. 'Oh my God, Mel, this is incredible. Incredible. I didn't even know Dad had that kind of money. I knew things would work out OK.'

'You did not,' she teased.

'OK, I didn't. But . . . fuck, this is the best news ever.'

As the door slammed behind him, Mel felt a huge swell of relief and sent up a silent prayer of thanks. Marshalls was back in business so that meant La Femme, Le Homme was safe and – thank you, thank you – Josie and Cammy's jobs were safe too.

And Joe . . . it must be such a weight off his mind. She realised that she was happy for him. Truly, truly, happy. What was it he'd said? Oh yes, the best news ever. It was great. Amazing.

And no, she wasn't going to give in to churlish or negative thoughts. Or petty gripes. No, she wasn't. Definitely not.

But, if she did, she might stop to think that the best news ever should actually have been the fact that she'd agreed to give him another chance.

Thirty

Zipping through the streets into the city centre, Suze realised that at that very moment hers was probably the only car in Glasgow with the roof down. And it felt great. She took a massive breath in and felt giddy relief as her lungs filled with cold, crisp, fresh air. They'd done it. They'd somehow managed to put their whole lives back on track. With – she threw her head back and laughed at the irony of it – a little help from the mother-in-law from hell. A woman previously regarded as Satan's force on earth, but who now, for services above and beyond the call of duty, would henceforth be referred to as 'the lovely Virginia'. The strange thing was, she actually meant it. She'd seen something in Virginia that afternoon that she had never noticed before – a fierce love and protective instinct towards both her husband and sons that transcended her inherent evil.

In fact, she had almost – with the emphasis on *almost* – been human. Who'd have thought that Virginia Marshall could ever have been a candidate for mother of the year?

That, more than anything that had happened over the

last few months, made her want to . . . she braked suddenly as an old lady pushing a supermarket shopping trolley stepped out in front of her. Bloody hell, why did people do that to her? And such a sweet-looking little grandmother. A sweet little grandmother who was now sneering at her, er, now growling, now going red in the face, now opening her mouth, now, 'Watch where yer going, you fancy flash daft bastard that ye are.' She marched over, gave the car a kick, then returned to her trolley and pushed it off to the other side of the road.

Yep, they don't make them as sweet as that any more.

Completely unfazed and more than a little amused (explosive, aggressive, irrational old woman – it was like looking at a snapshot of her future), Suze put her foot back on the accelerator and . . . What had she been thinking about? Oh yes, mother of the year. Mother. The word stuck. It was time. As soon as Karl got home tonight, she was going to put the baby issue on the table and, for the first time in years, she had absolute faith that they would be able to work it out.

They'd both come out of this whole horrible stage of their lives more mature, more grounded and more responsible – perfect criteria for them to move into the realm of people who spent Sundays wandering up and down Mothercare and getting whipped into raptures by the sight of three-wheeler buggies. She and Karl could do that now. They could.

Maturity. That was all it took.

She slammed on the car brakes for a second time, pulled the key out of the ignition and jumped out of the car.

Yes, she'd definitely grown up because of this experience.

Head high, trying to ignore that her five-inch Jimmy Choo heels were sinking into the turf, she strutted across the grass in the direction of the small crowd of people who were gathered at the side of the boating pond.

Yes, she'd moved up to another level, and from now on in she'd be more responsible in her actions.

The first person to spot her was Avril, who was now waving in her direction. She went over to join her, glad that she'd got the venue right. This was Avril's occasional second job, doing the make-up for fashion shoots for the city's newspapers. Suze had always encouraged it because Avril was so good that it invariably led to more business for the shop.

The shop that was run by a newly matured, responsible boss.

'Hey, Suze, what are you doing here?' she asked, with a definite overtone of suspicion.

'Oh, nothing. Just passing. I remembered you said you'd be here so I just thought I'd stop and say hello.'

'Just passing?' Avril retorted disbelievingly, pursing a set of bright-green lips and forcing the flash of lightning that was painted on the side of her face to distort into more of a squiggly line.

'Just passing. Good outfit, by the way – has Ziggy Stardust called to ask for it back yet? Oh, excuse me one second, sweetie.' Without moving a step, Suze called over to the figure that had just materialised from a portable tent used for storing and changing into the clothes. Maturity. Serenity. Responsibility. 'Hey, Anneka!'

As the model turned around, Avril closed her purple eyes and whispered a low 'Oh fuck.' Anneka, on the other hand, didn't even get time to come up with a suitable reply.

'I had a chat with Karl about your offer . . .'

There was utter stillness on set as everyone waited for the next instalment. Glasgow was a huge city but its fashion circle was a tight incestuous group in which there were few

230

secrets. Every single person there knew Suze, and knew that Anneka had got far too intimate with Karl's zoom lens.

'. . . but we've both agreed that we'll pass. You know, even something mildly attractive can lose its appeal when you realise that everyone in town has been there.'

Several sets of top teeth bit into bottom lips and several shoulders were now starting to shake with suppressed laughter.

Eyes blazing, Anneka finally managed to open her mouth to speak but Suze got there first.

'Now, now, don't argue, hon – I know you're disappointed, but please try to understand. We're five-star kind of people . . . and slumming it just isn't our thing.'

Suze leaned over and gave Avril a kiss on the cheek. 'Bye, sweetie. See you tomorrow.'

'You're a complete maniac, do you know that?' Avril whispered, her lightning bolt stretching with her smile.

'I know. But you love me.'

With a wink, she turned and strutted off in the direction of the car, knowing that the whole event would be recounted in bars, restaurants and ladies' toilets for the next fortnight. It was all down to maturity. Because Suze knew that responsible, grown-up adults always tied up loose ends.

Thirty-one

One episode of *Desperate Housewives*. Tick.

Double bill of *Curb Your Enthusiasm*. Tick.

One episode of *America's Next Top Model*. Tick.

Second half of a two-part episode of *Blaggart*. Tick. (And no, she no longer felt quite the same lust for that new detective sergeant.)

Two large glasses of Cava. Tick.

Elevated mood? Tick. Tick. Tick.

In fact, by the time darkness began to fall and she popped into the kitchen for a refill, she realised that this was the first time she'd felt anything approaching relaxed and normal in almost two months. Life was good and it was only going to get better. Her previous devotion-to-husband levels would soon return; she'd revert to feeling safe and secure in his care, trust would be fully restored, and in the meantime she had a shop that she loved, where she worked with two great friends that she adored. And she was having a gloriously rare afternoon on the sofa with just the remote control for company. Yep, life was good. Sunny. Oh, and that thing with Cammy? Gone. Pfffff! Away. It was a stupid crush born of unhappiness and now that she'd rediscovered happiness it had completely receded. Disappeared.

Except ... why had her feet crossed the room and deposited the rest of her body next to the window, where she could clearly see that the light was still on in La Femme, Le Homme across the road? She glanced over at the old wooden clock on the thick oak fireplace. 6 p.m. He was working late. Normal opening hours on a Sunday were eleven to five, but with Josie gone it must be taking longer than usual to clear up, cash up and lock up.

Poor Cammy. He worked so hard for her and never, ever complained. He came in early, he stayed late, he worked his days off if required. As with Josie, it was more than just a job to him, and Mel was eternally grateful that she'd taken him on, not just for his dedication but also for the friendship that had developed. Yes, friendship. It hadn't gone any further than that and that's exactly how it would always be.

There still wasn't any movement in the shop. He must be in the office cashing up the till. Or perhaps he'd decided to replenish the stock and was sorting out inventory in the storeroom. The thought suddenly came to her that a good friend – yes, *friend* – would go over to help. She could even take him a bottle of wine as a thank you. Nothing wrong with that – bosses did that kind of thing all the time.

Of course, she should change first – navy velour trousers, a bright-red Radio Clyde 261 T-shirt and a scrunchie would never win a prize in the chic outerwear category. The pink furry yeti slippers would have to go too.

In the bedroom, she slipped on her favourite black Vivienne Westwood basque, over black boot-cut jeans (gratifyingly loose after her stress-induced weight loss of the last few weeks), with a long, silver, fine-knit waistcoat that

Cammy just happened to have brought her back from New York when he'd been over there for a long weekend.

The scrunchie was removed and a wave of red curls immediately cascaded down her back. Just the face now. Picking up her powder brush, she gave her cheeks a subtle layer of matt bronzer, added a coat of mascara and a dab of lipstick. Done.

Ready. Back in the lounge, she collected the wine, picked up her bag and left a scribbled note for Joe.

Just popped over to the shop to help Cammy close up – won't be long.

Out of habit, she drew a smiley face underneath. Of course, she'd probably be back before he got home; after all, she was just going over there for ten minutes or so on a purely professional basis to aid in the relevant administrative tasks that were required at the close of business. She slipped the wine bottle into her bag and headed downstairs.

For a long, long time after, she wished that she'd just stayed on the couch and watched the second part of *Blaggart*.

Thirty-two

She'd known that she would see him again. Closure. There had to be closure and she knew without doubt that's what this was about, saying goodbyes and moving on, no harm done, no love lost.

'Hey,' he'd greeted her with an easy smile. When he looked at her like that, his eyes like dark pools of raw sexiness, it was tempting to make this last just a little longer. They'd been good for each other. They'd come together at a time when both of them had been looking for something, and they'd found it in all its breathless, orgasmic brilliance. But could it ever have been a permanent thing? No. Because he'd never belonged to her and, if she was being completely honest, she'd understood that from the start. Theirs was a passing thing, a momentary aberration and now it was time . . .

'So it's time for goodbyes,' he murmured softly.

It wasn't a question, more a statement of fact, and he wasn't in the least surprised when she nodded slowly, almost sadly. He realised that it had been an incredible ride, the kind of affair that should go down in textbooks as being perfect − explosive attraction, amazing sex, compatible attitudes. In fact, in another lifetime . . . Actually, there was no point in even thinking that way because he wasn't convinced it was true. Despite everything that they'd had between them, they'd never fallen in love. But then, how could they?

'Am I the only one who will never regret this?' she asked.

'Nope.'

She knew he wasn't lying. OK, so he'd never fallen madly in love with her and begged her to gallop off into the sunset but what they'd had had been enough to keep each of them sane while they were in a holding pattern of figuring out what they wanted to do with their lives. Now, she knew what she wanted and she had a strong hunch that he did too. But . . .

'And I've no doubt that there will be the occasional moment when I will miss it. But it's done. Can I ask you something?'

He nodded.

'Do you love her?' she said.

Surprise caused him to flinch. That was the last thing he'd expected her to say . . . Love wasn't something that he'd ever heard her mention. But then, hadn't she always had a propensity for the unconventional and unexpected.

'I do.'

'Then you're going to have to work it out.'

'I know.'

The pause stretched, both of them knowing exactly what to do but somehow reluctant to do it. Yes, it was over and she felt they'd been lucky to have experienced something so amazing. But they'd also been lucky that the fall-out from their relationship hadn't destroyed them.

'So . . .'

He walked towards her for the last time and, even though they both knew that nothing would happen, the raw sexual attraction between them would always be there.

'I have to go, before I do something I regret — like hang on to your ankle and force you to drag me around like an old boot.'

He laughed, glad that she was joking. 'OK. Just as long as you understand that I might occasionally miss you so much that you could open your curtains in the morning to find my face pressed against the window.'

It wasn't true. They were just consoling each other, shifting the relationship back on to a plane of casual acquaintance so that when they met in the future there would be no discomfort.

Even the way that his arms went around her was less intense than it had ever been: no heat, no anticipation, no clothes dropping to the floor in seconds. She looked up to him and it was only natural that their lips met. She ran a finger down his cheek, then kissed him again. 'You take care of yourself. You know, I'll never admit it again, but I think you're a pretty cool guy. Oh, and an utterly incredible shag.'

'That feeling is definitely mutual.' He laughed as he leaned down to kiss her again, a little longer this time, one final goodbye.

There would be no emotional reunion, no second instalment, this was done.

And all he felt was . . .

The noise was unmistakable: a violent cacophony of smashing glass that made them both exclaim as they jumped back.

That's when she realised that her earlier statement had been somewhat premature. Their relationship might be over – but there was still every chance it could destroy them.

'Mel! Oh, holy fuck, Mel, what are you doing here?' Suze gasped.

Thirty-three

Suze never realised that it was possible to stay upright or alive
after the heart had completely stopped, but apparently it was.

'Mel, I . . .'

She what? *What?* She ransacked her mind for appropriate things to say in this situation and came up with the
sum total of precisely fuck all. Really. What could you say
when your best friend/sister-in-law had just walked in and
caught you saying fond farewells by sticking your tongue
down the throat of her employee of the year?

Hopefully, she hadn't seen or heard anything too incriminating. Perhaps the bottle smashed just as she came
through the door and all she saw was her and Cammy
having what could have been construed as an innocent
hug. Yes. That kind of thing happened all the time. They
were a very huggy kind of company. Dear God, please
make it be true.

'How long have you been . . . ?'

'Long enough.'

And that was why she didn't believe in God.

'I'm so sorry, Mel.' That came from Cammy, who was

now completely ashen faced and wearing an expression of utter horror.

Suze quickly realised that she had to explain, but apparently no one had filled Mel in on that plan because she was now spinning around in a puddle of wine and heading back out of the door.

Cammy lunged over and threw his hand on Mel's arm to stop her but she calmly pulled away.

'Please, Mel,' he begged, momentarily glancing at Suze for support, but his plea went unanswered, given that she was still too busy being rooted to the spot in shock, fizzy alcohol now spreading under the soles of her shoes.

Composure regained, Mel spoke first, her voice sitting somewhere between stunned and strangled. 'I just came over to help you close up but I guess I interrupted something. Sorry about that. I'll see you guys tomorrow.'

Oh, bloody, bloody bollocks. Only Mel would catch someone in this situation and react like that. Why, oh why did she have to be so bloody civilised? Suze would have felt a lot better if Mel had just punched Cammy in the face and scudded Suze with her handbag. But no, she had far too much class for that.

'Look, please, let us explain.' Cammy again, pleading now.

Mel just looked from one to the other, and Suze's stomach lurched as she realised that the emotion in her eyes wasn't anger or rage, it was sorrow, with maybe a little bit of hurt thrown in.

'It's not necessary.'

Finally, Suze rediscovered her voice. 'It is, it really is. You've seen us so now you have to let us explain. Talk to us.'

'I don't. It's none of my business and, trust me, Suze, the last person I feel like talking to right now is you.'

Mel made a second attempt to leave.

This time Suze jumped in her path. 'Come on, don't

239

do this! Please, hon, I know that we don't deserve it, but hear us out. Please.'

Urgh, she hated begging. In fact, this was the first time in living memory that she had resorted to it but the situation didn't exactly lend itself to nonchalance or indifference. There was a hesitation, a momentary stillness as Mel deliberated what to do.

Suze went for the presumptive close. 'Come on, it stinks of wine in here. Let's sit out in the shop and at least they won't discover we died of alcohol inhalation at the postmortem. If we move some seats into the gents' section, no one passing by will be able to see us.'

Oh, crap, why? Why did she always have to resort to ridiculous humour when faced with awkward situations? As they trooped out into the shop, she realised that, in the category of 'areas used for the purpose of confessionals', a small space between a rail of Calvin Klein boxers, gents' animal-shaped novelty G-strings and a display case full of Prada pants had to rate up there with the more unusual.

Cammy slid down the wall and sat on the floor, Mel perched on the edge of a mannequin base and Suze sat in one of the French armchairs.

Surprisingly, Mel was the first to speak. 'So, how long?'

Cammy stared dolefully at his black leather biker's boots as he answered, 'A few months.'

'*What?*' Clearly not the answer Mel had been expecting. 'So you two were seeing each other before you accused Karl of having an affair? Before you did the whole honeytrap thing? Before . . .' She was getting louder and louder, clearly losing the battle to remain dignified in the face of blatant twatdom.

'Yes!' Suze blurted. She then took a moment to readjust her tone from screeching to calm and matter-of-fact. Why did she never have a tranquiliser to hand when she needed one?

'Dear God, Suze, what kind of messed-up individual are you?'

Suze had no answer. None. It was difficult to argue with sound reason. She knew the only way out of this was to confess all and beg for mercy . . . and, for that, she was definitely going to need some liquid courage.

'Hang on a second.' She disappeared into the office and returned with three miniature bottles of champagne, an act that undoubtedly won a prize in the 'Most Inappropriate Beverage Awards'. 'I brought these to refill the salon fridge, but our need is greater.'

She passed them around.

'OK, so I'm just going to start from the beginning and please remember that I know I've been a disgrace and give me some warning if you feel like punching me at any point.'

Mel looked like she wanted to be anywhere on earth except right there. 'You know what? I really don't give a toss. You don't owe me any explanations. What you two do is up to you and I'll just be grateful if you could try in future not to fuck up my life when you're playing your messed-up games.'

Ouch. It was a definite body shot and Suze could see that she was using reason as a precursor to another attempt to flee the premises so she headed it off by launching straight into the history of Suze and Cammy, chapter one.

'It started when Karl first put pressure on me to start a family. It completely freaked me out.'

'You don't want children? But you once asked me if I wanted children and I got the feeling it was something you wanted?' Cammy interjected, puzzled.

'No, it was something I wanted to *avoid*,' Suze hissed. She remembered that night, in a car park not long after they'd started seeing each other. He'd obviously completely misread her. Bloody hell, they really did not know each other at all. 'And anyway, is this helping?' she asked, exasperated at the interruption.

He had the grace to shut up and let her get back to fumbled explanations and requests for mercy.

Sticking to stereotypical behaviour had never been her strong point. Usually it was the thirty-something woman who succumbed to the relentless thudding of the biological clock but in this case it had been Karl. The clock hadn't even hit midnight on his thirtieth birthday when he announced that he thought they should start trying for a baby, an idea that Suze had dismissed instantly. No, no, no, life was for living recklessly, not for sleepless nights and small creatures with demands. The thought terrified her. She had been brought up by her father, and she loved him, but she had absolutely no experience of being a mother. What if she was rubbish at it? What if she couldn't do it right? What if it changed everything?

No, she had a business to run, and shopping to do, and fun to have, and gossip to revel in and . . . she loved her life. That was it. She just loved her life and had no desire whatsoever to change it.

Karl, on the other hand, had flipped into full-on wannabe-daddy mode. The fights had been frequent, the sulks endless, until he just stopped communicating with her. Had she had the benefit of hindsight and the services of a good shrink, she would have realised that that was right around the time that the business was failing, and perhaps the obsession with having children was his way of trying to salvage something good out of a terrible time. But . . . well, she couldn't read minds and had taken a different perspective on the whole thing completely. Karl was a sexual guy who needed almost daily servicing and, if he wasn't having sex with her, then it made perfect sense in her mind that he'd gone elsewhere, probably to some biological-clock-thudding thirty-something who held a similar desperation to breed. And where had that left her? Lonely. Suspicious. Defiant. Angry. Furious. Hurt. Bitter. Spiteful. And stupid.

Her toes curled at the thought and the mortification was so strong it was almost impossible to speak. Oh what an idiot she had been. Eventually she forced her larynx back into operation. 'That's when it started. Remember the night in The City bar last year to celebrate Josie's birthday?'

Mel nodded.

'We were all far too drunk and far too crazy and Cammy offered to get me a taxi and then he was in the taxi and then we stopped the taxi and . . .'

'OK, I get it!' Mel blurted. 'It was a whole late-night-taxi situation.'

Cammy decided to enter the conversation. 'And since then we've just had . . . a thing. Not very often. Just every now and then. Just . . . I dunno, just a crazy distraction from the shit that was going on in our lives.'

Suze took a long slug of the champagne. 'And a bit of self-preservation to be honest. I know it doesn't make any sense to you, Mel, and I know I should have tried to work harder to sort things out with Karl, but in my own bloody-minded stupidity I figured that, if Karl was going to go off with someone else, then I needed something to dull the pain. And Cammy was it.'

Where the hell had that come from? Suze took another drink, more to stop herself from talking than anything else. This was not the time to discover hidden depths and emotional insight, not after an adulthood in the relentlessly shallow and superficial camp.

Mel, on the other hand, was a black belt in those hidden depths and emotional insight. 'You know, in a really messed-up way, Suze, I actually think I get that. I just can't believe you didn't talk to me about it.'

Every word Mel uttered was steeped in disappointment.

Suze responded by staring at the floor, unable to meet her gaze. 'Because I knew what you would say. Speak to Karl. Tell him how you feel. Be honest. At no point would you have suggested that I deal with my problems by shagging your assistant manager.'

Cammy threw her a look of irritation, but she batted it right back at him. 'What? It's a bit bloody late to try to wrap it all up in warm and fuzzy language, isn't it?'

He took up the infidelity relay baton. 'But it's over now, Mel. Suze and Karl are back together and there's no question of anything more happening between us, not ever.'

Suze started to chew on her thumbnail, then spat it out when she realised that it was a hundred per cent plastic and tasted disgusting. Instead, she glanced at Mel, who had reverted back to a mute setting. She was just sitting there, hugging her knees, looking like she was ten and had just discovered that her puppy had been put down.

Suze changed tack and tried to distract herself from yet another excruciating silence by staring at the crotch of the model on the Calvin Klein poster, but the tension soon overwhelmed her and she had to ask the question that was hanging in the air.

'Are you going to tell Karl?'

Mel's head snapped up like she had been shot. 'Of course not. Why would you think I would do that?'

Suze sighed. 'Because you're truthful. And good. And it would be the right thing to do. And to be honest, I'd understand if you did. But please believe me, as soon as Karl and I sorted things out, Cammy and I stopped our ... thing.'

Well, *almost*. It seemed petty to mention that day in the hotel and, technically, yes, that had come after she and Karl had reunited but she had tried to end it then, to say goodbye – it had just come out a little, er, bendy. Again, what the fuck had she been thinking?

244

'I'm also loyal to my friends,' Mel answered, sighing with irritation. 'It's up to you to handle the issues in your marriage, not me or anyone else. Didn't the honeytrap disaster teach us that?'

Ouch, direct hit! Score one for the Campaign Against Outside Marital Interference.

'So you won't tell him?'

'No.'

'Thanks, Mel. And I'm sorry. I'm really sorry and I hope you don't hate us for this.'

Mel chewed on her bottom lip for a few seconds before saying, 'I don't. I don't hate either of you. I get it, Suze. I'm not some angelic, self-righteous militant evangelist for sexual restraint. I make mistakes too.'

For the first time, Mel and Cammy locked glances, but Suze was too busy making her next point to notice. 'But when Joe made a mistake you found it so difficult to forgive him.'

Score one for the Campaign For Uncomfortable Truths.

Mel nodded thoughtfully. 'You're right. But that's because he'd made promises to me and he'd trashed them. Or, at least, I felt he did. I'm not going to judge my friends, Suze, but I think I've got a right to judge my husband when he betrays me.'

It was getting cold now. The automatic timer had switched off the heating and the freezing Glasgow winter air was seeping under the door and in through the fabric of the huge store-front window.

'So where do we go from here?' Cammy asked.

'Back to normal.'

Suze tried not to show any surprise at Mel's response. Back to normal would be good. Great, in fact. And, now that all the secrets were out in the open, she was sure they could do that. Full disclosure. Secrets out. From here on in she resolved – yet again – to be a new Suze: a measured, honest, thoughtful Suze who made wise decisions and carefully thought things through before she spoke or acted.

'What else can we do? It's not like I can tell the two of you to piss off and never see you again. Look, I'm tired. I'm tired and I'm going home,' she announced wearily, pushing herself up from the floor and heading for the door. She was almost there when she paused. 'You know, the only thing about this that I don't understand? It's you, Cammy,' Mel pondered.

'Why?'

'Well, you said that this was a distraction from problems in your life, but what problems did you have? You were seeing Anneka and Anna, you were always out on the town. You were having a great time.'

Aw, do not do this to me. Suze looked heavenwards and resolved that if indeed there bloody was a God up there she was going to have a serious word with him about his twisted sense of humour. He could not throw this at her when she'd just vowed to live a life of honesty and intelligent decisions. Oh, cruel, cruel, cruel. That's it, she was just going to keep schtum.

Even though she knew the answer, it was time for lies by omission. For denying the facts. For keeping her mouth shut in the name of restraint and common sense.

But hadn't she just made a promise to herself to be honest and true? This turning-over-a-new-leaf stuff wasn't getting off to a great start. She looked at Cammy, but he was too busy doing a rabbit/headlights thing to answer. Mel deserved the truth.

'Because –' she could feel her buttocks clench as she forced herself to spit it out '– and trust me I hate to say this because I've done enough interfering in your and Joe's lives, but Cammy? He's in love with you.'

Thirty-four

It was time to be thankful for small mercies, Mel decided.

She had her health.

She had an incredibly fulfilling job.

She shared her life with a husband she loved.

And who loved her.

But the biggest blessing of all? That she'd just returned home and realised that the flat was still empty.

When had her life turned into a soap opera? It was ridiculous. Surreal. Until not so long ago, every day just bobbed along in a little bubble of contented bliss, love and laughs, and now? Carnage.

So far, if she was keeping pace with everything, and as far as she understood, developments within the Marshall clan went something like:

Suze thought Karl was having an affair.

Joe almost had an affair.

Their company almost went bust.

Karl then did have an affair.

Mel contemplated having an affair.

And the whole time, the object of her affections was already having an affair.

With her sister-in-law.

On what planet would any of that constitute acceptable standards of behaviour?

She took a bottle of wine out of the fridge and filled the largest glass she could find, then took it through to the bedroom, pressing the play button on the CD player as she passed. The intoxicating melody of track five on Seal's *Soul* album immediately tugged on her heart strings. 'I've Been Loving You Too Long' and apparently he ain't gonna stop now.

It was like a subliminal message from the spirits of HMV.

The fresh scent of the newly washed sheets consumed her as she flopped down on the bed. She could quite happily have crawled under the duvet and stayed there until the memory of this night dissipated. Of course, she'd have to arrange for someone to bring her food and water because that was likely to be a long, long time away . . . somewhere around her Zimmer years.

'He's in love with you.'

No, no, no, no. That wasn't the kind of thing that got blurted out in the middle of the male-underpants section of a Glasgow shop. It just wasn't done.

And poor Cammy (yes, there was an irony to calling him 'poor Cammy' when it was now blatantly clear he had been shagging almost every stunningly beautiful woman that he knew) – he'd looked like he wanted the earth to open up and swallow him.

'You're . . . you're . . . what?' she'd gasped, mouth flailing like a large goldfish in a drought.

At that point Suze had got up from her chair and announced that she was going home, although she did stop on the way to crouch down in front of Mel and hug her.

'I hope you know how sorry I am for everything. And I know I'm a useless, unlovable trollop but you have to believe me when I say I'm really sorry I kept this from you and . . . oh, bugger, I'm just sorry for *everything*. I never meant you to get caught up in my madness. If it happens again, you have my permission to shoot me.'

Despite still having both feet in the shocked and disappointed camp, Mel had smiled and returned the embrace. 'You're absolutely nuts, do you realise that?'

'Indeed I do.'

'And I think you have to tell Karl, Suze.'

'Indeed I don't.'

That was Suze – self-centred, occasionally unhinged and completely devoid of a conscience. Yet, somehow all those combined to make eight years of unbreakable friendship in what had been one of the best relationships of Mel's life. Would this damage it? Not in the long term. Unless, of course, there were more secrets to come out. She couldn't promise she'd react as well if it turned out Suze was a serial killer, a serial shagger or had siphoned off enough money from the company to buy the Bahamas. But, barring those things, Mel knew in her heart that they'd be OK.

She and Cammy, however, were a different story.

'Do you want to run too?' he asked her as the door closed behind Suze.

'No.' Actually, she did, but they would have to have this conversation at some point so it might as well be now. For a moment she didn't know what to say so she was glad when he took it out of her hands.

'Are you completely freaked out?'

'Yes.'

'I'm sorry. I've just been a complete fuck-up.'

'Yes.'

OK, she was going to have to make a concerted effort to go for two syllables. Maybe even progress to sentences; otherwise, this was going to be a very long night.

'How long?' There we go – two words. It was almost a soliloquy.

He'd shrugged sadly. 'Since the night we kissed. Actually, I think for a long time before that but I didn't admit it to myself until then. Before that night, I knew marriage put you out of bounds. You and Joe were always so happy that I guess I never imagined we could be together. So I just got on with things, messing around with Anneka and Anna . . .'

'And Suze,' she'd interjected, to a rueful grimace.

'Yep, and Suze. I'm so sorry about that one – far too close to home,' he'd apologised.

Her forehead had fallen on to her knees. Dear God, did she know nothing about the people in her life? She hadn't spotted that Joe was unhappy, that Suze was having an affair or that Cammy was, it would seem, in love with her.

'So why didn't you say something after that?'

Shrugging was becoming his action of the day. 'I had to sort stuff out first, end it with Suze. I did pluck up the courage to tell you once but then you went off to Mar Hall with Joe and I bottled it. So I just carried on and waited for how I felt about you to wear off, or change, or . . . something. Don't hate me for this, but I was so hoping that the two of you wouldn't work it out.'

'Thanks.'

'I'm sorry, but it just seemed like there might be a chance. So I just wanted to wait . . .'

'Didn't look much like you were waiting tonight.'

'Look, I'm sorry,' he'd said. Again. 'It's just that, well, Suze and I are similar. We think the same in a lot of ways.

And we really were just closing it down tonight. It's been over for a while now.'

Cramp had set into her left buttock so she'd slid off the mannequin stand and on to the floor. There had been a silence, a lull in the conversation while they both processed this new situation, one that was only broken when Cammy had, inexplicably, burst out laughing. 'I'm sorry, Mel, but it's just . . . well . . . how messed up is this? I'm more nervous than I've ever been in my life and I've no idea what to say to you. There was definitely no training for this in men school.'

'Toilet seats. Flatulence. Declarations of love. None of it on the curriculum.'

They'd both laughed, as much in relief that they'd managed to slide this excruciation back on to a more familiar level of humour and banter.

More silence, this time a more comfortable, easy break in the conversation until a memory had flashed into her head. 'But that night in The City – I kissed you and you freaked out.'

This time the shrug had come with a simultaneous groan and a nervous slide of the hand through his hair. 'I know, but it was just so unexpected and you were so drunk and I just –' he'd struggled to find the words '– I just didn't want you to think that I'd pounced on you.'

'I think it was more a case of me pouncing on you.'

'Well, I didn't think it was the right time to let you. Although if you want to have another go at that . . .'

She'd grabbed the first thing that came to hand and threw it at him. Luckily it missed or she'd have forever retained the memory of him sitting there at this poignant moment wearing an Ernie the Elephant thong on his face.

'I think I might have been coming over here tonight to kiss you again.' That one had hung in the air for a while until Mel factored in her inherent personality and faced the reality. 'I don't know. I probably wouldn't have. I mean, random snogging has never been my thing.'

'Was that a dig because of what you saw earlier?'

'Absolutely.'

The time had come to settle this, to bring a reality check to the situation and achieve some kind of resolution.

'Cammy, I'm not leaving Joe. I owe it to both of us to stay and make it work and that's what I'm going to do.'

'I know. It's one of the things I love about you – you're strong, loyal. Far too good a person to be hanging out with immoral cretins like Suze and I.'

'You're right.' She'd smiled. 'Note to self: must find moral, upstanding friends. I'm thinking that the Paisley Six will do.'

The laughter had been mutual and, recognising that it was wise to leave on a high, Mel had scrambled to her feet.

'Just leave the cashing up and I'll get it tomorrow.'

He hadn't argued. After grabbing his jacket from the office, he'd walked her to the door, set the alarm and then locked it behind them.

'We'll be fine, you know. I promise I'm not going to turn into some weird, adoring psycho.'

'Good, because Josie is one psycho enough in this shop.'

'Oh shit, Josie – promise she will *never* find out about any of this?' he'd begged. 'It's as much for Joe's sake as mine. If she even had an inkling about how I feel she'd bump him off in a second. I think she wants to make it her life's work to get you and me together.'

To passers-by, they would have looked like any other colleagues leaving work for the evening, relieved after a long day, sharing a joke and a quick hug.

'I'm sorry, Cammy.' Explanations weren't necessary.

252

'Me too.'

'We'll get past this, I promise. There's a six-foot model out there somewhere with your name on her.'

Now, in the warm safety of her bedroom, she pulled one half of the duvet over her, hoping the comfort would be an antidote to all the conflicting thoughts and uncertainties. In fact, the only thing she was certain about was that Joe should have been home ages ago. Where was he? She rang his mobile, but it was switched off.

The huge big purple alarm clock on the bedside table said nine o'clock. Even if the nurses had let them stay for the second round of visiting in the evening, it would have been over ages ago. Perhaps he and Karl had gone for a drink. Mmm, that was it. They must have gone out to celebrate the salvation of their company. Would have been nice if he'd given her a ring though and asked her along. Or at least just let her know when he'd be back.

In saying that, maybe it would be a good thing if they stayed out as late as possible. At least then Suze would have more time to recover. Suze and Cammy. A twinge of . . . something . . . fluttered in her stomach and her heart started to beat just a little faster. Never in a million years would she have suspected that there was something between them. But then, with regards to others, oblivion *was* the recurring theme of her life lately.

It had to change. Maybe it was a fatal flaw in her personality that compelled her to take everything at face value and never dig too deep beneath the surface. All these crazy things had been going on and she'd had absolutely no idea. Maybe she'd been too wrapped up in work, too consumed by the trivial stuff to really pay attention.

It was definitely time to change that.

If there was anything good to come out of this, it was that she now knew, unequivocally, that she and Joe were back on the same page, both committed to the same future. No more freak outs, no more surprises, just a steady, consistent path towards family, contentment and the whole happy-ever-after thing. And this time it was what they both definitely wanted.

The door slammed and shook her from her contemplations, and just a few seconds later his frame filled the doorway.

'Hey, gorgeous, sorry I'm so late.' He tossed his jacket on the cream rattan chair in the corner and joined her on the bed, kissing her briefly on the lips before sliding off and settling flat on his back, just his head turned towards her. 'So, what have you been up to tonight, anything exciting?'

She shook her head and waited for the bolt of lightning to be sent down from the heavens. 'Not much. Popped over to the shop to help Cammy close up but that was about it.'

Nope, nothing exciting. Not a thing. Oh, but, by the way, Cammy is apparently madly in love with me. Especially now that he's stopped shagging your brother's wife. Yep, he likes to keep it in the family. If he ever discovers he's bisexual, you might want to prepare yourself. She was glad that the semi-darkness was disguising her scarlet face. Unlike everyone else in her immediate circle, she'd always been pathetically bad at subterfuge and lies.

'What about you – was Karl thrilled? And did you fall at your dad's feet and thank him profusely.'

'Definitely yes on the second one. One hundred and fifty grand, Mel – that's how much he's given each of us. We're going to each put fifty grand into the business to pay off the rest of the company debt, and that will leave another hundred each to do whatever we like. Can you believe it? A hundred grand. Apparently, Mum's frugality and his lack

254

of materialism have combined to make them loaded and they've decided now is the time to share.'

'So we won't complain any more when your mother gives us her usual ten-quid Marks & Spencer voucher for Christmas?'

'Definitely not.'

He was grinning as he rolled over on to his side so that his whole body was facing her. This was nice, she decided. Almost like old times. Just the two of them chatting, laughing, just happy being together. They should make a point of doing this at least once a week. An early-bed night, perhaps phone in some food, and just chill out and ponder the world. Now that they were completely back on the same page again, she resolved to do everything possible to keep them there.

'And Karl? Was he excited too?'

Even in the dim lighting, she could see that something flickered in his eyes. Hesitation? Fear, perhaps? No, she chided herself, she was just being ridiculously oversensitive. All the drama had left her a little highly strung and melo-dramatic.

'Erm, no, not really. Karl wasn't exactly thrilled tonight. That's why we were so late – just talking things through.'

Hang on, by the tone of his voice, it was now very obvious that there was something going on. See! One reso-lution to be more attentive and perceptive and already she'd discovered her first hidden drama. What was going on? What could Karl possibly be unhappy about? Unless . . . oh, bollocks, no – had he found out about Suze and Cammy? Oh no. Anything but that – just anything. She could hardly bring herself to ask.

'What's the problem? What's he upset about?'

If Joe noticed that her voice was a few notes higher than normal, he didn't mention it.

'Erm, me. He's upset with me.'

Actually, come to think about it, Joe's voice seemed on the choirboy side of normal too.

'But why? What happened?' Probably a brother thing. You know, the resurgence of a twenty-year-old grudge involving Scalextric.

'OK, babe, I'm just going to blurt this out, but don't panic because I can explain and it's a good thing, I promise.'

This no longer sounded like anything concerning Scalextric. Panic on.

'You see, the thing is, Mel, I've been thinking and you know I said that I realised something wasn't working in my life?'

She nodded fearfully. Hang on – weren't they supposed to be on the same page? He'd told her he was over all that insecurity and uncertainty about the meaning of his life. It would seem . . . wait, he was talking again.

'Well, I've realised that my job was a big part of that too . . .'

Phew, that was OK then. Everyone went through phases of unhappiness at work and he'd soon flip back to enjoyment and fulfilment. Joe and Karl were a great team – always had been and she knew that they would stay that way for the rest of their lives.

'. . . so I quit.'

Thirty-five

'Karl, I'm so sorry to have to tell you this but I've been having an affair.'

She barely had the last word out when she hit a pothole and the car skidded across to the kerb, just missing a terrified cyclist in fluorescent yellow Lycra. Even the Glasgow roads department would seem to be cosmically telling her not to be so fucking stupid.

It wasn't lost on her that a few months ago – hell, a few *weeks* ago – she wouldn't have dreamed of confessing. But that was before . . . God, she'd been such a fool. Such an arrogant, stupid, self-obsessed fool.

It was Mel's bloody fault. She loved her dearly but why did she always have to be so spectacularly decent? It should be illegal or punishable by something terrible to have that much integrity. And the thing was, when she spent too much time in Mel's company, that inherent goodness developed into some kind of airborne virus and seeped into Suze's pores.

Logically, she could see that confessing was crazy and would only hurt Karl even more. Not to mention the damage to their relationship. She and Cammy had escaped relatively unscathed from their fling, no casualties, no prisoners, and it seemed insane to voluntarily take a wee jaunt along death row.

Tomorrow. She'd think about it tomorrow. There was no point telling him tonight, not when he was on such a high about his dad coming to the rescue. In fact, maybe she should wait a week or two until everything calmed down and got back to some semblance of normality. She would tell him, she definitely would – but not yet. For now, she just wanted her husband and her normal life back.

Turning into the street, she spotted Karl's car in the driveway. Excellent. With any luck, Virginia would have buggered off to bed and she could curl up on the couch with her husband, drink wine and, if he got really lucky, she'd let him lick some chocolate Nutella off her nipples. Oh yes, she was feeling like it was going to be that kind of night.

As she neared the house, she automatically lowered the electric windows, then flipped a switch on the steering wheel. A zillion decibels of Queen's 'Bohemian Rhapsody' shot out into the atmosphere and . . . Kerching, another winner! Right on cue, Mrs McNee's house lit up like a Christmas tree and a huge Mrs McNee-shaped shadow appeared at her front-room window. Revenge was definitely a dish best served with a large dose of noise pollution. Compared to the hours she spent under intensive police interrogation, it was a small, but oh-so-rewarding victory.

Please let Virginia be in bed, please let Virginia be in bed. The woman might have been ultimately responsible for pulling them back from the brink of financial ruin, but this was a time for marital celebration, intimacy, utter joy and Nutella.

However, when she threw open the front door, she realised that no one had passed that message on to Karl.

Number one, he was sitting at the kitchen table, a peculiar choice of location because he was more of a sofa guy and – to the best of her recollection – only ever used the kitchen table for eating or having sex. Occasionally both.

Number two, his bleary eyes, dishevelled appearance and slumped posture indicated weariness with the possibility of intoxication.

Number three, the assortment of empty beer bottles in front of him would appear to confirm the intoxication theory.

Number four, his mother was sitting across from him, and they seemed to be deep in conversation.

'Karl, what's wrong? Is it your dad?'

All she could think was please, *please* do not make the earlier predictions about the shock of the financial situation killing Donald come true. Karl would never forgive himself for that.

'He's fine, Suze, he's fine,' Karl replied.

Oh thank God. She crossed the room and ruffled his hair as she passed him on the way to the fridge. 'So what's up then – you look like shi—'

Her mother-in-law's eyebrows shot up.

'Tired. You look tired. Is something wrong?' Chardonnay. Cava. Chardonnay. Cava. Cava. She finished with an executive decision and removed the Cava from the chill shelf just as his face crumbled into utter dejection.

'Joe quit. He quit the company.'

Thankfully (unlike Mel's earlier shock-related reaction), her grip on the bottle of Cava was tight enough to avoid a puddle situation.

Why on earth would Joe ever want to leave Marshalls?

'He says that he wants to take the money and go off to discover what he really wants in life.'

And how could it possibly be so sudden?

259

'He said it was an instant gut reaction that just felt right.'

How could Mel not have mentioned this?

'I don't even think he's told Mel yet.'

Despite the lack of joy/intimacy/celebration, she was gratified to see that at least they were back on the same mental wavelength. Poor Karl. He and Joe had been together all their lives and Karl would miss him so much. Unless . . . *did Karl want to go with Joe and find himself too?*

'I can't believe it, Suze. I mean, how could he leave? It's completely nuts.'

'Not to mention insulting and so absurdly ridiculous that I can only surmise that he's not thinking straight. Perhaps he too has developed an over-fondness for alcohol,' Virginia interjected.

Suze ignored the dig. She didn't know what to say. It was just so unexpected. Joe, the brother that had been left with reliability and predictability after Karl had inherited all the excitement, dynamism and ambition had somehow morphed into Mr Free Spirit.

Virginia threw her a disapproving glance. 'You know, dear, I've noticed that you do drink rather a lot of alcohol and it's not always the most productive way to handle a situation. Not to mention what it does to the skin. It'll be like bloated leather by the time you're forty.'

All earlier cash-related goodwill instantly dissipated, leaving only those old, long-held feelings of distrust and loathing. She had a sudden thought that the one and only bonus that would have come from splitting with Karl would have been that she might one day meet someone else and gain a new mother-in-law. Every cloud.

Moving over behind Karl, she slid her arms around his shoulders and leaned down to kiss the back of his head, not caring a jot that the public display of affection incited a Virginia eye roll of the most disapproving level.

In a saved-by-the-bell moment, the phone rang and Virginia tutted, said, 'I'll get it,' before swiftly moving off, obviously keen to escape before she had to witness further repulsive activities like possibly hand squeezing or – gasp, the world is going to hell – the nuzzling of necks.

'Marshall residence,' Suze heard her declare. Who even talked like that any more?

She slipped around and sat on Karl's knee, hoping that Virginia would glance over and the shock would put her in the bed next to Donald for the foreseeable future. At least then she and Karl could have their lives and their privacy back.

'I'm sorry about Joe, honey, but, you know, maybe it'll be a good thing. Maybe you'll enjoy working on your own. Or –' she was struggling to come up with any other possible plus points '– or maybe he'll be gone a fortnight and realise his mistake and come running back.'

Poor thing, he looked so distraught. Thank God, she hadn't come barging in, confessing all and devastating him for the second time in one day. Now, she just had to be there for him, to listen, to support him, without judgement or making things worse with her own opinions.

She'd dodged one bullet today, so she wasn't going to walk right into the target range of another rifle.

'But what if he doesn't, Suze? I don't want to do this without Joe. We've always been together, always done everything side by side. I just . . .' Oh feck, he was getting choked up. 'I just don't know if I can handle not having him around every day.'

Supportive wife. Supportive wife. Supportive wife with more than a little bit of irritation creeping in. So Karl couldn't live without Joe. He was filling up at the very thought of it. Distraught. Gutted. Couldn't go on.

Yet when she'd left he'd dusted himself down and gone and shagged an evil-tongued, not-so-fucking-super-model!

Biting her lip was the only way to stop the roaring in her head from escaping. Come on, they'd moved on from that. They'd got over it. They were a new couple, reborn, and there was no point in dragging up the horrors of the past.

Instead, she settled for a whispered, 'Don't worry, babe, it'll be fine, I promise.' Which it probably wouldn't and she didn't, but it was all she could manage while locked in a battle with her outraged inner self.

She was just about to go for serious neck nuzzling when she realised that Virginia had returned to the table and her demeanour was saying that whatever had happened in the last minute and a half hadn't sat well with her.

'Karl Marshall, can I ask you a question?' she said in what was very close to the tone of Helen Mirren in *Prime Suspect*. 'Is there any reason that you know of that a woman called Anneka would be calling you at home?'

If it was possible for Karl to win prizes for taking 'stressed' to a whole new level, then he'd just hit the jackpot, closely followed by Suze.

'Why – was that who was on the phone?' Karl stuttered.

'Indeed it was.'

'What did she want?'

The pause was interminable, the tension not helped by the fact that Virginia had now pulled her shoulders back, while looking at Suze in a very strange manner.

'Apparently, Anneka is concerned that you might be missing some items of clothing and toiletries that you left there on your last visit.'

That snide, nasty, devious little cow. Suze's teeth began grinding in fury. She should have expected this. Anneka was every bit as conniving and vindictive as she was and she should have known that the skinny slapper would never let Suze's little stunt in the park go unpunished. But calling their house? Bold. Proceeding with bitchy meddling when she realised it was Karl's mother on the phone? Now that was true mastery in the retribution stakes.

'And she took great delight in informing me – although obviously I only have her word to go on – that you and she had some kind of relationship fairly recently.'

'She's lying,' blurted Suze, desperate to make this go away. 'She does that kind of thing all the time. She said she was having it off with Gerard Butler last week.'

Virginia stared at Karl for a second, then flicked to Suze, with that same expression from a moment before. It took Suze a minute to compute that it was . . . bloody hell, it was *pity*! Virginia was actually feeling sorry for her.

'Suzanne, darling, that's an admirable stance to take –' she turned back to Karl '– but I know my son and I know guilt when I see it. How could you, Karl! How could you! You are a married man and I did not bring you up to behave that way. It's a disgrace. *You* are a disgrace.'

'But –' Karl started, but she cut him dead.

'Do *not* answer me back, young man, or you will live to regret it.'

Suze had another go at derailing her mother-in-law's ire. 'Virginia, really, I –'

Virginia's hand shot up and froze in a 'STOP' move- ment. 'Suzanne, please don't,' Virginia interrupted, before turning on her son again. 'Karl Marshall, I am thoroughly disgusted by your behaviour and I will be passing this infor- mation on to your father.'

Karl closed his eyes, realising there was absolutely no point in arguing. However, Virginia wasn't finished. She leaned over and placed her hand on Suze's shoulder. 'Suzanne, it's no secret that you and I have never been close and that for many years I have questioned Karl's decision to choose you for his wife. Well, I now realise that

I owe you an apology. I'd also like to apologise to you on behalf of my son. No woman should have to discover such a terrible thing about the man she loves. I'm sorry. Very, very sorry for you.'

Nooooooo. Suze could feel all her remaining powers of restraint and reason slowly ooze right out of her body. She could cope with many aspects of Virginia's behaviour towards her. She could handle the disapproval. She accepted the animosity. She even, in a bizarre way, relished the blatant bitchiness and verbal wars.

But she couldn't, just couldn't, on any level, handle the utter degradation and humiliation of Virginia Marshall's pity. Nor could she let her think that her son was the only one to blame here. It had been her fault too – perhaps even more than his. She couldn't throw him under the Virginia bus and let him take all the flak. Something snapped inside her, and in a split second she decided there was only one thing she could do.

'Virginia, I appreciate your defending me, but there's something you should know. Something you should both know.' She turned to Karl, her heart breaking at the prospect of hurting him. But it was the right thing to do. The fucking crazy, absolutely stupid, certifiable right thing to do.

'I had an affair too.'

Thirty-six

'You what?'

'I quit.' For the first time in her life Mel wished that Joe smoked, drank to excess or had a burgeoning gambling addiction because then he might be revealing that he'd given one of those things up instead of . . .

'You've left Marshalls?'

Why was he grinning like he'd just discovered he'd won the lottery? Or Angelina Jolie in the bath?

'But why?'

'Doesn't it ever get to you? Doesn't it ever piss you off that for the last eight years we've got up every morning and done exactly the same thing with exactly the same people? There must be more to life, Mel, and now we've got the money to go find out what it is, take a year out, travel to places we've never been before.'

He leaned over and playfully ran a finger from her shoulder down to her hip. Somehow she managed to conceal her feelings and fight the urge to react in a way that would result in a finger requiring plaster.

'Let's just see where life takes us.'

Casualty department, Glasgow Royal Infirmary.

'What do you think?' he asked with all the giddy restraint of a five-year-old on Christmas Day.

She thought about it, considered it from all angles, gave it thorough contemplation. For about ten seconds, before blurting out, 'Joe, I think you've lost the plot. You love your job, you love working with Karl. Why isn't that enough any more?' She caught his eye and instinctively knew that the truth was actually a little deeper than that. 'Why is *nothing* enough any more?'

'You are, Mel, I swear. I'm just ... I don't know.' He flopped back on to the bed and sighed. 'It was that night in the bar, Mel, it changed things. I hadn't realised how stale life had become and I just don't want to go back to the monotony. I want more. But I do know that I want you to be with me.'

So much for being on the same page: she was on page 34 of How To Overcome Marital Blips and he was on page 56 of the Thomson's Summer Sun brochure.

The strangest thing was that deep inside there was a part of her that wasn't surprised. If she was honest with herself – and ouch, that hurt – the fallout from the honeytrap had fundamentally changed how she felt about him and, much as she tried to remanufacture the feelings she had before, she wasn't sure that she could. The most telling testimony to that was her reaction right now. The old Mel would be devastated, would beg him to change his mind, or would immediately drop everything to do anything he asked of her.

But the new and not necessarily improved version? She just felt, well, sad.

Taking her silence as contemplation, Joe regrouped and came back with more arguments for the defence. 'We could tick off all our ambitions as we go. You always wanted to learn to scuba dive.'

'The swimming pool over at Bellahouston Sports Centre would be just fine for that.'

He grimaced, and ploughed on, an edge of desperation creeping into his voice. 'We could walk on beaches, visit the wonders of the world, sleep late, do anything we want to do.'

'But none of this is what we planned, Joe.'

'Plans change.'

'Not like this. You can't just rewrite the script of our lives and expect me to jump. I had plans too, hopes, things I wanted to do this year – do none of those matter? And what do your parents think? Aren't they devastated that you want to leave the company?'

He shook his head. 'Mum's none too pleased, but Dad understood. Think he regrets not doing something similar when he was younger. And I know you had plans, Mel, but this could be so great. Just think, we could just try to get pregnant in lots of different places. Beautiful places.' He laughed as the prospect gained momentum in his head. 'We could even do a Beckham. How does Galapagos Marshall sound?' He chuckled.

Honestly? Like the kind of dumb thing the old Joe Marshall would never have said. She'd already told him that she wanted to put off starting a family this year but he obviously just hadn't accepted it. It was like he was being so deafened by the call of whatever it was he felt was out there that he'd lost the ability to hear her.

'Joe, I don't want to go anywhere. I'm happy where I'm at right now,' she told him softly, aware of what she was really saying and realising that, for the first time in a long time, she felt sure about something. 'I love my life here.'

For a long, long moment, he was silent and she could see that he was deciding whether to argue more or concede defeat. 'Do you love your life here more than you love *us*?'

She buried her head into his chest, desperate to put off the inevitable for just a little longer.

'Do you?' he repeated, his hands stroking her hair now, softly, lovingly.

'It's not a question of loving my life more than us, it's just a question of accepting we've changed. I think we want different things now.'

She knew that she was reverting to her typical behaviour patterns, trying to put a positive spin on things, trying to cushion hard blows and keep everything on an even non-confrontational plane.

But she also knew, just knew, that this was one confrontation that there was no escaping.

His hand was on her face now, tracing confused, tangled lines across her forehead. 'Please come with me, Mel, I have to do this. Don't ask me to give it up.'

. With a sad, low exhalation, she nuzzled into the crook of his arm and rested her head on his chest.

They lay like that for a long time, the silence punctuated by the ticking of her big purple clock.

Eventually, in soft, gentle tones, he spoke. 'I feel that this is a crossroads and if I don't make the right decision then I could regret it for the rest of my life.'

As he said it, Mel realised that, if she was really, truly honest with herself, that was how she felt too. Perhaps they were both on the same page after all. She pushed herself up to face him, his eyes and the shadows of his body visible in the column of light from the lamppost outside their bedroom window.

'Joe, we have to accept what's really happening here.' She leaned over and kissed him, as if the loving touch would soften the blow. 'The truth is that you don't love me enough any more to stay. And I don't love you enough to go.'

Thirty-seven

Had it really come to this? Twenty-four hours ago Suze had been ecstatic, riding the crest of a wave and now, once again, her spontaneous, reckless gob had her drowning in a huge big ocean of crap.

I had an affair too.

Even now, almost twelve hours later, the echo of that statement made her tremble. What had she been thinking? The obvious answer was *nothing intelligent*. She shouldn't have told him like that. She should have waited until they were alone, until she could explain properly. However, while she did accept a portion of the blame for this royal cock-up, she still maintained that an element of responsibility must belong in a bloody big way to Virginia. If Virginia hadn't been so utterly patronising and condescending (and, yes, she did realise that in the last twelve hours she'd taken Virginia's blatant pity and embellished it, giving it sinister undertones and exaggerated malice), then her ridiculously childish and immature pride would never have tried to fend off the embarrassment by spouting the adult equivalent of 'Well, I chucked you first, na na na na boo boo.'

So much for this whole experience having taught her that maturity and composure were crucial in a crisis. Repeat after me – I. Am. A. Fuck. Up. Albeit, she mused, a fuck-up who was looking deadly. Realising that she'd need every single weapon in her not-insignificant armoury, she'd pulled out the stops when it came to dressing for the day. Her favourite low-rise 7 For All Mankind jeans, the ones that looked like they'd been spray painted on. Towering tan leather bondage sandals. And Karl's favourite top, a white vest with inner support that somehow made her look like she'd shoplifted a couple of cantaloupes from Tesco's fruit aisle and was attempting to smuggle them out on her person. And of course, her hair was left loose and flowing the way he liked it best.

I had an affair too.

She shuddered as the flashback – by its very definition – flashed back once again.

The world had stopped the minute she'd blurted it out. Virginia had just sat there, stunned, giving her the stare of death, while Karl had jolted back, sending her sliding right off his knee and on to a very undignified pile on the floor. It was difficult to kick herself, put her head in her hands and scramble to her feet all at the same time, but somehow she'd managed – just in time for Virginia to give her a verbal battering.

'There have been very few times in my life when I have been rendered speechless, but this is most certainly one of them,' she'd spat. 'Karl, Suzanne – I have no idea what goes on in your lives but it appears to have sunk to a level of debauchery that I, frankly, find abhorrent.'

With that she'd picked up her Liz Claiborne clutch, spun on her heels and marched out of the door. Actually, she didn't so much march as glide. The woman was the picture of well-bred posture and decorum even when confronted with a scene right off the *News Of The World*'s front page.

Suze stared after her. Where was she going? Her room was upstairs so why was she leaving?

'Should I go after . . .' she blurted to Karl, but got headed off at the pass with an incredulous '*You had an affair?*'

'I'm sorry, Karl, but I had to tell you. It was a mistake and I regret it so much, but if we're going to start again then I want you to know everything.'

'*You had an affair?*'

He really was going to have to move past that bit if they had any hope of working this out. Which they did. They had to.

'You are fucking priceless, Suze!' Shaking his head now, still staring at her, he did the last thing she expected: he laughed. 'Fucking priceless,' he repeated, still laughing, but it had now morphed into a pseudo-evil laugh like the bloke from *The Shining*.

It stopped as quickly as it had started, sliding into more incredulous head shaking and ultimately another challenging stare. 'With who?'

'I don't think . . .'

'With who?' he'd repeated, his tone chilling.

'Cammy.'

He visibly reeled at that one. He and Cammy were by no means mates but they'd always got on well at group nights out and had occasionally gone for a few beers together, mostly – Suze suspected – because Karl got a bit of a kick out of hanging out with Cammy's 'beautiful people' crowd.

'When?'

'I don't think . . .'

'When?'

What did it matter? Surely what mattered was that she'd

271

confessed and now they just had to find a way to deal with it and move on? 'It's not important, Karl.'

'*When?*'

Apparently, it was to him.

'It started a few months ago – when you stopped sleeping with me and I thought you were having an affair. Before the honeytrap.'

'So let me understand this – *you* were having an affair so you set *me* up?'

She nodded shamefully. 'I was so sure you were having one too and, to be honest, I think I was looking for something to justify what I was doing. I swear that, for what it's worth, if I could go back and change it, then I would. Karl, you have to believe that I'm sorry. And what's important here is that if I wanted to stay with him then I would have but I don't. I never did. I was just destroyed and irrational because I truly thought that you'd checked out of our marriage and in somewhere else.'

'So that's how it works? Whenever we hit a bump in the road, you go off and fuck someone? Well, we've had plenty of bumps on our road, Suze, so how many times has this happened before?'

'Never! Karl, come on – you know that! This time was . . . it was different. We couldn't agree on the kids thing . . .'

'Don't you dare use that as an excuse!'

She stood up, unable to stop her knees from shaking and deciding that furious pacing was a better way to deal with this. 'It's not an excuse, it's a reason! Just another one of many. Look, Karl, you can't do this,' she demanded, a sudden flash of anger searing across her eyes. Sod being repentant and begging for mercy, it was clearly getting her nowhere. Yes, she'd messed up but he wasn't exactly blameless in this whole debacle either and she was damned if she was going to let him continue to lord over her.

'I made a mistake. A huge one. But it's the first time that it's ever happened and I promise you it will be the last. At least apply a little equality to our fuck-ups. I did what I did because I thought I'd lost you. When you thought I was gone, you did exactly the same thing. So don't come all high and mighty fucking sanctimonious with me when you are exactly the same. That's always been both our strength and our weakness, Karl – we're exactly the same.'

Wow – where had that come from? The pacing was obviously sending blood pumping to her brain cells. But every word of it was absolutely true. Were they both to blame for everything that had happened? Absolutely. This wasn't a one-way trip down Infidelity Road. Actually, given the amount of activity, it was more of a dual carriageway. However, she'd made her point and he should just accept it as accurate and they could both move on. She wasn't going to labour any further. There was absolutely nothing to be gained by dragging this out or attacking him further. Her speech was done. Over.

So why was he still sitting there looking at her like she'd just announced she was a serial killer and had a collection of thumbs in Tupperware dishes in the fridge?

Come on, Karl, accept this and move on. Don't make me come over there . . .

'You just tell yourself whatever you have to, Suze,' he said in a flat, weary monotone. 'But you're a liar. And I hate liars.'

'*You* hate liars?' she bit back incredulously. 'You were lying to me for months about the business, so don't go all moral high ground on me, Karl Marshall, because there's blame on both sides. We're equally at fault here.'

'You think? Don't fucking kid yourself, Suze. Business is one thing, shagging someone behind your husband's back is another. That's about as low as you can go.'

273

With that, he stood up, ignored the chair as it tipped over and crashed to the ground, and walked towards the stairs. Halfway there he stopped. 'Oh, and Suze – we are absolutely *nothing* alike,' he sneered.

Aaaaaargh! How fucking dare he judge her like that? He had fucked up. He'd lied to her. He had had an affair too – albeit after they had separated. As far as she could see, that made them quits. In fact, more than that . . .

'You're absolutely right, you self-righteous git,' she yelled. 'There are a couple of core differences – the main one being that I run a successful business whereas you lost all our money. And how did I react to that? I accepted it, Karl. I forgave you. I pitched in and tried to find a way to help. But not once, NOT FUCKING ONCE did I castigate you or belittle you for it. I stuck by you, you ungrateful shit, because I love you. So pardon me for thinking that this one time, just once, you might overlook the fact that I'm fallible and do the same.'

And with that, leaving a stunned husband standing in the middle of the room, she grabbed her bag and followed the path already travelled by her mother-in-law to the door.

There was a certain irony that she'd been the one who'd confessed to being unfaithful yet had stormed out in fury at *his* behaviour, but nonetheless she felt that she had ample justification. How dare he? How bloody dare he react like that when he'd made so many mistakes too?

She was in a bath in room 343 of the Hilton (paid for by Karl's credit card) before her fury had left her and she'd realised that – once again – she'd been so far down the reasonable-behaviour scale that she'd actually slipped on to a different scale altogether. The 'I'm An Irrational Twat' scale? Or how about the 'My Hormones Have Taken Me Hostage' scale? She'd done it again. She'd let her temper and her self-preservation run the show and what had it achieved? Nothing – other than slamming doors, a hotel bill and yet another unresolved problem. When would she learn? When? She wanted her husband and, if she and Karl were ever going to have a chance, then they had to break a ten-year habit and learn that screaming, shouting and storming off would get them nowhere. If Mel had taught her anything, it was that sometimes you just had to suck it up and be the bigger person. That's why this morning, she'd woken up, nipped over to the shop before anyone got in, changed into the clothes she always kept there for emergency nights out, and headed back to the house.

When she arrived, there had been nothing but silence so she'd crept up the stairs and there he was. Flat out on his front, a white sheet covering half his body but leaving some of his back bare, one rugby-ball-shaped buttock and one finely toned leg exposed. Her libido responded accordingly. Her stomach flipped and she wanted nothing more than to strip off and climb right on top of him. Hopefully they'd be at the tickly bit before he fully woke up and realised that it was his adulterous traitor of a wife who was impaled on his privates. But she didn't.

Instead, she took a pair of scissors out of her bag, followed by something that had meant so, so much to her and then she'd ceremoniously started cutting. After a few moments, there was a definite twitch from the Adonis's direction. And another. A stretch now, and a scratch (why do men always scratch their bollocks first thing in the morning?) and then a . . . wow, he shot upright and, when his eyes focused enough to absorb the scene, he was clearly perturbed.

'Suze, what the hell are you doing?'

OK, perhaps she hadn't thought through the wisdom of his waking up and seeing her sitting over him clutching a large pair of potentially lethal scissors.

His eyes went from the scissors, to her, to the scissors, his expression somewhere between confusion and disbelief. 'Is that . . .'

'My diaphragm,' she confirmed. 'I'm hoping that you'll realise that I'm the best thing that ever happened to you, beg me to come back and in return I promise that there will be no more diaphragms, just plenty of activity geared towards making us parents. Although I have to warn you that you will regret it when I'm fat, with swollen ankles and the general demeanour of a psychopath with PMT.'

He sank back on to the pillows and for a second Suze was worried. Come on, he had to forgive her. He *had* to. He couldn't let their marriage go.

After a few long, terrifying moments he sighed deeply as he ran his fingers through his hair. 'Suze,' he began softly, sadly, 'you . . .'

Yes?

'. . . are absolutely . . .'

What? Right? Beautiful? Adorable?

'. . . certifiable.'

He was rewarded with a wide grin and a playful nudge with a leather bondage sandal. 'But completely cute and irresistible, right?'

Although obviously fighting it, he eventually gave in to a brief burst of laughter. Of the non-*Shining* variety.

It took him a few seconds to regain some modicum of gravity. 'But you know, Suze, I still can't believe what you did.'

'I know and, believe me, I will never stop regretting it, Karl.' It was just a small white lie. For his own good. 'But remember, you did it too.'

He held his hands up. 'You're right. And I don't say that lightly. After you left last night I thought about what you said and you had a fair point.'

'Good.' She kept it brief, not trusting herself to keep on the sane and intelligent side of calm reason and methodical thinking.

'Just tell me that you didn't go to him last night.'

She hadn't even considered that he might be worried about that. 'Karl, I promise it's over. It has been since the moment we sorted things out. It wasn't even a relationship, it was just a –'

'No.' His hands shot up again. There were some things that he could clearly live without hearing. It was time to change tack.

'I love you, Karl.' For the first time she was solemn, sincere. 'You are the only man I've ever been in love with and I want it to stay that way.

'I want to be with you. I want to have your children. I'll do whatever you need me to do to believe that. And I swear on your mother's life I will never, ever be unfaithful to you again.'

'You hate my mother.'

'I know – I was hedging my bets.'

His laughter was louder this time, thick with relief and release.

Time to cross her fingers and go in for the close. 'I know that I will never love anyone else more than I love you. Could you honestly imagine loving anyone more than me?'

It was a little cocky but her heart was thumping so hard she knew she had to wrap it up into a yes or no scenario.

He looked at her, paused . . .

Her internal impatience gene shouted for a little less time on the deliberation side.

'No. I couldn't. We've both been stupid. We've both been wrong. But I do love you, Suze.' He reached over and pulled her towards him, his hand cupping her neck in the way that made her knee-tremblingly horn-tastic. His lips

277

were at her ear when he whispered, 'I think we deserve each other.'

If there had been a spare philharmonic lying around they'd have burst into a spontaneous rendition of the 'Hallelujah' chorus.

Turning to kiss him, she felt total all-consuming jubilation and lust, emotions that were joined by rampant desire the minute his hand found her jeans, flicked open the button, lowered the zip and slid inside.

Karl loved Suze.

Suze loved Karl.

And they were already on their way to adding a third name to that equation.

But this time it was mutual.

The weekend that decisions had to be made . . . then changed . . . then made . . . then changed . . . then . . .

Thirty-eight

'That'll be £69.99 please and if you'd like to give me your loyalty card I'll give it a quick stamp, love.'

Mel watched as the customer handed over the little pink passport-sized booklet and Josie thumped a bright-red lip-shaped kiss in the next free box. 'You're almost up to Silk Level – that's a twenty per cent discount or a free La Femme Dangereux corset and matching knickers.'

'Oooh, I think I'll go for one of those then. See you next week.' The very tall, very broad customer gathered up the assorted purchases and teetered out in four-inch heels throwing a cheery wave behind him.

'That bloke from *Blaggart* must be earning a fortune – and the love of his life is spending most of it in here,' Josie pondered, as she made her way over to Mel and threw her arm around her. They stood and stared out of the window for a few moments, before Josie thrust out her free arm. 'We're out of tissues but if you're desperate you can use my sleeve. This jumper's due a wash anyway.'

Mel smiled and put her arm around Josie's shoulders, not breaking the stare that was fixed on the door across the street.

'Has he gone yet?' Josie asked. 'Only I've got the balloons and the hooters in the back and they're ready to go.'

'Josie . . .' Mel replied, a hint of warning in her voice.

'OK, OK, I'm not being a good friend. You're right. How about if I fall to my knees and wail uncontrollably for ten minutes due to the pain of your loss and then wait a good half-hour before getting out the balloons and the hooters.'

Just as Mel was about to answer, a taxi pulled up. She held her breath and . . . Nothing. No activity. Had he changed his mind? No, he wouldn't. For the last two weeks, he had been researching and planning this trip, preparing everything he'd need and saying goodbyes. Karl had finally come around and wished him well. Although he was still gutted by Joe's leaving, he was trying to do the big-brother thing of being supportive and understanding. His mother, on the other hand, was still outraged at what she considered a completely ridiculous waste of time and money that she likened to those 'dreadfully unhygienic hippies' in the sixties.

Still no movement. Perhaps he was on the phone to the airport checking his flight. France, Spain, Greece, then over to Indonesia, Malaysia, Thailand, China and then on to wherever the journey took him. There was no return ticket and why should there be? The lawyer had commented that they were possibly the most amicable couple to have sat across the table from him. What was the point in arguing? Legal separation now, no-hassle divorce in two years' time. Just like that.

The taxi beeped his horn yet again and every inch of her started to tremble. Josie said nothing, just pulled her arm tighter around Mel's waist and delivered some moral support by osmosis.

Still no movement. They'd said their goodbyes that

morning with tear-soaked hugs and promises to stay safe, keep in touch every few days and not eat anything that didn't look like it was thoroughly cooked. Then she'd left for work, aware that if she stayed even a second longer she'd beg him to stay and it would be for all the wrong reasons: the security, fear of change, uncertainty about the future, sadness at saying goodbye to someone that she loved. Still no . . . She gasped as suddenly the main door to their building opened and there he was.

'Cammy,' Josie shouted in the direction of the stock-room, 'get out here and help me hold her down in case she makes a run for him.'

He was saying something to the taxi driver now, then he stood up, stopped, looked over towards the shop and realised that she was watching him. Her heart thudded as he smiled at her, then . . . then . . . don't go, Joe. Just don't go.

He stepped off the pavement, past the back of the taxi and . . .

Josie's arm tightened, could have been for comfort or restraint.

Another couple of steps and then he stopped . . .

Her ribs threatened to crack under the pressure of the relentless thudding coming from her heart.

Oh. My. God. He was going to . . .

'Come,' he mouthed to her, his eyes pleading.

Josie repositioned her arms around Mel's shoulders and adopted a stance that she'd seen on an American crime show, one that was recommended for use when performing a citizen's arrest on a potentially armed suspect.

Mel's whole body tensed as a physical blast of pain hit her in the chest. She wasn't sure if it was her heart aching or Josie preparing to take her down.

She should go. She should. Why was she just standing there when . . .

It was only when he waved that she realised her head had been shaking from side to side.

Beside her, Mel heard Josie tut, 'Always said he was a knob.'

And then the knob was gone and she was standing there, tears streaming down her face, watching a taxi disappear down the street with what she'd once thought was her future sitting in the back seat. He hadn't even turned the corner yet and already she felt a violent pang of missing him.

Josie put her arm in front of Mel's face again, but her wool/acrylic-mix sleeve was saved by Cammy who appeared on the other side of Mel with a large box of tissues. 'Brought these in – thought it might be a Kleenex kind of day.'

Mel smiled and took one from him and wiped her face. Neither of them had the heart to tell her that the result was on the Yang Yang side of panda.

'We could shut up shop and go get drunk,' Josie suggested.

Mel shook her head. 'Can't. Single woman now with a mortgage to pay. There'll be no slacking here, troops. In fact, if you want to give me that whip out of the display cabinet, I plan to start using it.'

A single woman. Joe was gone. Gone. Her husband had left her. Should she have gone with him? Perhaps she should have. It wasn't too late. She could catch up, take a later flight. But no . . . She'd made her decision and she had to stick to it, even if it meant more things would have to change.

Joe had offered to leave her a portion of his windfall but she'd refused. She'd done nothing to earn it and she had her shop. That was all she needed. It would be tight, but she'd make it work. And, if it didn't, well, she could always get another job. Another involuntary shudder over-took her as that thought struck home, but it was a definite possibility. She could leave Josie and Cammy to look after the shop and find something else that would give her enough flexibility to manage both. Her fallback position of opti-mism kicked in and she shook off the worry. She'd be fine. She had to be. In a way, it was quite exciting. For the first time in her life she didn't have to answer to anyone. Not her parents. Not Joe. No one. She was a free spirit, an independent woman, a keeper of her own destiny, a . . . whoa, she was getting a bit *Lord Of The Rings* there. Time to calm down and figure out a way to increase sales by thirty per cent.

She slipped into pensiveness again. Maybe she *should* have gone. After all, how many people ever got the chance to have such freedom, to go wherever they wanted to go and do exactly as they pleased? Maybe this would have brought them closer together, solved their problems, cemented their lifelong commitment? Maybe . . .

Josie tugged her in the direction of the back office. There was one bloke over in the male section of the shop so Cammy hung back to take care of him. Poor Cammy. He'd been a little subdued for a few days after she'd caught him with Suze, but they'd got over that by clearing the air one night over a bottle of wine. There would never be anything between them. Her crazy crush had disappeared as quickly as it started, and, although she'd reinforced how much she loved him, they both realised that it was never going to be more than platonic. They were great friends, but they both accepted they'd probably make lousy lovers. Mel was always going to want committed monogamy and a quiet life; Cammy needed a bit more excitement in life than that. His affair with Suze proved that and it was just too big a hurdle for her to overlook. They just weren't right for each other and deep down they both knew it. From that day onwards, they'd slowly climbed back on to a stable emotional plane and it was beginning to feel like their old easy friendship and mutual affection had returned – without the longing for perks or nudity on either side.

Besides, there hadn't been too much time for ruminating over events because they'd been kept really busy playing a new game called 'Avoid The Disgruntled Husband'. Every time Karl came within fifty yards of the shop Cammy was sent to the storeroom until it was safe to come out. And since part of Karl's new devotion to his wife involved popping in to Pluckers next door at least twice a day, Mel was thinking that they were going to have to fit the cupboard out with a supply of tinned goods, water, a Portaloo and a PlayStation.

She checked her watch. He'd been gone for less than five minutes. He wouldn't even be out of the city yet. There was time to join him, time to go after him . . .

As soon as they got into the office, Josie filled the kettle and plonked it on the desk. 'Right then, I need to know exactly how long we have to wait before we can start broaching sensitive subjects with you,' she asked, flicking on the kettle switch and liberating a packet of chocolate digestives from her handbag.

'How sensitive? Mildly embarrassing or borderline excruciating?'

'Neither. Just very personal and possibly intrusive.'

And hello again worry! Mel experienced definite trepidation before she answered. With Josie, personal and intrusive could cover anything from asking to witness your next colonic to discussing how to have sex in a train toilet.

'OK, go, but, if it's anything to do with porn, the answer's no.'

Josie could have gently led into her question, she could have wrapped it up in fluffy language, she could have thrown out some comforting words to prepare Mel for the situation. But she was Josie, so she went for the brutally straightforward approach. 'Now that Joe is gone, can you afford to keep this shop and still have some kind of a life? Sorry to ask, Mel, but we cash up at night and we know how much it takes and how all the profits have always gone back into the company accounts. Can you afford to start taking a wage?'

Oh, poor Josie, she was worried about the shop closing and losing her job. Mel felt a surge of guilt – she should have sat her down and talked to her before now, reassured her that no matter what happened Josie's position was safe. Sometimes she was just such an indomitable spirit that Mel forgot that when it came right down to it she was a woman of pensionable age who must have fear and worries about her own future.

'Josie, I'm so sorry, I should have spoken to you before about this. Listen, you need to know that your job will always be safe here. Please don't worry that you will ever be unemployed.'

'Aw, bollocks, I'm not worried about that, my darling, I've been headhunted three times in the last month. I swear if that bloody woman from Thongs & Tongs comes in here again I'm going to have her done for harassment. Besides – hair products and knickers in the same shop? She must have been sniffing hairspray fumes when she came up with that one.'

Mel was puzzled – if that wasn't her concern, then what was? And note to self: that stroppy, staff-thieving bint from Thongs & Tongs was now barred.

Ten minutes he'd been gone now. He'd be on the M8, the motorway that headed straight to the airport. She could

287

call him. He still had his mobile phone with him. She could just press the numbers and . . .

'So can you afford this, Mel?'

Mel looked up at her, so tall and fierce, standing there like an extra from Jackie Chan, the Elderly Years.

'I don't know, Josie. I really don't know.'

A large, perfectly symmetrical round tear squeezed out of one eye and plopped down on her lap. What had she been thinking? This was the most stupid, the most reckless thing she had ever done. What if business dropped or if there was any kind of problem that involved a large outlay? She had no contingency, no fallback position. The holding company for Marshalls might be out of overdraft but there was no way she could ask Karl and Suze for money even if she desperately needed it. She just couldn't. Optimism, blind bloody optimism had made her do this. However, now that Joe was gone and the reality of it was sinking in, she realised that it made no sense at all. It was insane. Stupid. She could have steered her life in a direction that involved the man she loved, sun and a life-changing adventure, and instead she'd shackled herself to loneliness, poverty and worries.

He wouldn't even be at the airport yet. There was still time, still a chance . . .

'Oh, sweetheart.' Josie leaned over and hugged her, ignoring the kettle that was now shooting steam into the air above them.

Eventually, Josie pulled back, and took a deep breath of assertiveness. 'Right then. Come with me, I need to talk to you next door.'

Confusion replaced Mel's fears. 'Why?'

Why would Josie want to speak to her next door? Josie had been less than chipper with Suze since Cammy had taken her into his confidence and confessed to her about the affair. He'd thought it was only fair that he put an end to her burning wish to see him and Mel get together so he'd told her everything. It was the first time he'd been thudded across the back of the head since he'd reached adulthood.

But this would appear to be no time to argue. Josie had her by the hand and was yanking her out of her seat. 'Come on, hon, I promise it'll be worth it.'

'Cammy, we'll be back in ten,' she yelled as the two of them cut a track across the shop.

They were almost at the door when it swung open and an exceptionally tall, dark-haired guy with the kind of tan that women pay fortunes for walked in.

'Perfect timing!' Josie announced, as she reached up and kissed him on the cheek. 'Right, you're coming with us too.'

Mel stopped dead, mortified, seriously contemplating whether Josie might require sedation until whatever mania had possessed her blew over. 'Josie, you can't just kidnap customers like that.'

Josie wasn't listening. She now had hold of the guy's hand and was steering him back out and towards the entrance to the salon. And bizarrely, he wasn't even putting up a fight.

Why on earth had she ever thought that staying in this madness would be worth giving up Joe for? She checked her watch again. And knew that she still had time to call . . .

Thirty-nine

'So let me get this straight, you lot want to invest in our company?' Suze asked sceptically, clearly waiting for the point where everyone laughed and confessed to a wind-up.

'I know, we must be fecking mad,' Avril replied, not even looking up from the peacock-blue enamel that she'd been painting on her toes for the last ten minutes.

It was a squash in the salon staff room but somehow they'd all managed to get in there: Josie, Mel, Suze, Avril and the very tall man with the tan, the colour of which she vaguely recognised as being the same shade as the creosote used to paint her garden hut.

Josie had made the introductions as soon as they'd congregated, or rather, after Avril had looked at the guy and muttered, 'Skank,' and he'd returned the compliment with a murmured, 'Trollop.' Then they'd both collapsed into fits of giggles and hugged each other for a good ten seconds. Suze had made a note to reprimand Avril about drinking before she came into work.

'Everyone, this is my son Michael. He flew in from Rome this morning,' Josie announced, pride oozing from every word. 'And we've got a proposition to put to you ladies. Now, there's absolutely no pressure . . .'

'Has she got a weapon in her bag?' Suze whispered to Mel.

'Dunno, didn't get time to frisk her.'

Josie rewarded them with a pause and a disapproving stare, then continued, 'But we think we might have a suggestion that could help out everyone. And, Suze, would you stop rubbing your back and making those pained expressions.'

Suze's hands immediately dropped to her side. She'd become so obsessed with getting pregnant that she was already having phantom back pains.

'Oh, are you pregnant? Congratulations,' Michael said with a friendly smile.

'No we're just trying, but I will be soon.'

Avril harrumphed disdainfully. 'They've been trying for a fortnight. She's already organised the decorator for the nursery and won't go anywhere that she can't pee at ten-minute intervals.'

Michael started to look a little scared. 'Mum, is it always like this?'

'Absolutely, son,' Josie replied with a maternal beam.

Looking at both of them, Suze could see the similarities. Michael had obviously inherited his mother's height gene, yet he didn't stoop like so many other tall blokes. He must have been about six foot four perhaps? She briefly wondered whether the propensity for larger than average extended to his . . . No! How could she think those things? She was a married and soon-to-be very pregnant woman.

She figured he was probably in his mid-thirties, maybe a little younger, but he had one of those inscrutable, younger Robert De Niro faces that made it hard to tell. In fact, that was it! He actually did look Italian, with his jet-black hair and brown eyes and a nose that definitely veered towards

291

Roman. Suze thought him . . . interesting. Not classically handsome, not in the same phwoar category as Karl or Cammy, but definitely not too shoddy at all.

She didn't have time to ponder any further because that's when Josie launched into her business proposition.

'Right, so here's what's going on. Michael here –' cue yet another maternal beam '– is moving back to this country now that his neurotic slut of a wife has buggered off with a baker.'

Suze shook her head. You couldn't make up this stuff, you really couldn't. She cast a sideways glance at Mel and realised that she was looking rough. And sad. Damn Joe for cutting out on her like that. She still couldn't believe that Mel hadn't gone with him and she couldn't help thinking that this wasn't the end of the story. Those two had been made for each other, hadn't they? It just didn't seem right that Mel was sitting here bereft and Joe was on his way to God-knows-where and probably feeling exactly the same way. It didn't seem right that their marriage had been blown apart by a mistake that was undeniably far less serious than the mistakes made by her and Karl. If they could find a resolution, then surely Mel and Joe could too? But then, what did she know? Hadn't she already proved that her ability to understand relationships was up there with her ability to, say, give a ten-minute speech on the merits of her mother-in-law. In Cantonese. There was no point getting involved other than to offer support and unlimited nights out featuring cocktails.

'Hey, Ma Walton, are you paying attention?'

'I am, Josie. Sorry, carry on.'

'Thank you. Now, he has two daughters and has agreed to spend alternate months here and in Italy, so he decided to bring in a management team for his restaurants in Italy, and look for another business over here that he can invest in without any hands-on input.'

Suze was impressed. Who knew that Josie had spawned an international entrepreneur?

'So what we're proposing is this. Michael, Avril and I will form our own company and we'd like to invest in the salon and the shop as partners. Everything would run exactly the way it is now. Suze, you'll have Avril's eternal devotion and, Mel, you'll have mine,' she'd joked.

That's when Suze had primed herself for the revelation it was a wind-up, and had been astonished to realise that it wasn't. 'So let me get this straight, you lot want to invest in our company? But I already have partners. Karl, Joe, Mel and I are all in this together.'

'And you know how well that's been working for you so far,' Avril retorted.

The comment inflamed Suze's newfound sense of loyalty. 'Hey, don't you . . .!'

Michael jumped in. 'Look, ladies, if it's not for you, then that's absolutely fine. But – and I hope you don't mind, Mel – my mum explained the situation to me, they sketched out some rough figures . . .'

'That's industrial espionage, Judas,' Suze hissed in Avril's direction.

'Bite me,' came the reply.

Michael, looking very scared now, ploughed on regardless. 'It just seemed that it might be a possibility, especially for you, Mel. Both shops are in profit, albeit not a substantial one yet. But with the right marketing and investment that could change. My proposal would be to buy shares in each shop from Marshall Holdings – you ladies would still hold the majority shares either as part of the holding company or as individuals, and my mum and Avril would be your junior partners. But, as I say, it's just an offer. Mum and Avril love working with you so it seemed like a good idea . . . at the time.'

His expression made it clear that he was beginning to revise that judgement call.

Suze exhaled as she tried to kick baby buggies and Barney the Dinosaur wallpaper borders out of her head and replace them with pragmatic analytical skills.

At face value, the idea actually did have some merit. Since their construction, Karl and Joe had had no commercial input in the shops whatsoever, yet all profits from the shops had gone into the big black pit called 'Marshall Holdings'. There had been little investment over the last couple of years, and, although as a group they were back in the black, they still didn't have the luxury of setting aside funds for expansion or further development.

However, if the shops were run autonomously with a backer who was going to put his very large wallet where his very large, erm, *mouth* was, then perhaps that would be a great thing for all of them. Take all their eggs out of the one basket. Leave her and Mel to run their businesses as independent units, Karl to rebuild the construction side without the complexity of the other outlets and Joe could carry on wafting around the world until his money ran out or he caught some dreadful tropical disease and had to be medi-vac'd home.

Yes, it definitely had potential. Solid potential.

'And it also comes with another very real benefit for you, Suze,' Avril said with her trademark nonchalance.

'What's that?'

'You'll have a partner who's very understanding when it comes to maternity leave.'

Suze suddenly decided that it was the best idea that she'd ever heard.

However, it wasn't just up to her. She turned to the woman sitting next to her, the one who had been through so much over the last few months, none of it her fault.

After all the trauma of the last few months, Karl and Joe would agree to this if they knew what was good for them.

Mel, though, had always gone along with everything they wanted, gone with the flow to keep everyone else happy so, as far as she was concerned, this decision should be up to her.

'Mel, honey, what do you think?'

Forty

What did she think?

She thought that by now he'd be in the terminal building. He'd be sitting in the bar in the departure lounge with a beer in front of him, and a dozen girls waiting to go on a hen weekend to Magaluf would be nudging each other and pointing him out, egging on the prettiest one to ask for his phone number.

She thought that he'd have his phone in his hand and he'd be staring at the numbers trying to decide whether to call her one last time to say goodbye. Or perhaps even to make one more attempt to persuade her to go with him.

She thought that no matter how terrible he was feeling there was a little part of him that knew he was doing the right thing. And that was the part of him that would stop him picking up his bag, walking right back out of the building, jumping in a taxi and coming home to her.

She thought that a year ago she'd have walked across fire for him, would have gone to the ends of the earth just to see him, but now, despite missing him so much she felt a physical pain in her gut, she was sitting in the salon staff room instead of following him.

She thought that, if this was a romantic comedy starring Kate Hudson, Kate would be in a taxi right now, heading for the airport, looking beautiful despite the tears, and would get there just in time to stop him walking through the gate. She'd then kiss him passionately to a rousing chorus of applause from all the other passengers.

And she thought that if she left right now she'd be able to do the same.

Three months later. The weekend that lives were changed, hearts were healed and only one situation threatened to get violent . . .

Forty-one

Mel blinked and blinked again, then pushed the white sheet off her body. God, it was hot. Sodding tropical. She thrust her arm out to one side and swept it down the space beside her. Empty. Why was it empty? She sat up, realising that a thin trickle of perspiration was running down the space between her breasts. A familiar knot began to tighten in her stomach when a clanking from another room invoked a sigh of relief. It was OK. He was there. Exactly where he should be.

'You all right?'

It took Suze a few seconds to realise that the teenage hoodie with the questionable skin and the aggressive gait was talking to her. Bloody hell, he couldn't have been any more than sixteen – what was he doing here? Ante-natal classes were a place for adults, not marginally post-pubescent boys who should be congregated in wooded areas drinking cider while sucking on questionable roll-ups.

'Do I look like I'm OK?'

'Naw,' he grunted.

'Well done, son – you'll go far.'

Post-pubescent teen grunted and moved off, leaving her rooted to the spot, staring, just staring at the two people in front of her, deep in conversation, not even aware that she could see them. Suze felt a violent, hormonal surge of hysteria. It was bad enough that he'd got stuck in traffic. It was hugely upsetting that he'd missed the scan. But bringing his mother? Karl Marshall was about to be a dead man.

'I brought you coffee,' Joe said softly, handing over a bright-orange mug emblazoned with the slogan 'Sex is cardiovascular – time for exercise?'

'Is that an offer?' the girl asked, stretching out languidly, completely unconcerned that he could see every inch of her nakedness.

He reached right over and took the cup back off her, then slid on to the bed beside her. The last four weeks had been as amazing as they'd been exhausting. It was like he remembered it had been right at the start when he'd first met Mel. And he was determined to enjoy every sweet, orgasmic minute of it.

The hairs on the back of his neck stood up in the way he imagined criminals in a siege situation felt right before a sniper's bullet took them out. Karl stopped talking and slowly, almost painfully, turned around to see his wife's face and he knew. He knew that he'd made a mistake, but he'd been caught in the crossfire. Virginia had insisted that she was coming, Suze had insisted that she wasn't. In the end, it came down to a choice between which of the two would inflict the least damage. He was beginning to wonder if he'd made the right decision.

Virginia threw her arms as far round Suze as they would

reach and gave her an uncharacteristic hug. 'Darling, you are blooming! Positively blooming! That's those Marshall genes in there,' she said with a beaming smile.

Who knew that the prospect of grandparent status would turn Virginia into a gushing, representative from The Obsessive Granny Party.

'Now let's get you home because we need to discuss the nursery. It's never too soon to start planning.'

Looking at his wife's expression, Karl had a hunch that the nursery wasn't top of her planning list at this precise moment. However, bollocking him for bringing his mother definitely was.

'Karl, Can I speak to you?' Suze's voice was slightly distorted, given that she was speaking through what Karl could tell was a very false smile.

'Suze, I'm –'

'In private!' she hissed.

Reluctantly, unwilling to leave a public place where there would at least be witnesses, he followed her to a deserted fire exit.

'I can't believe you brought her here.'

'Suze, I'm so sorry, but she insisted. She wants to be involved.'

'I think I preferred it when she hated me. Let's not even discuss it because if we do they'll find your body in a skip. Anyway, I suppose I'm going to have to get used to there being other females around.'

He froze, shocked, astounded.

'Do you mean . . . ?'

Suze opened her bag and took out the small, grainy image that she'd been handed just a few moments before, then burst into tears as she nodded. 'It's a girl.'

Several jubilant yells and three rotations around the

fire exit later (she didn't mind – he'd soon need mechanical intervention to lift her up and spin her round), he punched the air. 'Bloody hell, another woman in my life.'

'Yeah, like you don't have enough problems.' Suze laughed. 'Now go back over there and break the news. And Karl . . .'

'Yes, babe?'

'If you ever bring your mother to another ante-natal appointment, your daughter and I will punish you until the end of time.'

Ominous words, but the huge grin that beamed across Karl Marshall's face made it obvious that there was nothing he'd love more.

'Hey,' Joe said, 'I've been calling for ages and getting the engaged tone. Who were you talking to?'

'Suze. They were at the hospital today and they've just found out they're having a girl.'

'That's amazing. Although . . . Not sure if the world is ready for another Suze.'

Mel laughed as she realised that was exactly what she'd been thinking too. She loved her best friend more than life, but, well, she just hoped the baby had enough of Karl's genes to dilute the drama.

'You still sound sleepy,' he said.

'I am. Bit of a restless night. Too warm.'

'You still leaving the heating on at night?'

'Sorry?'

'I said . . .'

'Yes!'

Mel laughed. The time delay on the line was only a second or so but it sometimes led to them talking over each other. And, of course, it didn't help that a sixteen-pound Labrador pup was attempting to chew the phone while it was still at her ear. So far that morning he'd demolished a bowl of fruit and eaten a kitchen chair. She loved the new male in her life. Even if he did hog the bed.

'I don't want Bob to get cold in the kitchen. Not that he's staying there. You were right – I gave in and let him sleep with me last night.'

'It was only a matter of time,' Joe replied, and, although he was ten thousand miles away, she knew he was smiling.

'Mel, I need to tell you something. I –'

'It's OK, I know.'

Even the delay couldn't disguise what he was about to say. She'd heard it in his voice the last few times that he'd called: the remnants of sadness had been replaced by a joy, an irrepressible enthusiasm that she remembered hearing many years ago on a Fuengirola beach. He'd met someone else.

'How?'

'Just call it intuition. Is she nice?'

'She is. Her name's Ellie, she's Australian. But Mel, a part of . . .' He paused, his voice thick with emotion.

'I know that too,' she whispered. 'Joe, you're exactly where you should be. And so am I. But a part of me will always love you too.'

As she hung up, she knew she was right. He was on a windswept beach and she was in windswept Glasgow, with a Labrador called Bob who had now moved on to eating a shoe.

And she had never, ever felt happier.

Epilogue

'I'm telling you there is no bloody way that's a 40DD. It's a nonsense. I blame that bloody European Parliament, you know. Useless bunch of cretins and the sole contribution to our society is that they've buggered up our bra sizes.'

'Aye, you're right, Senga. And sausages. Our sausages are definitely smaller since they made us use all that kilograms and litres rubbish.'

'I'm going to have a word with my Edwin about it. If there's anyone who can set those politicians right on the size of their sausages, it's my Edwin.'

There was a cacophony of hilarity as three of the Paisley Six shrieked with amusement. Mel rubbed her jaw, trying to prevent it setting into a deranged grin caused by laughing almost solidly for the last two hours, since Senga and her posse had descended on them. This time there was a double celebration: another bingo win (eight hundred quid to Montana this time, but split between six) and a shopping spree to get everything they'd need for Senga's hen weekend.

306

Yes, to the astonishment of everyone who knew them, the local Conservative party members and Councillor Edwin Davidson's constituents, he and Senga Summers, aged forty-nine, a voluptuous 44–40–56, had been whipped into a whirlwind romance, culminating in his breathtakingly romantic proposal in the middle of a public forum meeting regarding the management of the city's landfill sites.

To the astonishment and delight of the audience, she'd accepted by running screaming up the centre aisle, throwing herself over the speaker's table and sucking his face for approximately two and a half minutes. It had made front-page headlines in the *Daily Record* the next day.

There was a commotion at the archway and Mel leaned over a display of nipple tassels to see what was going on. The archway had been Josie's idea, opening up the wall between the two shops so that they benefited from each other's passing trade. It was genius and Mel couldn't believe that she and Suze hadn't thought of it before.

Taking on Josie and Avril as partners had been the best thing they had ever done. Karl and Joe had willingly signed the shops and all related assets over to the girls, allowing them to form 50–50 partnerships that had flourished from the start. Josie had been the brains behind the fashion shows, spectacular joint ventures with other top-class independent retailers in the city. Avril had created stunning catalogues and introduced a pre-event service, partnering with PR agencies to obtain the guest lists for all red-carpet events throughout the city, then inviting the attendees to come to the shops to be made up, styled and then taxied to the venue looking fabulous. At a cost, of course. She'd also used her contacts in the modelling world to secure a makeover slot on a weekly, teatime TV show. It was the kind of advertising that no amount of money could buy and that, together with the increased spend on marketing and promotion, had made the shops so busy they'd had to take on far more staff to cope with demand.

Michael, too, had been a revelation. He spent every second month in Scotland and during that time had worked away in the background, dedicating himself to setting up websites for the shops so that they now had an online merchandising service that allowed them to sell underwear and beauty products via the internet. If Mel had realised how astonishingly profitable that would be, she would have done it from day one.

In just six months they'd gone from a modest profit to the kind of figures that would have been like a lottery win this time last year.

'Dear God, Jean, what's wrong with you – you look like you're about to keel over.'

The commotion from the archway had now worked its way across the room in the shape of Jean and Ina, Ina holding on to Jean's arm as she shuffled painfully along, wincing with every movement. Montana jumped out of her seat to make way for her and she slowly, gasping with pain, lowered herself into it.

'I feel . . . I feel . . . In the name of Jesus, Senga, why did you tell me to have a Brazilian? That's an affront to womanhood, so it is.'

Senga's hand flew to her mouth. 'Jean, I said a *Swedish*! A Swedish massage. Were you not paying attention?'

Jean's devastated expression said it all. 'I just remembered that it was the name of a country, so when I saw "Brazilian" on the price list . . .'

The rumbles of suppressed amusement were starting now, all of them trying desperately not to laugh in the face of Jean's obviously chronic adversity.

'Right enough though,' Jean commented solemnly, 'I

should have known something wasn't right when they told me to take my knickers off and open wide.'

The dam burst and there wasn't a ribcage in the house that wasn't bent over, howling with laughter.

'Aye, and I better warn my Angus tonight – shock like that could kill a man with his angina.'

Suze arrived and caught the last sentence, then immediately stopped and crossed her legs. 'Oh don't, Jean, or there'll be another indignity coming up over here. I watched a really funny old episode of *Will & Grace* the other night and let's just say it should have come with a health warning involving pregnant women and bladders.'

Ida got up this time and gave Suze her seat. Not that she needed it really, but, since the whole piles/sore back/hormones of a maniac combination had convinced her that this would probably be the only time she'd allow Karl to get her knocked up, she was milking it for everything it was worth.

'Oh and, girls, I forgot to tell you – Cammy sends his love. Our Stacey said she got him a bit part in a Fried Chicken advert and they reckon that it's only a couple of steps away from mega-stardom and his first Oscar. Apparently, that Orlando Bloom bloke is shitting himself.'

Suze's and Mel's eyes met and they both smiled. Cammy. A couple of weeks of playing Avoid The Husband and Heal The Unrequited Love had been enough and he'd headed over to LA for a fortnight of rest and relaxation. Two weeks. Which made him, oooh, three months and twelve days late in coming back.

Mel didn't mind. Actually, she did – she missed him terribly. But when he'd called to explain that he loved it there and thought that perhaps he could pick up some work, she'd encouraged him to stay. He had a big future in front of him. Just not with her.

WILL GALLOWS
& THE ROCK DEMON'S BLOOD

Across the sea of heads, she noticed the door open and a familiar mop of black wavy hair ducked down under the lintel to enter. It was second nature to him now, after several bruises and a couple of borderline concussions in his first couple of weeks as their backer.

His companions elicited a whole chorus of oooohs and aaaahs from the assembled customers. At the very same moment, both Abrielle and Josefina spotted their grandmother, broke free of their daddy's hands and ran screaming towards Josie's outstretched arms.

'I'm sorry, do I know you girls?' Josie had said sternly.

'It's us, Nana, it's us!' they screeched, loving this game.

'Nope, sorry, I've no idea who you are. Although, of course, that might change if I get ten kisses from each of you.'

The girls fell upon her, sending Josie flying on her arse, whereby they jumped on top of her and slavered her with huge sloppy kisses.

'You know, my mother really does need to loosen up a little and take life a bit less seriously,' Michael observed.

Mel grinned. 'Indeed she does.'

'Are you still OK to get away? Only, it looks pretty busy.'

'No, no, these aren't real customers. I mean they are of the paying variety, but they prefer the self-service method of purchasing. And, besides, they've already got more than they came in for –' all eyes spun towards Jean '– so they're just waiting here until happy hour starts at the pub round the corner.'

'Go on, you two, hurry up before I change my mind about letting my partner finish early,' Josie interjected with accompanying shooing gestures.

Mel reached into the office for her bag and slipped it on to her shoulder, then leaned over to give Josie, who was scrambling to her knees, a kiss.

'And stay out late. If I hear either of you got home alone before midnight, there'll be serious disciplinary action.'

Michael waited for Mel to join him, face flushed because the scariest collection of women he'd ever seen were all staring at him with dewy eyes and huge grins as if he'd done something far more magnificent than walk in the door and offer to take Mel away from all this.

'Yes, Mother,' he shouted to Josie, before turning to Mel and whispering, 'You think at my age there could be nothing more she could do to embarrass me and yet . . .'

'Oh and, Michael, do we need to have the birds and the bees conversation?' Josie cackled, hugely entertained by the whole scenario. This was the best outcome she could ever have hoped for. The son she adored and the woman who was like a second daughter to her. She'd never admit it but she already had her hat and shoes picked out for the wedding.

'. . . and yet, there we have it,' Michael added.

Mel breathed a huge sigh of contentment as she crossed to the door. She loved her life. She loved her job. She loved her friends. And she definitely had a growing fondness for the tall guy beside her with the gorgeous manners and the crinkly brown eyes.

Nothing could be better and she knew, just knew that it was going to stay that way.

'Oh, Mel, I forgot to tell you,' Suze shouted just as they reached the door. 'You know we were talking about ways to monitor the service our clients get when we're not here? Well, I discovered that there are these agencies you can go to and they send in secret . . .'

With a smile and a wave, Mel let the door bang shut behind her.

Acknowledgements

As always, a million thanks to my agent, the fabulous Sheila Crowley, who was simply magnificent every step of the way – especially the bit right before deadline that involved author hysteria. Also at Curtis Brown, Katie McGowan, Tally Garner and Sarah Lewis have been fantastic. Thank you all.

Emma Beswetherick continues to be the most inspirational, insightful editor a writer could have. Thank you, Emma – you are truly a blessing.

Huge gratitude to the rest of the team at Piatkus: Donna Condon, Lucy Icke, Paola Ehrlich, Mary Tobin and all the others who played a part in the road to *Temptation Street*.

My husband claims that when he married me, he didn't realise that I came with several women sitting around my kitchen table at all times. Thanks and love to the brave souls who are always on hand with advice, laughs and an assortment of high-calorie indulgences: Frankie Plater, Jan Johnston, Gillian Armstrong, Janice McCallum, Linda Lowery, Wendy Morton, Pamela McBurnie, Sylvia Lavizani, Mitch Murphy, Carmen Reid, Gemma Low,

Emma Vijayaratnum, Sadie Hill, Rosina Hill and Liz Murphy.

Thank you so much to all the journalists, booksellers and bloggers who said such nice things about my previous books. And I'm eternally grateful to all the readers who have supported me throughout the years.

And finally, to my gorgeous, funny, adorable menfolk (one large, two small) – thank you, thank you, thank you. I know how incredibly lucky I am. But no, just because there's another book, doesn't mean we're going to live in Disneyland.

Love,
Shari x